KEEPER

A KNIGHTS OF ROSEWOOD NOVEL
BOOK 1

DANIEL A. PETRANGELO

DANIEL A. PETRANGELO

ACKNOWLEDGMENTS

Cover by Youness El Hindami
Edited by Marthese Fenech
Proofread by Joe Pierson

Thanks to Alayna and Mike.

Special thanks to Mark M Bulmer. It all started with the Portuguese chicken.

PROLOGUE

Andars Demeter stepped off his private helicopter and crossed the main deck of the deep-sea oil rig Poseidon's Trident. The pilot remained seated per his employer's decree. Demeter drew the salty sea air into his lungs and savored it for a heartbeat before entering the elevator. The doors opened at the bottom of his descent, and he emerged onto the rig's second deck. The awful glow of yellowish fluorescent light bathed his skin in a jaundiced hue.

He despised his oil rigs. Not the profits they produced, of course. Rather, he hated the smell of metal and grease and the sour stink of old sweat. He especially disliked the sounds. The constant whirring, buzzing, rattling, and banging of machines. The crew's incessant arguments, profanity, laughter, and bawdy jokes.

A huge man by any standard, Demeter's head almost touched the seven-foot ceilings. His broad shoulders brushed against the walls of the rig's steel corridors, sullying his perfectly tailored suit with each step.

The *Trident*'s general manager ensured the crew never

entered this section of the rig, guaranteeing Demeter peaceful passage to the second elevator secreted behind a high-security, reinforced door that only he could access. His ears popped from the pressure change as the elevator bore him down to the rig's third deck beneath the ocean waves.

The doors slid open to reveal a study in contrasts. Unlike the decks above, the ceilings here rose fifteen feet, and recessed fixtures suffused the area in soft white light. Demeter strode through the wide corridors comfortably, satisfied by the cleanliness and, most importantly, the silence. The third deck more closely resembled a spa than an oil rig, thanks to the sophisticated noise- and vibration-dampening technology he'd paid an obscene amount to procure. The deck's planning and construction proved an extravagant expense that required clever financial misdirection to prevent audits from nosy regulators and activist investors.

He entered a lounge area and found an attractive woman in an armchair typing something into a smartphone. She stood at his arrival.

"Andars," she said without formality.

The woman wore flat shoes, a black pencil skirt, and a white blouse beneath a fitted blazer, her black hair cropped short. She stood at least five feet ten but looked minuscule compared to her host. If he intimidated her, she hid it well. Practically all who met him showed some measure of fear, revulsion, or deference—usually all three. No one would call him handsome. Far from it. Overlapping scars and welts covered Demeter's entire body. Even the bones in his face appeared uneven. His coarse skin and cold blue eyes invited the wrong sort of second glances. The not-so-subtle running joke among the world's financial elite anointed Andars

Demeter the ugliest man on the Fortune 50, a distinction he had grown to savor.

"Impressive facility," she said in his native Hungarian. "Though, arriving here by underwater craft was rather unpleasant."

He smiled, genuinely impressed with her grasp of his language. They had met once before, and he had barely noticed her. Demeter suspected that he should have paid closer attention.

"You are certain of its privacy and security?" she asked.

He clenched his jaw, annoyed by her question. Demeter did not like when others second-guessed him. He answered in the same language. "I am quite positive that in the brief time you have been here, you have performed an assessment. How are my privacy and security?"

She regarded him for a moment, then glanced down at her smartphone. "I located an electronic record in a contractor's secure database that referred to a 'third deck of unknown purpose.'"

Demeter's eyes widened at the news. "Which contractor?" he asked, his anger manifesting in the veins that suddenly protruded on his neck above his white-collared shirt and navy-blue tie.

"Hong Kong Advanced Networks. Ah, I see from your bemused expression that you don't know that particular contractor. You, or should I say, your project manager, Johann Karlson, hired HKAN to install server farms."

"I will deal with this— lack of discretion."

"No need. An unidentified group bombed HKAN's offices not thirty-five minutes ago." She delivered the revelation without the slightest change of tone or cadence.

"A gruesome, senseless attack," she continued. "About two dozen casualties, not including collaterals in the adjacent offices. Most of the company's records were destroyed. Furthermore, hackers managed to wipe all its data from the company's cloud-based servers. Coincidentally, Johann Karlson died of a heart attack just this morning. His poor wife made the discovery. Very sad. He was so young. Just forty-one years old. I sent condolences on your behalf. An expensive but tasteful bouquet shall arrive later this afternoon."

Demeter stared at the woman as his rage boiled up inside him. He well understood cruel necessity. Despite the tragedies and the betrayals—both those he committed and those committed against him—this woman's ruthless efficacy left him disoriented. He grunted angrily, then reached out and grabbed the front of her blazer. He lifted her off the ground and drew her close until his scarred face was mere inches from hers. He could break her in half.

"What gives you the right to kill one of mine?" he growled.

Again, the woman showed no fear. She stared back into Demeter's snarling face. Her composure in the heat of his anger gave him pause, and he put her down. They both knew that he couldn't harm her. As much as he hated to admit it, he needed her.

"Never," she said slowly, "touch me again."

They glared at each other briefly before she continued the conversation. "We require absolute discretion, Andars. If the Knights of Rosewood discover our plans, we are dead. Do you understand?"

"Don't tell *me* of the Rosewood, woman. If not for me, you would know nothing of its existence."

"That's not quite accurate. You need to trust us, Andars."

"I trust no one."

"And look at you. You're a poor reflection of your much-vaunted noble house."

Despite the woman's mockery, Demeter made no rebuttal. The treaty had reduced him to a beaten beast, fearful of kicks from his master's booted foot.

"Together, we will return your house to its glory. Come, let us check on my man."

He didn't move. The ease with which this woman commanded him left him outraged. He stared down at her and considered tossing her into the sea as a light snack for the sharks, but as she returned his gaze, Demeter wondered who might eat whom.

Reluctantly, he led her out of the lounge. They walked down an immaculately clean corridor, passing climate-controlled glass rooms filled with state-of-the-art computer servers, graphical processing units, and exabytes of data storage.

They entered the control room together. A screen dominated an entire wall of the enormous rectangular space. The soft light and sterile ambiance that characterized the third deck's corridors and lounge were also present here. The room was devoid of people except for a young man seated at a large desk in the room's center. He was surrounded by two keyboards, two laptops, and a smartphone. Opened cans of energy drinks were strewn about his location. His fingertips flew frantically across the keyboards. Lines of code shot across and down a section of the main screen.

Before the woman or Demeter could speak, the young man began talking at a ragged pace. "I just hacked into the National Security Agency's bulk metadata collection database. Check out the notes I added to my profile."

The main screen displayed a high-resolution mugshot of

the young man. *'Large and in charge'* in bold pink comic sans lettering marred the photograph.

Now wearing a playful smile, he turned to look at the woman and Demeter. When they showed no amusement, he faced the screen again.

"Wow. Tough crowd," he remarked before moving on. "Building an oil rig on this spot is genius. We've hijacked the transatlantic fiber-optic cables on the ocean floor without anyone knowing. I've hit god-tier hacker status."

"I told you to delete your criminal file," the woman stated coldly, "not play with it."

She didn't wait for the young man to reply. Instead, she turned to Demeter and made the introductions in flawless English. "Andars Demeter, this is Avinash Salem. He will live on this rig for the foreseeable future, reporting to and taking orders directly from me."

Avinash pulled his eyes away from the code and data streams to look at Demeter. "Are you like eight feet tall?"

Demeter sneered at the hacker, then turned to the woman. "He looks like a Dickensian street urchin." He paused to sniff the air. "Smells like one too."

Avinash frowned. "Huh?"

"How he looks is irrelevant," the woman replied. "When he was sixteen, this *street urchin* hacked into the secure customer records of the world's second- and third-largest credit card companies. A year later, he did what most people thought impossible and hijacked the flight computers of a passenger jet—mid-flight."

Avinash grinned up at him. "I made them go up and down like a half-billion-dollar yo-yo. I wish I could've seen the one-percenters in first class while they bounced around in their cush seats." The moment the words escaped him, Avinash's eyes shot open, and his smile evaporated. "Ah, not a one-percenter like you. You look like you work out."

Demeter snarled. "People like me don't fly commercial, fool."

Ignoring the argument, the woman continued. "He accomplished that with a two-hundred-dollar laptop and a Wi-Fi hotspot at a coffee shop."

"Where did you find him?" Demeter asked.

"A juvenile detention center, awaiting a judge's decision to transfer him to an adult criminal court," the woman responded.

Avinash interjected, "The idiot prosecutor. He wanted to send me away for multiple life sentences. Something about cyber-terrorism and using me as an example. It was a joke. No one on the plane got hurt!"

"We intervened on Avinash's behalf," she continued, but the urchin interrupted again.

"Next thing I know, I'm free! I walk out the gates of juvie hall to a tricked-out black limo and a chauffeur holding the door for me like I'm Bollywood royalty. You should've seen the guards' faces."

Avinash spun around in his swivel chair before he righted himself, then turned his attention back to the screen and keyboards. Demeter's scarred face grew hot with anger.

"He was caught once, and here he is hacking government agencies from my oil platform. You don't see this activity as risky?"

"No way I can get caught with this gear. Even if those Luddites detect an intrusion in their networks, I'm routing the attacks through so many other countries and organizations, including their allies. It'll take them a few years to figure out who it *wasn't*. Don't worry. You're clean."

"Regardless, Avinash isn't here to steal government

secrets." She turned to look at the screen. "Show Mr. Demeter our next acquisition target."

"Huh?" Avinash asked uncertainly.

The woman's jaw tightened. "The robotics project," she snapped.

"Oh!" His hands moved swiftly across one of the laptops, and a webpage appeared. It contained videos and images of smiling law enforcement officers carrying various high-tech gadgets, including body cameras and strange-looking sidearms.

"Deus Ex Mechanika Inc.," Avinash began. "They manufacture nonlethal equipment for police agencies around the world."

Demeter nodded. "I'm aware."

The main screen displayed the street urchin's actions as he executed programs and navigated past authentication portals at a rapid-fire pace. He clicked through numerous folders, including one called *Tier Alpha Research and Development*. Avinash opened a confidential folder, breached the additional safeguards meant to prevent unauthorized access, and then located and played a video clip labeled *K9SA Prototype 347 Mobility Demo 12*. Demeter watched the recorded demonstration of a sophisticated quadruped robot moving about an obstacle course with unprecedented speed, strength, and agility.

"Looks promising." Demeter downplayed his excitement. "You said 'acquisition.' Why spend billions to acquire the company when we can simply steal the plans and build it ourselves?"

The woman answered immediately. "Because we need the people who make the tech to make the tech work for us."

Demeter thrust his chin toward Avinash. "Is that not what he is here to do?"

Avinash snorted. "I'm a hacker, dude. I write code and scripts. I'm no engineer."

The woman walked toward the laptop on the desk and gestured toward it. "Avinash will help us catch another kind of prey. Bring up the profiles I asked you to locate."

The young man began typing on the laptop's keyboard. The screen flashed, and images appeared. Demeter grunted upon recognizing the individuals in the pictures.

"Finding information on most of these people was quick and dirty. These two," Avinash said, using his mouse to move the cursor over the faces of two men, "are successful Grand Prix motorcycle racers. The Innocenti brothers. Their family is absolutely loaded. Mommy is some super-wealthy Italian high society type. She owns a bunch of swank hotels, resorts, cruise liners, and a collection of ugly but expensive paintings. All the people you told me to find are beyond rich. Like the 'I-use-ten-thousand-dollar-bills-as-toilet-paper' kinda rich."

The woman turned her face up to look at Demeter. "Any chance with the brothers or their mother?"

He shook his head. "Not likely. Carla, I'm sure, is as recalcitrant as ever. Age reinforces such traits, not diminishes them. The boys, I understand, take after both her and their dead father. They're full of preposterous notions about nobility and honor. On the other hand, their very public personas and dangerous vocation present other opportunities."

She nodded, seemingly satisfied. "Agreed."

They ran through the list of other targets, evaluating the risks and opportunities until only one remained. Demeter pointed at the final image on the screen: a portrait of a distinguished-looking gentleman in his sixties or seventies. Demeter's mouth twisted into a sneer. "What of my old friend here?"

"Same MO as the others," Avinash explained. "Wealthy? Check. Influential? Check. Another interesting tidbit. He's been missing from public life for at least ten years."

"Do you know where he's been hiding, urchin?"

Avinash blinked a few times at the insult, then shrugged. "Yeah. Some little nowhere town called Bethel."

1

WHEN THE WIND IS IN THE EAST

Robbie Noble squirmed in his chair, wishing he were anywhere else. Girlish giggles and hushed sighs traveled up and down the rows of seats inside the gymnasium at St. Boniface Catholic High School. Most of the student body, from freshmen to seniors, regarded the action on stage with keen interest. Teachers stood like sentries with backs against walls, eyes roving over the hundreds of students assembled to watch the spectacle. Despite the dim lighting, Robbie noticed that some of the teachers were more attentive to the action on the stage than the potential mischief among the students seated throughout the large auditorium.

What sounded like a cat-call from one of the female students closer to the stage brought Robbie's head around again. For all the impressive set designs, costumes, and other student actors on the stage, one figure held the crowd's rapt attention. Drake Gallant—honors student, captain of the football team, and most popular senior in school—sat on a stage riser wearing a tight white T-shirt and blue jeans. He expertly strummed an acoustic guitar in a soft, haunting melody. Then he began to sing. The audience murmured as Gallant's voice complemented the stringed instrument perfectly.

"Ah, c'mon," Artie Rutherford scoffed beside Robbie. "He can sing and play guitar, too?"

A loud shush came from Ms. O'Reilly, who leaned against the wall to the boys' right. She glared at them until they returned their attention to the stage. Artie settled into his chair, but not before quietly uttering another thought.

"Drake won all the events at the genetic Olympics."

Robbie shot his friend a hard look to shut him up. Artie responded with a shrug. Besides his short stature, curly reddish-blond hair, and freckles, Artie was most famous around the school for his unlimited supply of signed permission slips that excused him from school-organized physical activities. Artie and Gallant existed at opposite ends of the physical specimen spectrum. Robbie was somewhere in the middle. Not tall. Not short. Somewhat broad-shouldered but skinny with a mop of almost-black hair.

Whispering swept through the audience as the black-painted door on the left side of the stage opened, and *she* emerged. Blake Brooks, the first sophomore ever to land the coveted starring role in a St. Boniface stage production. This year, Mr. Elam, the drama teacher, had adapted the ancient Greek myth of *Eurydice and Orpheus*. Blake, tall and stunning, her golden blonde hair pulled back into a long, tight braid, wore a wispy, spaghetti-strap white dress that flowed down to her knees. Barefoot, she made her way onto the stage. Each step emphasized her litheness and athleticism. Tentatively, her version of Eurydice stopped before Gallant's seated rendition of Orpheus. Gallant's singing faded, and he lowered his guitar. A hush hung over the auditorium. Robbie knew this scene from reading the story in class. It was meant to dramatize the lovers' first meeting in the underworld after Eurydice's untimely death. Robbie grabbed at the sudden discomfort in his stomach and willed himself to look away, but he failed.

Blake reached out and clutched the head of her stage husband to her abdomen. When Gallant cried out, the audience let out a collective gasp. Blake collapsed over Gallant's head, running her hands down his chiseled back, then dragged them back up again. Gallant stood, holding Blake in his muscular arms without strain or effort.

Robbie slumped back in his chair and looked up at the ceiling. Artie patted his shoulder sympathetically. The play continued for another thirty-five excruciating minutes. Blake flowed across the stage, graceful and lyrical like a ballad come to life, while Gallant stomped about like a drunken professional wrestler. Robbie looked at the girl sitting to his left to validate his internalized review of Gallant's performance. He was disappointed. She sat on the edge of her seat with pursed lips and softly fluttering eyes.

Is she swooning?

The play progressed toward its fateful final scene. Spotlights tracked the two leads. Gallant walked toward a white door at the opposite end of the stage meant to represent passage out of the underworld. Blake followed, but much more slowly. In the story, the god of the dead placed a single prohibition on Orpheus. He mustn't turn back to look at Eurydice until they reach the surface. Gallant arrived at the door but did not exit. His deep voice rang out through the silent auditorium. "Eurydice? Eurydice, where are you?"

Blake continued forward, moving between the large props on the stage, seemingly unaware that her lover called out to her. She was two steps behind him. Recognizing her imminent return to light and life and freedom, tears fell from her eyes, and her mouth formed into a joyful smile. She reached out to touch Gallant.

"Am I deceived?" Gallant asked, then turned to look for Blake. Their eyes met, and they shared a sharply inhaled breath.

A pause. The audience watched, transfixed. No one moved. No one made a sound.

"My love," Blake whispered.

The two spotlights winked out. A moment passed, and a single spotlight returned. Gallant held Blake once more, but her body was limp and lifeless. He fell to his knees. "Noooooo!"

The spotlight faded until the stage went dark. Several seconds later, the audience erupted into whooping and loud applause.

After the curtain call, Robbie remained in his chair as the noisy exodus from the auditorium began. Artie gave him a light shove to knock him out of his stupor.

"I love half-day assemblies, even when I'm forced to sit through another pubescent melodramatic slaughter of a classic."

Robbie didn't answer.

"C'mon, Robbie. Father Flynn awaits. We're finishing the section on heraldic orders. History may not always be the most interesting subject, but learning about all those knights is pretty cool."

"You go on ahead without me, Artie. I'm gonna stick around for a few minutes."

His friend rolled his eyes. "*Mein freund!* No point getting all sad and mopey because the prettiest girl in school has eyes for the letter jacket–wearing jock."

Robbie sighed. "Blake isn't just pretty."

Artie nodded. "I know, man. She's awesome—literally,

one of the nicest and smartest and funniest people in the world. You gotta admit, though. She and Drake make a good couple."

Robbie's eyes narrowed at the comment.

Artie laughed. "I'm just goading you. Don't make it so easy. I'll tell the good padre you're helping stack the chairs. Later, Roberto."

A commotion sounded from the stage. Robbie turned to see Blake in conversation with a group of her girlfriends. They tittered and whispered about her 'hot scene' with Gallant. Robbie rolled his eyes and tried not to listen.

"You and Drake have so much chemistry!" Blake's best friend, Valeria Anaya, looked at Robbie as she made the pronouncement.

The gnawing in the pit of his stomach intensified. He wasn't sure if the nausea was a byproduct of standing so close to Valeria and her overpowering floral perfume or because she described Blake and Gallant's intimate reunion scene. He ignored both the comment and the commenter.

"Robbie!"

Blake rushed over and hugged him. They looked at each other through brown eyes, hers light, his dark.

"Hey, Blake. Your performance was great today."

"You think so? I know you're not a fan of this story."

"Well, what can I say? The play is about a guy who condemns his wife to eternal damnation because he can't remember basic instructions. Don't. Turn. Around. Orpheus!"

His comment set off an angry response from Valeria. "You're so dumb, Robbie. You don't get the play because you're still a little boy."

Robbie looked at his only nemesis. Her perfectly blown-dry, long brown hair fell halfway down her back. Her dark eyes and brown skin could have graced a thousand fashion magazines. Physically, she was beautiful, but spite and pettiness twisted her malformed soul. Robbie, Blake, and Valeria had known each other since first grade. Valeria had turned hostile toward him when they started high school for reasons that remained unknown to Robbie.

"It's okay, Val." Blake smiled and laughed nervously, clearly trying to disarm the tension between her two friends. "When you think about it, Robbie's not wrong."

His face flushed with embarrassment as Blake spoke up in his defense. He appreciated her intention, but it often fueled Valeria's attacks even more.

Robbie replied to Valeria without looking at her. "Are you disappointed you couldn't livestream your reaction to the play for all your followers? The whole school knows how desperately you crave those likes."

His retort must have struck a nerve, as Valeria made a crude gesture with her right hand, which prompted a loud reaction from Ms. Fortier, one of the school's two vice principals. Ms. Fortier's eagle eyes had witnessed Valeria's response to Robbie's insult.

"Ms. Anaya, St. Boniface has a long and proud tradition of producing proper young women and men who do not resort to such undignified expressions. You will go to class immediately and see me after school to discuss your detention."

"But I have cheerleader practice—"

The vice principal cut off Valeria's protests. "Enough, Ms. Anaya. My classroom, at three thirty sharp."

Valeria snatched her bag—an ugly, multicolor monstrosity she had undoubtedly photographed and shared on social media—from the chair beside her, shot a death stare at Robbie, and stormed out of the auditorium.

Ms. Fortier looked expectantly at Robbie. "Well, Mr. Noble? Don't you have a class to attend?"

"I'm helping with the chairs," he answered.

She looked at him through narrowed eyes before nodding. "Hurry up, then go straight to class."

Some students loitering near the stage seemed to catch Ms. Fortier's attention. She headed off to intercept them.

Blake tilted her head to the side in a disapproving look. He shrugged and tried to look innocent. Then she smiled.

"Come on, Robbie, Valeria's a good person. The three of us were inseparable. I've never figured out why the two of you stopped getting along. It's lonely, playing the peacekeeper to your two best friends."

"I didn't come to talk about Valeria. I just came to say that you did a good job."

Blake's laugh was warm and melodic. "Robbie Noble, you are such a terrible liar! I can't imagine how much you hated the play."

She was right. He had hated it. But not because of her.

"Hey, Blake," came a deep, booming voice from the stage.

Robbie cringed. "Annnnnd cue the oafish halfwit."

Blake gave Robbie another disapproving look—a real one this time. Gallant approached them but didn't spare Robbie a glance. The play's co-lead towered over them both. His damn T-shirt showed off every bulge and ripple on his chest, arms, and shoulders. How could anyone compete against a human growth hormone like Gallant?

"Think we can practice that reunion scene again before tomorrow night's big performance?" Gallant smiled coyly, waiting for Blake's reply.

"Oh, Drake, enough," Blake chastised, but her smile

suggested she wasn't upset. "You know we don't need to practice that scene anymore."

Blake glanced at Robbie, her cheeks crimson. He wanted to vomit all over Gallant's big, stupid muscles.

"We can never practice too much." Gallant smiled again, then turned and walked away.

"Sorry, Robbie. The cast is meeting to discuss the performance. I'll see you later."

She disappeared behind the stage curtain, and Robbie was left to help clean the auditorium.

2

THE STORM STRENGTHENS

Robbie rode his mountain bike west, through the center of town and into the sun as it blazed its unstoppable path toward the horizon. The journey from St. Boniface High School to the Feist Reference Library took him thirty minutes. He crested over the next hill, and part of the library came into view directly before him. The building's dark stone columns and deeply shadowed arches stood resolute against the clear blue sky. A peculiar structure, the library was one of the oldest and largest buildings in Bethel. Thanks to its incongruous gothic architecture and mysterious history, it remained a popular subject of speculation and conspiracy theories among the locals.

He cruised into the sparsely populated parking lot and locked his bike outside the central hex. The three-story library consisted of five hexagonal buildings linked together by long corridors, with the central hex designated as the hub of the spoked wheel. He climbed the stairs to the entrance and pushed through the metal-latticed wooden doors. He entered the large atrium and approached the beautifully ornate rosewood reference desk. Bas-relief carvings along each side of the desk depicted a different library from history.

Robbie scanned the two staircases on opposite sides of the atrium that led to the other floors and determined from the lack of activity that he'd likely finish his shift early tonight. Besides the desk and the staircases, the rest of the space was filled with study tables and massive X-shaped shelves containing reference books, including encyclopedias, atlases, and dictionaries, some dating back at least a hundred years. The library boasted an extensive collection of nonfiction books in the northern hex, while the eastern hex contained fiction. The western hex housed a secure storage area for special collections, a sophisticated restoration room for book repairs, and the administration offices. Dozens of individual computer stations were situated in the southern hex.

Mr. Breton stood behind the reference desk, talking to a patron. The librarian pointed to the eastern hex. The patron nodded and left, presumably to find whatever book she sought. William Breton was a tall, powerfully built man with a full head of gray-and-black hair and a neatly trimmed beard. As always, he wore a dark suit. Today, it was navy blue. Robbie received a warm smile as he approached the desk.

"How was school today?" Mr. Breton always asked him about school. He seemed almost as interested in Robbie's grades as his parents were.

Robbie shrugged. "I sat through a dress rehearsal of this year's drama production."

"Ah, yes. *Eurydice and Orpheus*, correct? Truly, a classic."

"It was classic something," Robbie uttered unenthusiastically.

The librarian smiled slightly but didn't press any further.

"Did the elementary school kids come for their field trip?" Robbie inquired, hoping they hadn't. Their visits usually resulted in a huge mess for him to clean.

"They did indeed. The school buses whisked them away thirty minutes ago."

Robbie sighed.

So much for leaving early.

"How bad is it?" he asked.

"Disorder and destruction on a scale unprecedented." Mr. Breton smiled and laughed, enjoying his joke too much for Robbie's liking.

"Great," Robbie responded sarcastically. "Who else is working tonight?"

"Ms. Stevens requested the day off, and Shawn called this morning to inform me that he felt unwell."

Robbie groaned. "I better get started."

The librarian nodded and spread his hands. "Alas, this is why I pay you such riches, isn't it?"

"Riches? Mr. Breton, you don't even pay me minimum wage."

"I don't? Is that legal?"

"You pay me a student wage," Robbie replied flatly.

"Ah, yes. You're a student, after all. Fortunately for you, Mrs. Davis stayed behind to help tidy. Off you go. Everything has a place, and every place has a thing."

Robbie rolled his eyes at the comment. He had certainly heard Mr. Breton say it enough over the years.

"I'm pretty sure you're wrong about that, Mr. Breton."

"It's a worthy debate for another time, Robbie."

The librarian turned to help a visitor who approached the opposite side of the reference desk. Robbie recognized her as one of the library's semi-regular patrons. The woman appeared to be in her late twenties and dressed in a long skirt and blazer. Robbie wondered if her perpetual sternness was a performance to convince Mr. Breton to hire her as an assistant. She was pursuing a postgrad degree at the nearby university and frequented the Feist for its extensive rare book collection.

Robbie headed for the West hex. He doffed his school dress shirt in the washroom and replaced it with a plain white polo from his backpack. He didn't bother changing his pants. Mr. Breton preferred that library staff wore collared shirts and frowned whenever he saw a pair of blue jeans. Robbie had swapped out his black dress shoes for a pair of white sneakers before he left school. He hated riding his bike in dress shoes. Finally, he went to the staff room on the second floor of the West hex to stow his backpack and helmet and call his mom.

"Hey, Mom. I'm at work."

"Hi, kiddo. How was school today? I heard the dress rehearsal was amazing!"

He took a deep breath before answering. "School was fine. The play was fine."

"So, everything is fine?" He heard the teasing tone in her voice. "What time will you be home tonight?"

"Mr. Breton and I are the only ones here, so I won't be home until around nine."

"Okay, well, call before you leave so we don't worry. Wear your helmet and make sure the lights on your bike are working. Ride safely, okay? No trails at night, Robbie."

"You know, Mom, I'd be much safer riding home in the dark if I had a cell phone. I can even pay for it myself."

"Uh-huh. *Maybe* when you turn sixteen. The money you're making is to pay for college, not so you can text your friends, play video games, and watch videos all day instead of doing homework."

Robbie sighed. Arguing with his parents about this topic was futile.

"We love you, kiddo. Don't forget to remind William about dinner at our house this weekend."

"Sure thing, Mom. I love you, too. Bye."

Mr. Breton had no family of his own and was like a grandfather to Robbie. He visited the Nobles' home a few times every month to play chess with Robbie's mom, and he had an open invitation to holiday dinners. Robbie's mom said that the librarian reminded her of her late father, who passed away when she was a teenager.

He left the staffroom and rode the elevator to the third floor of the West hex. Robbie cursed when he saw the state of the open reading area customarily reserved for elementary school outings. Dozens of children's books littered the floor, tables, and desks. Scrap paper was strewn from one end of the area to the other.

He found Mrs. Davis loading books onto a cart. She had taught Robbie in third grade. He now stood several inches taller than the bespectacled teacher.

"Hi, Mrs. Davis."

She smiled brightly when she recognized him. "Oh, hello, Robbie. I have tried to clean up after the kids, but I'm sure I failed to meet Mr. Breton's standards. He's a rather meticulous man."

"It looks great, Mrs. Davis," Robbie lied, wondering if

she needed new eyeglasses. "Thank you. I'll take over from here."

"I hope this job isn't interfering with your studies."

He shook his head. "It's not. My parents make sure of that. Besides, I enjoy working here. It's usually pretty quiet, and I like the smell of old books."

She left soon after, and Robbie continued sorting and stacking.

He returned to the staffroom a few hours later to eat the dinner his dad had packed for him that morning. While rifling through his backpack, he remembered eating the meal before last period.

"Ah, c'mon," he muttered to the empty room.

Confident that his book stacking was ahead of schedule, especially now that the library was closed, Robbie considered riding his bike to the coffee shop down the street for a quick sandwich.

Boom.

A sound echoed through the building, rattling windowpanes and causing him to jump. Then the power went out. The library fell into darkness except for the battery-powered emergency lights near the doorways and the muted twilight from the setting sun that filtered through the windows. Robbie picked up the staffroom phone and dialed the extension for the front desk. The phone was dead. He needed to find Mr. Breton, and the best place to look was the central hex.

Robbie moved unhurriedly down the stairs and through the perfectly silent corridors. Navigating the building in near darkness was a new experience, however. Robbie passed a series of windows with a decent view of Bethel. He thought it strange that the shops and traffic lights in the distance had not lost power.

He heard voices as he approached the central hex and stopped outside the doorway. Though dusk was giving way to night, Robbie could make out two figures conversing inside the entrance to the library. One of the men was Mr. Breton. The other man was almost a giant. The stranger was even taller and much broader than Mr. Breton, who was a large man in his own right.

Robbie hesitated at the edge of the room, uncertain about interrupting their conversation. He was sure that the two men hadn't seen him yet. He nervously bit his lower lip, contemplating whether to wait for an opportunity to catch Mr. Breton's attention or return to the staff room. He chose to wait for the librarian instead of heading back through the darkening corridors.

"The intervening years and this quaint town have treated you kindly." The stranger spoke in a deep voice with an accent that Robbie couldn't identify. The librarian didn't respond. Instead, he watched the man through narrowed eyes.

"Imagine my surprise when I learned you had chosen to live among these peasants, pretending you are a benevolent, old librarian. It's brilliant, in a way. And these simpletons are unaware of your true station."

"You should not be here, Andars." Mr. Breton spoke with an imperious tone Robbie hadn't heard from him before.

The stranger, Andars, walked further inside the library and stopped beneath a slant of dim light from a window. Robbie saw him properly for the first time. He was bald and looked younger than the librarian, though his age was hard to judge at this distance. Angry red scars and a noticeably asymmetrical bone structure marked his face. Like Mr. Breton, Andars was impeccably dressed in a dark suit and tie. He carried a lacquered cane in his left hand, though *cane* was insufficient to describe the object, which was almost as tall as Robbie and the diameter of a thick stairway baluster. With each step, he thumped his walking stick on the marble, creating reverberations that echoed loudly through the air. Robbie jumped at each impact. Peering around the doorframe, Robbie noted that the man did not walk with a limp.

Why carry a cane if you don't need one?

"No interest in exchanging pleasantries? How discourteous of you." Andars made a show of looking around the library. "Hiding it here was bold. I give you that. My father would not have appreciated the irony, however."

The man's sharp, mirthless laugh cut through the silence of the nearly empty library. "He despised old man Feist. Was that why you chose this place? Another way to denigrate my father, even as his bones rot beneath Son Doong? One more affront to my House."

The librarian stood tall, unmoving. His voice was steady. "Leave now, and the treaty is preserved."

Andars walked toward the reference desk.

Thump, thump, thump.

"Treaty! Indeed. Modeled after Versailles, correct? Except we all know how that turned out, don't we."

Silent, Mr. Breton returned the man's gaze.

Andars would not relent. "Implacable as always, despite your vaunted secrets revealed by the harsh light of truth. Give me the scroll, and I will leave. Simple and bloodless."

A broad, garish smile split the huge man's face. "I see that you've unencumbered yourself of your cane. I understand that the Rosewood has made many advancements since the massacre."

Demeter frowned suddenly, and a look of insincere

concern transformed his face. "Oh, did you forget your phone, Breton?"

Robbie was more than passingly confused by their dialogue, but this last question seemed especially incongruous. Mr. Breton's jaw appeared to slacken at the comment. The stranger made a show of checking a large gold watch affixed to his left wrist.

"While I'm disappointed you won't accept my offer, I'm not surprised. I want to say this has been fun. Though, not in the way of two old friends seeing each other after many years."

The man walked to the door but turned before exiting. His gaze lingered on Mr. Breton a few seconds longer before he spoke again. "You know the problem with getting older, Breton? All that supposed wisdom we acquire is for naught if we can't adjust to the modern world."

As soon as he left, the librarian closed the door and secured the locks with an emphatic slam, betraying his unease.

"Robbie," Mr. Breton called with a tone that startled him. Although the librarian's voice was composed, it contained an undercurrent of tension that sent a chill up Robbie's spine. "Get out of here. Take the emergency exit."

He returned to the reference desk, disappearing beneath the counter momentarily. Robbie remained rooted to the floor, his heart racing. When Mr. Breton reappeared, he gripped the steel crowbar they kept behind the desk for prying open the atrium's stubborn metal window frames.

"What's going on?" Robbie asked.

"You need to go. Now!"

The librarian's vehemence frightened him. Mr. Breton picked up the desk phone, listened briefly, and then slammed it down.

"Foolish old man." Though he spoke quietly to himself, the words were loud enough for Robbie to hear.

Something heavy hammered into the door from the outside, sending dust into the air. Robbie and Mr. Breton braced themselves at the sounds of each impact. The door held against the first and second assaults, but the third snapped the hinges off the frame. The wood blew inward, and Robbie watched as a midnight-black four-legged creature bounded into the building. Larger than a full-grown German shepherd, it swung its head from left to right and back again, scanning the atrium. Its glowing red eyes settled on Mr. Breton.

Then it pounced.

"Go!" Mr. Breton shouted.

Robbie sprinted down the west hex corridor, fueled by adrenaline and terror. He arrived at the administration hallway, the emergency lights providing just enough illumination to guide him safely past the stairs, elevators, and two closed doors directly across from each other. The door on the left led to Mr. Breton's office, while the door on the right led to a storage room.

Robbie ran until he reached the short hallway that housed the emergency exit. He stepped forward, then quickly shrank back as something clawlike tore through the fire door from the other side.

No exit!

His heart hammered in his chest as a wave of panic consumed him. He retreated hastily down the hallway, wondering if he should return to the central hex. Mr. Breton's distant cry helped him decide.

I need to hide.

Robbie returned to the section of the administration hallway with the two doors across from each other. He tried the storage room first, only to find it locked. He crossed the hall and tried the other door. It clicked open, and he rushed inside. He locked the door behind him. A large window at the opposite end of Mr. Breton's office cast subtle shadows around the dark room. A neatly organized desk sat beneath the window, and wooden bookshelves lined the walls to either side of the desk. On the left side of the room, the librarian's huge gold and lapis globe glinted faintly in the dimness. Robbie hid behind the desk. He strained to hear noises from the hallway over his own heavy breathing.

He didn't wait long. The door handle rattled loudly. He shut his eyes and tried to quiet his ragged breaths. The rattling continued.

A quiet mumbling came from behind the closed door. "My keys—"

Robbie recognized the librarian's voice.

What do I do?

He knew he couldn't leave Mr. Breton in the hallway with whatever nightmares stalked the library. Robbie willed himself to cross the floor.

"Mr. Breton?" he whispered through the door.

"Robbie?"

The librarian sounded surprised, and something else, too. Robbie unlocked the latch, and Mr. Breton stumbled into the office. Robbie caught the man before he fell. After steadying the librarian, his hands came away wet and tacky, and a distinct metallic scent filled the air. He glanced at his hands and realized they were smeared with blood.

"You're bleeding!"

The staccato rhythm of metal charging across the marble floor was almost too quick to process. Something struck Robbie from behind, slamming him to the ground. The impact drove the air from his lungs, though he managed to turn over onto his back to see his attacker. His senses shifted away from the blossoming pain to focus on the creature that leaped at him a second time. He cried out as its two front limbs crashed into his shoulders. Robbie tried to move, but the four-legged creature pinned him down.

He stared into the face of a mechanical beast, unlike anything he had seen before. Its head was hard angles and black metal. In place of eyes, it looked at him through a half-dozen lenses of differing sizes placed symmetrically on its head. A reddish light pulsed ominously at the center of each eye cluster. Its broad barrel chest tapered back along the perfectly machined lines of its matte-black body toward a whiplike tail that lashed the air. The creature resembled a large cat, like a cheetah, rather than a big dog.

It raised its muzzle a few inches from Robbie's face. The black teeth were long and razor-sharp. The joints that affixed the jaw to the head were massive. Its mouth was large enough to crush a human head. The machine predator did not growl or breathe, but the whirr and whine of motors accompanied each movement.

Robbie grasped the legs that held him down. They were cold, metallic, and skeletal, like bones without muscle and flesh. The joints between the limb segments felt smooth. Robbie pushed against the metal beast but to no avail. He failed even to shift its weight. He gasped for air, partially due to fear but mainly because the creature restricted his lungs' capacity to draw breath.

Mr. Breton stepped forward and drove the crowbar like a spear into the metal beast's eye cluster. The improvised weapon sank deep into its head until it jammed. For the briefest moment, Mr. Breton loomed over Robbie and the beast like an injured avenging god. One arm, torn and bleeding, hung limply by his side while the other gripped the crowbar and pushed. Robbie saw the blazing firestorm of anger kindled behind the man's eyes as he forced the large metallic cat backward. The beast reared, and its tail lashed at the librarian before it toppled onto its side. It stopped flailing a moment later.

Robbie scrambled to his feet, and Mr. Breton crumpled to the floor.

3

SLEEP ON WITH NO FEAR

"Help me up," Mr. Breton wheezed.

The librarian struggled to stand. The blood on the floor made it difficult for his feet to find purchase. He gripped Robbie's shoulder with his uninjured hand and stood slowly. Robbie guided him to the desk, and Mr. Breton fell hard into the chair.

"Your arm," Robbie rasped. "So much blood—"

"I told you to leave," the librarian grunted.

Robbie shook his head. "I tried. That thing came through the fire door."

Mr. Breton looked pale and swayed unsteadily in the chair. Robbie's hands shook while he helped the older man remain upright.

"What's going on?" The tremble in Robbie's voice matched his shaking hands.

Mr. Breton ignored the question. "We need to get downstairs."

Downstairs? But we're on the first floor, and the library doesn't have a basement.

Robbie tried to say as much. "Um, Mr. Breton—"

"Check the bottom drawer of the desk."

Robbie complied, and he drew out a small first aid kit.

Everything has a place, and every place has a thing.

"Wrap my wrist and forearm with gauze, then bandage it as tightly as you can. I think that— thing nicked an artery. I feel lightheaded. No, don't bother with the antiseptic. We have to move quickly."

Robbie carefully removed the librarian's suit jacket, starting with the sleeve of his uninjured arm. He forced himself not to cover his mouth as he peeled the jacket off the other arm. One side of Mr. Breton's white dress shirt was saturated with blood, and torn strips of fabric were all that remained of his shirt sleeve. Blood trickled down in dense rivulets over his lacerated forearm and hand and onto the floor. Robbie gagged but managed to swallow the mouthful of bile before he wretched.

"The gauze," prompted the librarian.

Robbie shuddered and then did as Mr. Breton instructed. He dressed the wound in near darkness, which turned out to be a blessing. The librarian cried out and clenched his other hand into a tight fist. The rest of his body began to shake, but he managed to keep his arm still enough for Robbie to wrap the arm.

"It will have to do," he said through gritted teeth once Robbie finished dressing the vicious wound.

"Mr. Breton, what's going on? What are those things?" The words tumbled out of Robbie's mouth in a rush.

"Not now."

"We need to call the police!"

As the librarian tried to stand, he stumbled and fell to one knee. He grunted in pain, then climbed back to his feet. He limped to the ornate globe and did something out of

Robbie's view. A loud click sounded, and a section of the bookshelf swung open, revealing a hidden alcove.

Robbie didn't have time to marvel at the newly revealed doorway. His heart stopped at the sound of metal scratching against marble from somewhere outside the office.

"Come," Mr. Breton said, breathless from the exertion of walking. "The bookshelf is unlikely to buy us much time."

Once Robbie closed the bookshelf door behind him, the alcove was plunged into total darkness.

"Stairs in the floor." Mr. Breton's breathing became louder and more ragged. "You go ... first."

Despite his terror at the prospect of facing another machine cat or the giant man from the atrium, Robbie knew the librarian couldn't make it down the stairs on his own. He had to help him. "Together," Robbie whispered.

He closed his eyes and exhaled, then felt around until he found an opening in the floor. He slung the librarian's good arm across his shoulders. They began their descent into the floor of the library.

"How far?" Robbie asked, straining to keep the large man upright.

"Not close."

One foot after another, around and around the spiral stairway, without end. The suffocating darkness pressed in on Robbie, and the scratching sounds from above seemed louder. His legs felt like jelly. A painful cramp began to form just beneath his ribs. The librarian's disembodied voice distracted him a little from the pain.

"I am sorry. I hoped that maybe Lauren— someone to succeed me." Mr. Breton sounded regretful and strange, almost like he was far away.

"Lauren? You mean my mom?" Robbie asked.

"More like a family to me than my daughter, though

Elizabeth is not to blame. She never forgave me for her mother's death."

Robbie realized that the librarian wasn't speaking to him. The sentences came in fits and starts, the previous thought disjointed from the next.

"I thought I had more time. Imagine that. Almost seventy, and I thought I had more time. Undone by hubris. I should have seen this coming. It has ever been my job to prepare for this moment."

"I think I see light below," Robbie said, relieved by the sight as he led the librarian around the final turn of the spiral.

Assisting Mr. Breton, Robbie guided him down the last step, and together, they ventured into a dark hallway illuminated by a light in the distance. The temperature was noticeably cooler than upstairs, and the chill seemed to intensify with each passing step.

Several paces later, they passed beneath a stone archway and stepped into a room of indeterminate size and shape. Except for a small area lit by a single light source, the rest of the space was shrouded in darkness. At the center of the lit area sat a beautiful wooden reading desk and a matching leather chair atop a rug woven in threads of red and gold. A leather messenger bag was slung over one side of the chair. Illumination came from a banker's lamp on the desk's back edge.

"My phone, Robbie. On the desk. Hurry."

Slowly, he disentangled from Mr. Breton's arm and ran over to the desk.

At its center, he found a gold fountain pen. Some type of artifact – a thin, footlong silvery rod – sat near the top of the desk. Above the artifact was a letter opener with a reddish wooden handle. To the left of the pen, a handheld magnifying glass rested atop a partially unrolled scroll made of some kind of yellow paper. The top and bottom of the scroll were wrapped around elaborately carved wooden spindles. The scroll contained strange pictograms or characters drawn in black ink that made him think of the Egyptian hieroglyphs he'd seen in history class. Opposite the scroll, to the right of the pen, sat a sleek black smartphone, reflecting the light from the banker's lamp. He grabbed the device and spun around to return to the librarian, but Mr. Breton had reached the desk on his own.

The light of the desk lamp revealed the librarian's deathly pale visage and sweat-soaked brow. The bandages on Mr. Breton's arm had turned from white to dark red.

"You need a doctor! A hospital!" Robbie shouted desperately.

"The phone, Robbie."

He handed Mr. Breton the device, and it lit up immediately.

"Initiate emergency protocol message to the other Knights of Rosewood."

A female voice responded to Mr. Breton's voice command. "Biometric authentication confirmed. What is your message, William?"

"Demeter has come for the scroll. I require immediate assistance."

"Message sent," the phone voice stated.

"ETA on a tactical response?"

"Unknown."

"Isa, estimate the fastest arrival time based on location as the sole parameter."

"Drake Gallant is nineteen minutes away."

Robbie's eyes widened in surprise, his mind reeling. "What? Did it say Gallant?"

The librarian continued his conversation with the incorporeal voice of the smartphone.

"No, Isa. He cannot handle Demeter alone."

"I'm sorry, William. I have dispatched the message. Hamza Elsayed can be here in twenty-six minutes through the Junction."

"That's too long."

Mr. Breton's rapid breathing drew Robbie's attention. He gestured toward the phone in the librarian's hand.

No way the phone has reception down here, but we have to try.

"We need to call the police."

The librarian shook his head.

"This matter is not for the police. Isa, what are my vitals?"

"Your right forearm has multiple compound and comminuted fractures and lacerations. You have two fractured ribs. You've lost 29 percent of your blood volume and have entered hypovolemic shock. You will lose consciousness soon."

The phone voice stopped and then spoke again in a slightly different tone. It sounded almost human. "William, you're dying."

The final word hung in the air of that strange, surreal space. Robbie sat down on the floor and shut his eyes, overwhelmed by the fear and the adrenaline. He wrapped his arms around himself and tried to stop his body from shaking. So much had happened. Parts of his brain were picking up the second-by-second details. But none of it seemed real. He felt tiny and insignificant, entirely at the mercy of larger forces around him. He was powerless. Robbie heard Mr. Breton talking to the phone, but the words didn't make sense.

"Isa, estimate how long it will take us to reach the Station in my condition."

"Without adequate medical intervention, which is unlikely, you will bleed to death before you reach the Station."

He grunted. "I need you to give Robbie access to my kit."

"I'm sorry, William. I can't do that."

"Why not?"

"No protocol currently exists to provide a non-member of the order access to—"

"Dammit, Isa. In five minutes, Andars Demeter and his pets will come down those steps and take the scroll. They will cut down anyone in their path to do it. In my state, I cannot stop them. But with my kit, Robbie may survive."

"I cannot do that, William."

Breton glared at the phone as though he spoke to a real person. "By my authority, I make Robbie a Knight of Rosewood and give him immediate access to my kit."

"I'm sorry, William. He's an outsider. Making him a knight requires majority consent of the Conventus."

The librarian growled. As if to emphasize his frustration and urgency, a loud crash echoed down the spiral staircase.

"I need a way, Isa. We are out of time. Help me."

"William, you have sole authority to name the heir to your own house. By king's decree, your heir is a Knight of Rosewood."

The librarian's face contorted into anger. "Robbie will die because of a four-hundred-year-old rule!" He was shouting now, and his voice was full of both anger and despair.

Robbie's blood froze in his veins. "I don't want to die," he whispered.

Mr. Breton didn't seem to hear him. His expression

turned thoughtful. "I have no heir—" he said, his tone a mixture of hope and regret. "It's a loophole, isn't it? Isa, you brilliant, terrifying machine. A loophole that will be contested if the boy lives. But live he may."

"Yes, William," the voice replied gently.

Robbie watched as the jaw muscles in Mr. Breton's face relaxed. The librarian was quiet for a time. He regarded Robbie intently.

"You're a good boy, Robbie. Smart, curious, and trustworthy. Your parents are wonderful people. Ironically, this is not the first time I considered your family." He inhaled loudly, trying to catch his breath. "I ... I thought I had more time."

The librarian's downcast eyes struck Robbie as immeasurably sad.

"I don't understand, Mr. Breton."

"No, Robbie. But you will one day, I hope."

With great effort, the librarian stood to his full height. He slipped the phone into his pocket.

"We don't have time for the usual ceremony, I'm afraid."

Mr. Breton moved his uninjured hand across his body and toward his hip. Next, he closed his fingers as if to grasp the air. When he pulled his arm back, something extraordinary happened. An object coalesced from nothing, taking the shape of a long blade, a hilt, and a cross-guard, all composed of dark, swirling colors. Black, azure, and deep purples swam together within the solidifying lines of a shape that resembled a sword. Robbie was transfixed, and their present circumstances were temporarily forgotten, superseded by curiosity and awe. When Mr. Breton moved the sword, the blade left a momentary impression in the air wherever it passed. He held the sword horizontally between them.

"Robert Noble, I charge you with a great responsibility, passed down to me from my father, as it was passed down to him by his father and so on. Do you willingly accept this honor, this burden, with all its attendant sacrifices, to uphold the oaths of the Knights of Rosewood from now till the end of your days, understanding that the consequence of breaking your oath is death?"

The sword's enchantment over Robbie broke. Overwhelmed, his mind splintered into a thousand fragments at once as he tried to make sense of the librarian's senseless words.

What is going on here? How can I agree to this? What sacrifices?

Mr. Breton's legs buckled. The librarian stumbled forward but caught himself at the last moment and barely remained on his feet. Robbie could not deny this man who was so much like a grandfather to him.

"How? What do I say?" he asked uncertainly.

Robbie's words seemed to alleviate some of Mr. Breton's distress.

"Grip the blade of the sword and agree to the oath."

Mr. Breton used the desk to steady himself, then lifted the blade tip off the floor and returned it to the horizontal position between them. Robbie gripped the swirling blade of dark light carefully. It felt solid and dense. A slow, pulsing warmth spread into his hand. Wisps of what looked like black smoke seeped through his fingers and dissolved into the air. The librarian looked at him through heavily lidded eyes.

"I do. I agree," Robbie declared.

"Sealed in blood," Mr. Breton whispered. Then his voice rose. "Isa, on my authority as the head of House Breton, last of my name, I declare that Robbie is my heir in the Knights of Rosewood. Upon my death, he is to assume all privileges and responsibilities. Grant him full access to my phone and kit."

Isa responded immediately. "It's done, William."

The sword vanished, leaving the briefest afterimage in its wake. The librarian exhaled and allowed himself to fall into the leather desk chair. Robbie looked down at his own hands and saw thin lines of blood running across his fingers where he had gripped the blade. Mr. Breton took a few ragged breaths, then placed the phone back on the desk. He laughed. The sound was dry and hoarse. "If only Christophe could see me now, the joyless codger!"

"William," the phone's feminine voice began, "if you encode his DNA into the entanglement, his memories—"

Are they talking about me?

"Yes, Isa. I see no other way."

"It will likely kill you."

"Already the darkness encroaches, and my will grows insufficient to stay awake. I have only this left to do."

Mr. Breton began to strip the sodden dressing from his injured arm. Robbie required several seconds to comprehend what he witnessed.

"What are you doing?" He knew his voice sounded shrill, but he didn't care. "Mr. Breton, stop. Please!"

"Isa will guide you when I am gone."

The librarian stood with difficulty and then picked up one end of the silvery artifact from the desk. Robbie wanted to express the countless questions percolating in his mind, but Mr. Breton interrupted him.

"Take the artifact," the librarian said desperately, holding out the opposite end of the object.

Robbie reached out and gripped the artifact.

He blinked.

His legs almost buckled at a sudden bout of unsteadiness, as though the ground had shifted beneath his feet.

What just happened?

He caught the end of a conversation between Mr. Breton and his phone that drew his attention.

"—my notebook."

"Yes, William."

Robbie's eyes had trouble adjusting to the light. When his vision cleared, he saw Mr. Breton slumped back in the desk chair.

"Get up, Mr. Breton. Please," he implored.

But the librarian didn't answer. His sallow skin and rapid, shallow breathing sent a chill through Robbie's entire body. A new sound punctuated the near silence. A gurgle in Mr. Breton's throat. A rattle in his chest. The librarian's eyes darted around the room.

"The darkness— I can't hold it back anymore," he rasped.

Robbie wanted to cry out. He would be alone soon.

"Take the phone," Mr. Breton said between gasps. "It belongs to you."

Robbie picked up the device. The screen lit up when he touched it, unlocking immediately. Icons populated the screen.

"The others will understand, eventually. I am sorry, Robbie."

The sound of metal feet beating rapidly against the stone steps of the stairway shattered the relative quiet of the vault. Something was almost at the bottom of the spiral staircase. He saw nowhere to run except the black void beyond the light of the banker's lamp. He moved to help Mr. Breton up, but the librarian shook his head.

"Take this."

Clumsily, he gestured to a brown leather messenger bag. The zipper was open, and one end of a wooden spindle was visible within the pack.

The scroll?

Robbie secured the bag's strap over his head and across his shoulder, pulling it tight against his hip with both hands.

"Flee, Robbie. Into the vault. Keep it until the others arrive." Mr. Breton sank back into the chair and closed his eyes. Then he said no more.

4

BLEAK IN THE EVENING LATE

"Go, Robbie! They're almost here."

The phone voice jolted him from his trance.

"Wake up, Mr. Breton!" he cried.

"He's dead." The voice stated. "You must go now."

Dead!

"Where?" Robbie gestured at the darkness beyond the light of the banker's lamp. He immediately put down his arm when he remembered he was arguing with a cell phone.

"The vault extends below the entire length and width of the library structure, including the four satellite hexagons. Run, and I will guide you."

The scraping sound was so close now.

What choice do I have?

Robbie took the phone and messenger bag and ran, leaving Mr. Breton and the light behind. He ran without direction or destination, wanting only to escape from whatever was descending the spiral staircase. Almost immediately, the void enveloped him. He lost sight of the floor beneath his feet. He could no longer see his hands, and his breathing reached a panicked crescendo. His brain warred over which was worse, the unknowable darkness in which he found himself or Andars Demeter and his robot cats.

Hellcats.

He crashed into something solid. Robbie pushed at his attacker, anticipating the cold, metal limbs and the snap of jaws that would crack his bones into splinters. But the bite didn't come. Forcing himself to breathe, he realized he was fighting against the floor. He had fallen in his desperate flight. He sat up and looked around at nothing. Like a man thirsting for water in the desert, his eyes sought out light that wasn't there.

"Where am I going?"

"Based on your initial position, your eastward trajectory, and the speed before falling, you are beneath the central hex, moving toward the easternmost portion of the vault. I recommend altering your path seventy degrees to the left, increasing your chances of—"

Isa's voice was lost to the rhythmic sound of claws against a hard surface. Robbie ran. The scraping sound grew louder and louder.

"Robbie!" The phone voice was definitely shouting. "You must activate your kit."

"I don't know what that means!" he yelled back.

"Instruct me to activate your kit."

"Isa, activate my kit!"

Nothing happened. He turned toward the approaching noise and regarded the pair of fiery red eyes advancing on him. His breath caught in his throat. He couldn't think. He barely heard Isa's voice over the rapid pounding of his heart.

Suddenly, the rhythm of the scraping sound shifted. The

hellcat's hydraulics hissed loudly. He heard the beast claw for purchase before leaping into the air. Instinctively, he raised his arms over his head and closed his eyes, a futile gesture against the hellcat. A momentary flash of swirling indigo lit the darkness behind his closed eyelids. The air crackled violently, and the impact pushed him back, but only by a foot or so.

Isa continued speaking, but Robbie's brain prioritized the danger over all else.

The beast's terrible red eyes glared at him.

It leaped again, but something appeared between Robbie and the hellcat. A latticework of light exploded into the darkness and disappeared a moment later. The nature of that light was strange—deep blue shifting toward purple and fading into a shade of pink like the death throes of a summer sunset. He shut his eyes to protect his vision from the brilliant flash, but the after-image persisted.

Robbie lost his footing and fell onto his back. He scrambled away, trying to distance himself from the metal monstrosity. The beast halted its advance. The world condensed into two points of pulsing crimson. All was silence, except for Robbie's ragged breathing.

Thump, thump, thump.

The sound boomed through the emptiness, familiar and terrifying. Robbie recognized it immediately as the cane of the man who had confronted Mr. Breton in the library. Behind the red eyes of the hellcat, a light cut a slow path through the darkness. Robbie didn't move.

Andars Demeter stopped when he came abreast of the hellcat. He gripped his walking stick, except it was transformed. A shaft of sickly dark yellow light emerged from the top half of the stick. A long, curved blade of the same color topped the shaft, bathing the giant and the sleek metal predator in an ominous glow.

Robbie was close enough to see that Demeter's face was disfigured—scarred, pitted, and uneven from forehead to chin. The man looked Robbie over carefully.

"To which House do you belong, boy? Not Breton, surely."

Robbie remained silent and motionless. Terror held a grip on all the higher functions of his brain. The giant seemed to mistake his terror for defiance. A gruesome smile washed over his face.

"Breton is dead. Will you stand against me?"

Robbie tried to shake his head.

"Give me the scroll, and you may yet live."

Robbie wanted to comply, but his body remained inert. Not from bravery or a sense of obligation to the dead librarian. Terror paralyzed him. He lay unmoving, his breath coming out in gasps, on the cusp of hyperventilating. The giant man stepped toward him, then paused, turning his attention to the hellcat. The lights of its eyes flashed on and off, and its movement had gone from graceful and deadly a moment ago to fitful and erratic. Demeter's smile transformed into a sneer. The hellcat stopped moving, and its lights faded. Deactivated, it resembled a metal sculpture frozen in an aggressive, predatory stance. Demeter cursed in a language Robbie didn't understand and kicked the beast hard enough to send it skittering across the stone floor outside the light cast by the walking stick. Robbie jumped involuntarily at the violence. He remembered the weight of the machine on top of him. The hellcats were heavy and solid.

The kick should have broken the man's foot, but Demeter showed no sign of discomfort. He strode forward again until he towered over Robbie. He lowered the curved blade near Robbie's face as if to see him more clearly. Much like Mr. Breton's impossible sword, the weapon was solid along its middle yet insubstantial along its edges.

"Where is the scroll?"

The man's eyes alighted on the messenger bag strap slung over Robbie's shoulder. Demeter spun his weapon 180 degrees until the wooden side pointed down at Robbie. Without warning, he thrust the end at Robbie's chest.

The lattice of indigo flashed between the weapon and Robbie's body, surprising them both. Demeter tried again. He planted his feet and drove downward with the weapon. This time, he didn't relent. He pushed against the barrier. Robbie lay motionless, his eyes wide with shock, his mind uncomprehending. They remained locked in the pose for several seconds until Demeter grunted angrily and stepped back.

The reprieve was short-lived, however. Robbie threw his hands up defensively as the giant spun the sword-staff and struck, chopping at Robbie's shoulder with the curved blade of hard yellow light. The lattice appeared, lighting the vault in a brilliant coruscation. The point where the blade and barrier met sizzled and sputtered. The contact formed glowing rivulets of molten silver that pooled fleetingly and then vanished into nothingness as it dripped toward the ground.

Demeter leaned into the weapon with his massive frame, pushing harder and harder. Robbie heard the barrier as a loud hum behind his ears and watched in horror as it shifted through a gamut of colors, from indigo to brilliant pink and now a bright, ominous red. Though he knew nothing about the barrier, Robbie was certain it could not withstand this assault. Demeter's mad, grotesque grin told Robbie his attacker had reached the same conclusion.

Slowly, inch by inch, the glowing tip of Demeter's blade pierced the blood-red barrier at his shoulder, cutting through the bag strap, his shirt, and into his flesh. Robbie screamed.

Then the hellcat struck. It sprang from the darkness and closed its vicious jaws around Demeter's right arm. The man stumbled back, dropping his weapon. The glowing blade deactivated, and the world was again plunged into almost total darkness, except for the red light of the hellcat's eyes. They turned to regard Robbie for just a moment. The beast spoke to him in Isa's voice.

"Go!"

Robbie scrambled to his feet. He took a step, then tripped on something.

The messenger bag!

He picked up the bag by its severed leather strap. Just then, light bloomed somewhere behind him. He glanced up in time to see the blade of Demeter's sword-staff collide with a fast-moving shape, followed by a high-pitched shearing sound. The giant didn't spare a glance at the destroyed hellcat. He stalked toward Robbie once again.

I'm sorry, Mr. Breton. I can't do this.

He hurled the bag with all his strength into the darkness. A sharp, twisting pain lanced through his shoulder, but he managed to suppress a cry. He heard a clatter somewhere in the void as the scroll's wooden spindles struck the floor, followed by Demeter shouting something Robbie did not understand.

Robbie ran again. As he traveled deeper into the vault, he touched his shoulder and winced. The fabric of his shirt was wet and torn. His fingers came away slick with blood, and a burning sensation spread down his arm and chest.

Can Demeter track me in the dark?

Unlikely, as the man seemed to use his sword-staff as a source of light. On the other hand, the hellcat had no trouble hunting him. Demeter had destroyed the only one Robbie had seen down here. Were more stalking him right now? He slowed his pace, moving as quietly as possible, alert for any indication of pursuit. He heard none. He held his hands before him, mindful of unseen hazards.

"Isa," Robbie whispered the name but did not receive a response.

What had happened to it? He didn't even know what it was. Isa seemed much smarter than the voice assistants on any smartphone he'd ever seen. How had it taken control of the hellcat? At least, that is what he assumed had happened when the beast suddenly attacked Demeter.

Recalling that the device was in his possession, he tried to remove it from his pants pocket, but his hand was stiff and tingled strangely. He used his other hand to take the phone. It unlocked at his touch. Two messages were displayed on the screen.

SYSTEM ERROR: ISA offline.

SYSTEM ERROR: Overload Detected. Reactivation in 226 minutes. Please stand by.

A stabbing pain from his shoulder down to his fingertips interrupted his thoughts. He gagged on stomach acid forcing itself up his esophagus.

What's happening to me?

He slowed his pace even more to catch his breath. His

chest burned. Might the vault contain another way out? Where was the help Mr. Breton had promised? Even if help arrived, Robbie was skeptical that anyone could stop the giant who kicked a big metal robot cat across a room and carried a strange magic walking stick.

His hand brushed against something cold and unrelenting. He located the flashlight app on the phone and activated it for the first time, revealing that the object before him was a rounded column of rough stone. Robbie was grateful that he hadn't smashed into one of these columns while running at full speed.

He immediately deactivated the flashlight when he realized it might lead Demeter to his location. In the dark, he tried to determine which side of the column he had approached from. Then he sat down on the opposite side. He had to figure out what to do next, and this column seemed a good place to figure it out. Besides, he was so tired. Robbie touched his shoulder again. The flesh burned.

That can't be good.

His fingers grazed the open wound. He couldn't tell how badly he bled, but the throbbing had reached a point that forced him to notice it. The pain was ramping up, inching closer to unbearable with each passing second. He was tempted to use the smartphone again to look at the wound but didn't want to give his position away.

He rested his back against the column and listened for several seconds. Silence. According to Isa, the vault ran beneath the entire library. Would he end up lost in this dark place forever?

Exhaustion washed over him in a way he had never felt before, as though the overwhelming fatigue was itself a malevolent force that clutched him in its grip. A deep throbbing pain spread across his temples. He didn't remember closing his eyes but had no desire to open them. In fact, he didn't feel like doing much of anything except find a way to ease the agony. He gripped his injured shoulder, and pain spiked through his upper body, threatening to blackout his senses. Sweating now, Robbie felt his gorge rise but managed to keep down the contents of his stomach. He wanted to scream and then forced that urge back down as well.

A light glowed somewhere close. His eyes fluttered open. A man stood over him. He held up a dimly glowing blade that misted dark blues and purples along its edges.

"Who are you?" the man asked, his deep voice inflected with an unfamiliar accent. His skin was brown, and his black hair was tied into a ponytail.

Robbie remained silent. His eyes began to lose focus, and the burning feeling had spread to his stomach. Another figure, taller and darker than the first, approached the column. He held a weapon similar to his companion's.

"Who's this?" the new person wondered in a familiar voice. He stepped into Robbie's shrinking field of view.

"Robbie! What are you doing here?"

Gallant?

"You know him?" the man asked.

"I do. He's a student at my school," Gallant answered.

The man leaned in close to Robbie. "Did you see what happened to William? Where are the scroll and the notebook?"

Scroll? Yes. Mr. Breton asked me to keep it safe.

"It's gone. I'm sorry." Robbie heard himself answer, but his voice was so distant.

"What's wrong with him?" Gallant asked.

Robbie closed his eyes again.

"His shoulder! He needs help, Hamza."

Robbie clutched at his stomach and cried out. *Oh, God!*

He gagged, then turned his head to the side as noxious fluid sprayed from his mouth.

Robbie didn't notice when his face hit the hard floor or when the darkness swallowed him.

5

THE BUSTLE IN A HOUSE

lice Asher completed the final move of the sword form and swept the blade down and to the right as if to sheathe it. She opened her hand as the cross guard came level with her hip. The sword vanished. She could not understand Hamza's insistence on strictly adhering to traditional sword forms.

We don't have sheaths, so why practice sheathing our swords?

Hamza usually ignored these questions and made her practice the forms again. Today, however, Alice trained on her own. Instead of restarting the training sequence, as the assiduous master-at-arms would've insisted, she moved to the north-facing thirty-foot windows of the training room.

The view of Central Park from the 137th floor of her grandfather's condo tower never disappointed her, especially at sunrise. The light along the eastern horizon lit the trees fifteen hundred feet below the penthouse in a beautiful warm glow. She loved it up here, more so since moving to Los Angeles with her parents the previous summer. Though she had lived in Manhattan for just three years of her life, it was the place Alice most thought of as home.

The smartphone buzzed in her pocket. She grimaced before drawing it out to look at the screen. As expected, the training program that tracked and measured how well she performed the sequence of moves flashed disapprovingly. It scored her latest attempt at 27 percent, marginally worse than the 28.7 percent she averaged for this particular set of forms. Elsewhere on the screen, a vibrant red prompt indicated that she was late attempting the sequence again. Not for the first time, she cursed the absent sword master and his persistent training app. Alice often thought she executed the blocks, parries, and thrusts correctly, but Hamza's live evaluation and the training app usually indicated otherwise. She struggled with the sword. The weight and the length didn't feel right in her hands, but her confidence soared with two daggers. Unfortunately, Hamza remained steadfast that Alice master the sword before moving on to other weapons, so she trained with the smaller blades in secret.

Not that she wasn't progressing with the sword at all. After pointing out the innumerable flaws in everything from her stance to how she gripped the hilt, Hamza assured her that practice, hard work, and a will to succeed would inevitably lead to improvement.

Alice pressed a button to review the last sequence on the touchscreen, and the device began to play a recording of her most recent attempt through the forms. The figure that moved on the screen was a detailed three-dimensional rendering of her silhouette. Scores appeared beside each limb as she shifted from one move to the next. She could pause at any time and review in greater detail the moves she had executed correctly and those she missed. Alice watched one particular sequence where she scored a paltry 8 percent.

She paused the recording and pressed the "more information" button, which indicated that she was 1.3 seconds too slow in raising her right elbow to the next position and thirty-five degrees off the optimal angle. Alice might have thought the training app was broken had she not watched Hamza execute the form flawlessly.

She moved to the center of the training room's padded floor, set her feet, and took a deep breath. Instead of grasping at her right hip to make the sword rematerialize, she reached behind her back with both hands and made a downward pulling motion. She felt the warm hilts solidify against her palms. Alice swung the long daggers around into a fighting stance, the cool glow of each footlong black-and-indigo blade a contrast to the sunrise enveloping the trees far below. The corners of her mouth turned up as she remembered Hamza's disapproval upon learning about the twin daggers. He was likely more upset with Yasmin for programming the blades into Alice's kit than with Alice herself.

She began the forms again, adapting each move for two shorter blades instead of a single longsword. Alice completed each set of forms as quickly and precisely as her mind and body allowed. Panting hard and sweating through her workout gear, she sheathed the daggers to complete the sequence. This time, the training program scored her a perfect zero.

Of course.

With a long breath, she grabbed her towel and water bottle and lay down on her back. Alice wondered about the future of her combat training. Up until today, she had thought of it as a novel way to get some exercise. Sparring with Hamza or Domenico or Drake was better than jogging or squats in the gym, and she had grown fond of the two long daggers she could conjure into existence.

I just hope I never have to use them in an actual fight.

She watched the sun climb until it drew level with the training room windows. Without warning, the tears began to fall again. The temporary respite the training provided from the grief of her godfather's death collapsed suddenly. She looked at the picture on her phone's lock screen and remembered the captured moment with intense fondness. Eight-year-old Alice Asher stood backstage at the Palais Garnier in Paris, dressed in her finest clothes for such a special evening. Her face beamed with joy and awe as she posed with her favorite dancers from the world-famous ballet company. At the very edge of the photo, unaware that he was in the frame, stood William Breton, who had arranged to make a little girl's big dream come true.

She cried alone in the cavernous training room until her eyes were puffy and red. Unwilling to let anyone see her in such a state, Alice remained on the padded floor for a few more minutes and closed her eyes.

She started awake.

I can't believe I fell asleep.

She shivered, found her sweater, and zipped it to her neck. Making her way up the stairs to the penthouse's second floor, Alice reviewed the last twenty-four hours. How her parents had woken her in the middle of the night, breaking the news about her godfather's death. After the initial shock and tears subsided, they told her some of the details. Andars Demeter—a name shrouded in the mysterious past of her family's history—attacked and killed Uncle William at a library in a small town called Bethel. A boy around her age was gravely injured in the attack. Alice's father had gone to Bethel to help the boy, while Alice and her mom traveled to New York to be with her grandfather.

"Are we in danger?" she had asked. Her parents had been tense during their exodus from their home in Brentwood.

"No, sweetheart," her dad had answered confidently.

When Alice and her mom had arrived at the penthouse, her grandfather was in a state of agitation she'd never witnessed from him before. Deep furrows across his forehead and dark circles under his eyes had replaced the joyful expression he usually wore in her presence. Calvin Asher had hugged his granddaughter, and then her mom had sent her to bed. Alice had tried unsuccessfully to sleep for several hours before finally heading to the fitness room to practice the sword.

Though most of the details about the attack on Uncle William remained unknown to her, she sensed that something in her world was different now. Since her parents and grandfather had first told her about their family's connection to the Knights of Rosewood two years ago, she had struggled to take the whole thing seriously. They impressed upon her the need for absolute discretion, which she abided, but the sense of importance, duty, and gravity that pervaded her grandfather's conviction eluded her. Calvin Asher was clear; loyalty and duty to the Rosewood were paramount, and everything else—business, personal pursuits, and even family—followed from that first principle.

The Knights of Rosewood stuff wasn't just stodgy traditions and old-fashioned gibberish. At least, not entirely. Her phone and kit were a testament to that. Through a combination of high-tech wizardry gleaned from one of the scrolls and nearly limitless financial resources, the Rosewood had built a private and completely secure communications network using quantum *somethings* and decentralized *whatevers*. Alice didn't understand the technical details but noticed that her phone never lost connection to the network, regardless of location. Subways, airplanes, remote islands, wilderness—her phone always worked. The equipment that composed the private network infrastructure was distributed at various locations around the world in secure buildings controlled by the Rosewood. One such location was here, in a room on the main floor of her grandfather's penthouse.

Yasmin had explained to Alice that persistent and reliable connectivity weren't the only reasons for building a private communications network. Networks owned and operated by telecommunications companies were notoriously insecure, even when using sophisticated encryption to shield activity from prying eyes. The Rosewood's list of security threats was pretty straightforward. Everyone was a threat. More accurately, anyone not part of the Rosewood was a threat, including governments, corporations, nonprofits, and the remaining several billion people who lived on the planet.

Alice reached the top of the staircase and emerged into the penthouse entrance gallery. Two original paintings—a Rubens and a Klimt—hung on the walls to either side of the private elevator. To the right of the elevator and across from the staircase where she stood, her grandfather's latest acquisition from Sotheby's was on display. A tenth-century wooden sculpture of the Lord of the World, Avalokiteśvara.

Her arrival in the gallery coincided with the appearance of an unexpected figure who strode purposefully from the living room.

"Uncle Alden!" She exclaimed, surprised to see her grandfather's prodigal son.

He wore beige dress pants and a black blazer, with a white-collared shirt unbuttoned to the top of his chest. Face smoothly shaven and head full of dark-blond hair swept back with just a hint of glossy hair product, Alden Asher bore an uncanny resemblance to her father.

"Alice?" he asked when he noticed her. "My God! You've grown so tall since the last time I saw you. Have you graduated high school already?"

She shook her head. "No, I'm only in grade 10."

"Well, you are a perfect facsimile of your mother when she was younger."

Alice accepted the compliment with a smile. She had inherited much of her mom's appearance, from her reddish-brown hair to the delicate facial structure of her cheekbones, nose, and chin. Even the freckles that spilled over the bridge of Alice's nose resembled her mother's complexion. The color of her eyes—light gray flecked with amber—represented her father's only obvious physical contribution to his daughter. A common trait shared among the Asher men, including the one standing before her.

"It's nice to see you, Uncle. You're visiting Granddad?" Alice posed the question awkwardly. They both knew Alden was estranged from the rest of the Asher family. She hadn't seen him in person since middle school.

"I was made aware of William Breton's unfortunate passing. Do you know how he died?"

She stumbled over an answer. "Um, really, you should ask Granddad. I just heard about it myself not long ago."

"Yes, of course. How was such an early flight from LA?" He posed the question conversationally, but something in his eyes made her stumble over the answer.

"F— fine, I guess."

Uncle Asher smiled at her. This man and her father were so alike in appearance but different in the ways that truly mattered.

"I must be on my way, Alice. It was my sincerest pleasure to see you again."

"Thanks, Uncle Alden. You too."

He used the keypad on the wall to call the elevator. Seconds later, he descended to the building's main lobby.

Alice hadn't taken three steps before the patriarch of the Asher family entered the hallway from the direction she headed. Tall and slightly round in the middle, which even his tailored suit couldn't quite hide, Calvin Asher's hair and thick beard matched the gray of his eyes. A thundercloud of emotion gripped his face. He carried a small object wrapped in plain brown paper in his right hand.

"You met Alden on his way out?" he growled.

"Yes. He asked me about Uncle William's death and our flight to New York."

Her grandfather grunted.

"He didn't see you practicing the sword?"

"No."

Nor the daggers.

He spoke while striding toward the elevator. "I must attend to an unpleasant task. I'd like you to join me."

She nodded. "Where are we going?"

"London."

"Can I shower first?"

He seemed to notice her workout attire for the first time, and then he nodded. "Yes, but quickly."

"What's the occasion I should dress for?"

"Wear black."

Oh.

She turned in the direction of the living quarters. Alice had yet to take a step when her grandfather spoke again.

"Ah, I almost forgot. I was hoping to give this to you under different circumstances."

The tall man held out the paper-wrapped object. Alice accepted the gift.

"Please, open it."

Alice unwrapped the object without tearing the paper. Her eyes widened as she recognized the contents immediately.

"Granddad!" She was breathless. "A first edition of *Poems*? This box is pristine!"

Carefully, she opened the custom box and removed the book inside. She turned it over, reverently examining the sides and the spine. *Emily Dickinson* was embossed in gold on the cover.

"I've never seen a copy in this condition before. It belongs in a museum."

His eyes softened, and he smiled. "I am glad you like it, dear."

"Thank you!" She hugged him.

An hour and a half later, they traveled through East London in a fancy silver car with dark-tinted windows. Her grandfather opted to drive instead of using a driver, which was not unusual for him. The man loved his cars. She sat in what would usually be the driver's side at home. Slight disorientation accompanied the experience.

"It's strange," she began, "that Uncle Alden doesn't know about the Knights of Rosewood."

Calvin temporarily took his eyes off the busy early evening traffic to look at his granddaughter. "He knows more than he should."

They fell silent for a time, and then he continued.

"Introducing children into the Rosewood is perilous, especially when the children develop different values from their parents. Alden was not like your father or you. His petty cruelty and opportunism were a concern for your grandmother and me, even when he was a young boy, and it grew into something much worse after she died. He does not have the right temperament for the secrets we protect."

Alice could see the pained look at the admission in her grandfather's eyes.

"Alden was not the first child to reject his parents' values, nor the last. We are here to deliver news to another, in fact."

Her grandfather parked the car in front of a charming brick rowhouse. She exited the vehicle onto a well-maintained boulevard. Alice felt self-conscious when she noticed the staring passersby. She quickly realized that her grandfather's car was the main attraction. He didn't acknowledge the attention.

They approached the house via a walkway lined with manicured green hedges. Her grandfather rang the bell, and they waited. A few seconds later, a woman answered the door. She looked about the same age as her parents. Her hair and eyes were brown, and her clothes tasteful. Alice saw the woman's expression change from pleasant courtesy to disapproval as she recognized the man in the doorway.

"Uncle Calvin." The woman said with a tone that sounded suspiciously like contempt.

Though Alice had never met the woman, she knew William Breton's estranged daughter immediately.

"Good evening, Elizabeth. May we come in?" Calvin Asher asked. He responded to her barely veiled contempt with stoic politeness.

Elizabeth didn't answer immediately. She looked at Alice and then stepped aside for the pair to enter.

Natural light flooded the house's interior through large windows that highlighted the pristine white walls and polished wooden floors. The entrance opened into a large sitting room with stylish yet functional furniture that included a comfortable-looking gray sofa and chairs neatly arranged around a sleek driftwood table.

Alice and her grandfather stood in the front hallway. Elizabeth did not invite them further into the house.

"This is my granddaughter, Alice."

Elizabeth's eyes brightened, and her mouth turned up into what looked like a genuine smile. She offered her hand to Alice, who shook it.

"Of course! Michael's daughter. You have his eyes. I grew up with your father and uncle."

Alice tried to return the smile but faltered. She realized why they were there and wished her grandfather had warned her. "It's nice to meet you, Ms. Breton."

"I have some grave news, Elizabeth." Her grandfather wasted little time arriving at the purpose of their visit. "Your father passed away yesterday."

Though Alice expected the words, they still struck her all over again. She watched Elizabeth, even as her own eyes began to well up. William Breton's daughter did not faint or weep. If she shed a tear over the news, it happened after the Ashers left. Her only meaningful physical reaction was a hard swallow and fluttering eyelids.

"How?" she asked pointedly.

"William was living in a small town called Bethel. The authorities say a gas leak—"

"How dare you!"

Calvin stopped talking. Alice's eyes widened at the woman's sudden vehemence.

"A gas leak! You and my father with your self-important secret club of wealthy elites. You forget, Calvin. I am not like Alden. My father told me about the Rosewood Knights. I'm the one who rejected him!"

Alice noticed her grandfather stiffen at the harsh rebuke.

"Are you here to insist I take his spot in your precious Rosewood?" She spat out the last word like a curse.

Calvin's reply was calm but firm. "The line of Breton is broken, Elizabeth. I am here out of deference for my lifelong friend and for my fond memories of a smiling young girl who long ago sat on my knee and pulled my mustache. Your wish has been granted; your connection to the organization is severed."

Elizabeth Breton flinched this time, but her grandfather continued.

"You will have a place of honor at the funeral if you decide to attend."

He opened the door and motioned for Alice to exit. They stepped outside. He turned to face Elizabeth, who no longer appeared so sure of herself.

"William's executor will be in touch. I understand he left you his entire estate."

Elizabeth grabbed the door to steady herself.

Alice could understand the woman's reaction.

Hey there! Your dad, who you hated, is dead. Oh, and he left you billions of dollars.

The car maneuvered through traffic a short time later, the driver and passenger silent for much of the ride. Alice finally spoke as they approached the abandoned library in East Ham.

"Granddad, why did you ask me to come?"

He answered without hesitation. "I hope you will take my place as head of House Asher one day. You have much to learn."

Alice's jaw went slack. Her grandfather wanted *her* to lead their House? The idea had never even entered her mind. "What about my mom and dad?"

Her grandfather exhaled slowly. "Two things your father doesn't care for—running my businesses or the Knights of Rosewood."

Alice frowned, then shook her head. "That's not true. Dad is very careful about keeping the Rosewood a secret."

Her grandfather laughed, but it wasn't a warm sound. She heard more than a little bitterness. "When did you last train with your father, Alice?"

Never.

Her grandfather didn't wait for an answer. "The Rosewood is an anachronism to your parents. They're far more interested in living in grass huts and administering malaria vaccines to third-world farmers than protecting the world from men like Andars Demeter."

She bit her lip, then said what was on her mind. "Protecting the world? I thought the war was over."

"The war is never over, Alice. And one of our greatest enemies now possesses a scroll."

6

THE SKY IS BRIGHT WITH DAWN

The first time Robbie opened his eyes, he was awake long enough to understand that he lay in a strange bed in an unfamiliar room. The lights were dim, and a woman—his mom, he slowly realized—slept in a chair against the wall. He fell back asleep before finding enough strength to call out.

Warm sunlight streamed through the windows the second time he awoke. It felt good on his face, but the bright light hurt his eyes just a little. Again, he fell back to sleep before he could speak.

The third time he opened his eyes, the room was bright with natural light, but the sun no longer shone directly through the windows. He turned and saw his mom sitting in a chair beside his bed. She gasped when he looked at her.

"Hey, kiddo." Though she spoke softly, her eyes watched him intently.

"Mom," he whispered in a dry rasp.

His mom held up a glass of water from a nearby table, her hands shaking just a little. He drank weakly from the straw. The liquid felt good in his parched throat. Then she hugged him. The embrace was gentle, but he felt her tremble and knew she was crying. She helped him sit up.

"Mom, where are we?"

"Shhh. It's okay. We have plenty of time for explanations."

She reached behind his bed, and a female voice crackled from a nearby speaker. "Can I help you?" The voice was professional and clinical.

"He's awake." His mom's voice quivered slightly at the pronouncement.

"Excuse me?" the clinical voice asked.

"Robbie Noble in room 1-1-7. He's awake."

Silence followed for what felt like a full minute before the voice responded. "Dr. Asher hasn't arrived yet, but a nurse is on her way."

His mom reached out and smoothed his hair. She saw the concerned look on his face.

"We're at the hospital, Robbie."

"What am I doing here?" His voice sounded odd in his ears, as if he hadn't spoken in a long time.

His mom let out a long breath before responding. "You were sick, but everything is okay now."

Robbie shut his eyes and tried to remember. "I— I had a nightmare. A man with a sword and, ah, machines on four legs. Mr. Breton. He—"

Lauren Noble's calm composure seemed to fall away. She wrapped her arms around her son and held him tightly. After a time, she drew back, wiping her tears away with a tissue she must've kept in her pocket. "Do you remember what happened?"

The hospital room door swung open, and a nurse entered. Her eyes focused on Robbie. "Finally awake, I see."

The nurse ran through a series of physical examinations, concluding each test with a quick nod. "Everything looks good, Robbie. I see no reason to think you will experience any lasting effects from the coma."

Robbie's heart jumped at the word.

Coma?

"When do you think he can go home?" His mom asked.

"You can ask the doctor shortly." The nurse left the room, and Robbie's mom hugged him a third time.

"Mom, what was she talking about?"

She exhaled. "Your dad is on his way. Let's wait till he arrives."

Robbie shook his head. "I need to know, Mom."

She nodded. "Okay, Robbie. After school, you went to the library for your usual shift. There was some kind of gas leak. The firefighters found you unconscious in the staff room. Your shoulder was badly injured, but it's healed now."

He pulled the hospital gown down to look at the injury. It seemed okay, other than a new scar that didn't look new.

"They said you passed out and fell onto the glass coffee table in the staff room. Some of the shards cut you up pretty good."

He frowned as his mom recounted the story. "That doesn't seem right," he said uncertainly.

"There's more. The gas leak caused an explosion in the atrium. William didn't make it."

"No, that's not right," he whispered.

Fragmented memories flashed in his mind. Nightmarish black beasts with ruby eyes stalking him in the deep, unknowable darkness. A man covered in hideous scars thumping his cane against the rough stone floor. An injured and dying Mr. Breton whispering the words "Knights of

Rosewood." A glowing indigo sword illuminating Gallant's shocked face.

Did I dream it all?

His mom spoke, and his attention snapped back to the reality of the hospital room.

"It's okay, kiddo," she told him soothingly. "We don't need to talk about this now. Your dad has barely slept or eaten since the night of the accident. He can't wait to see you."

Despite the comfortable room temperature, his mom's words sent a chill through his body. He touched his healed shoulder again and asked the question that made him most afraid. "How long has it been?"

She took a deep breath. "I think we should wait for your dad."

"Please, Mom."

Another pause before she nodded with resolve. "Today is day eighty-eight since the accident."

He stared at her for several seconds, wondering if he remained in that nightmare.

"Robbie, you've been in a coma for three months."

He blinked as he tried to understand what she was saying.

She hugged him again. Tighter this time. "I'm so sorry, kiddo."

Robbie lay still in his hospital bed, in his mother's comforting embrace, thinking about what had happened and what it would mean. The school year was over by now. He would repeat his sophomore year. Blake, Artie, and all his other friends would be a grade ahead of him. They'd graduate a year sooner. He'd be in the same grade as this year's freshmen. Valeria would never stop teasing him.

"Excuse me." A new voice broke through the somber atmosphere in the hospital room.

Robbie looked up to see the visitor. The man was tall, with short, light brown hair and a neatly trimmed beard. He didn't look much older than his mom. He wore a navy blue suit and a white lab coat with dark blue-framed glasses. A stethoscope hung around his neck.

"Robbie's awake, Doctor!" The relief in his mom's voice was palpable.

The man smiled warmly.

"A wonderful development, Ms. Noble. Good afternoon, Robbie. My name is Michael Asher."

"Hi," Robbie managed to say while trying to process the news of his coma.

"How are you feeling?" the physician asked cheerfully.

Robbie took a moment to consider the question. "I'm weak. And my head hurts."

"Of course. All normal reactions under the circumstances. Your most recent blood work looks excellent, and the nurse's physical examination netted similar results. I still need to ask a series of questions, if that's okay with you."

"I guess," Robbie replied.

Dr. Asher nodded and walked across the room toward his patient's bedside.

"Do you mind stepping outside for a few minutes, Ms. Noble?"

"I do, Doctor. I'd rather be here with my son."

The man smiled and nodded. "I understand, of course. However, I must establish a baseline for Robbie's mood and cognitive function. If you are present, he may answer based on your subconscious facial expressions and body language."

"Mom, it's fine. I'm not going anywhere."

She exhaled slowly, looking between the doctor and Robbie. Clearly, she wanted to stay as close to him as possible. He wondered if she would ever let him out of her sight again.

"I'll be right outside." The words sounded like a promise.

Dr. Asher waited for the door to close, then removed a cell phone from his pocket and typed something on the screen. "I'm sorry about what happened to you, Robbie."

"You mean the gas leak?" he asked. His memory of the battle with Demeter warred with his mom's more mundane explanation.

"Fortunately, your parents appear to believe the official account of what happened that terrible night," Dr. Asher stated.

"Pardon me?' Robbie asked, surprised by the man's response.

"You have to understand," Dr. Asher continued. "Given the circumstances, the gas leak was an entirely plausible explanation for what happened to you."

Robbie stared into the doctor's gray eyes and asked, "You know what really happened?"

The man nodded, then approached Robbie's bed. "As much as we can piece together. The details are somewhat ambiguous given that William is dead, Isa is inoperative, and you've been in a coma."

"You're one of them?" Robbie asked. "Like Mr. Breton. One of these knights?"

Dr. Asher nodded. "I am."

The man's phone began to vibrate loud enough for Robbie to hear it. Dr. Asher pressed the screen and turned it to face Robbie. "It's for you."

On the screen, an older woman with short white hair and emerald green eyes stared back at him.

"We have been waiting for you to wake up," the woman declared, her face and manner projecting cold, steely authority. "I am going to ask you a series of important questions, and you will answer them. Am I clear?"

Robbie stared at the screen, not responding. After several seconds of silence, the woman called the doctor's name. Michael turned the screen back on himself.

"The boy's brain is addled." The woman snapped.

It wasn't a question.

"No, Augusta." Though calm, Dr. Asher's voice contained a strong note of irritation. "He's overwhelmed. A little empathy goes a long way."

"We need him to answer our questions, Michael. We don't have time for empathy."

Dr. Asher turned the screen to face Robbie once again.

"It's okay, Robbie. I know you're processing a great deal of difficult information, but we need your help."

Robbie looked at the screen.

"You had William Breton's smartphone." The woman named Augusta began. "How did you come to possess the device?"

"He gave it to me before, ah—." Robbie choked on the words, struggling to say them. "Before he died."

"Did William have his phone when the library was attacked?" she asked pointedly.

"No."

"Why would Demeter allow you to live?" Augusta asked.

The question triggered a memory of the grotesque giant standing over him with a glowing yellow blade, and the terror he felt that night returned.

"Who are you people?" Robbie asked, obviously frustrated.

"Answer the question!" the woman demanded.

"Augusta." Dr. Asher interjected. He turned the screen back toward himself. "Robbie has suffered tremendous trauma. Physical, and quite obviously, mental and emotional as well. I only agreed to this interrogation because of the danger my father *claims* Demeter poses and the assurances the Conventus gave me that you wouldn't cause him further trauma."

"Michael, your father was not hyperbolic."

"Perhaps, but my father is not a physician. Robbie is my patient, and I have a duty of care."

Silence shrouded the hospital room for five heartbeats before Augusta spoke again.

"Of course. I will not gainsay one of the world's most accomplished physicians. May I ask the boy a few more questions?"

Dr. Asher looked at Robbie, who took a calming breath and nodded. Augusta addressed him once again.

"Robbie, how did you survive Demeter's attack?"

"Mr. Breton's phone, I guess. Some kind of barrier kept appearing in front of me."

"Impossible," the woman replied.

Robbie agreed. "Yeah, I thought so, too."

Augusta wasn't finished. "What of the scroll?"

"The man you mentioned. Demeter. I— I guess he took the scroll."

Robbie burned with shame at the truth of what he'd done. He couldn't bring himself to admit that he'd thrown away the scroll after promising Mr. Breton that he'd keep it safe.

Augusta pressed on. "And the notebook?" Her eyes

seemed to bore into him. Robbie wondered if Dr. Asher's phone was glitching when she didn't blink for several seconds.

"What notebook?" he answered simply.

The woman's scowl indicated that she found his answer unsatisfactory. She looked ready to chastise him or ask another question.

"That's enough for today, Augusta."

Without another word, Dr. Asher ended the call and dropped the phone into his lab coat.

Robbie's head throbbed with pain. He wanted to close his eyes and go back to sleep, but he needed answers first. "What are the Knights of Rosewood?"

"I can't tell you that, Robbie. At least not right now." Dr. Asher looked Robbie in the eyes and nodded. "I know it's all very confusing. I'm sorry." His compassion sounded genuine.

"Confusing? Mr. Breton is dead!" Robbie half-spoke and half-yelled the words. "Someone tried to kill me."

The physician turned to look at the door, likely concerned that Robbie's mom would rush back into the room when she heard her son's outburst.

Robbie didn't care. He was angry.

"I lost three months of my life for some dusty old scroll?"

To his credit, Dr. Asher seemed to listen intently. He looked at Robbie throughout his tirade and then responded calmly. "You are right, Robbie. You should not be part of this."

Robbie kept going. "I deserve to know what happened to me, Dr. Asher. And what about Demeter? Where is he?"

"Andars Demeter has disappeared, but we are confident he will turn up soon."

So he's still out there.

"In terms of what happened to you, well, your health situation was complicated. You had a unique form of radioactive poisoning. When activated, Demeter's weapon emits a relatively harmless isotope. Usually, the isotope has a half-life of a few milliseconds. Unless it enters the bloodstream."

"Demeter's sword made me sick?"

"Yes, and the poison would have killed you. When the others arrived at the vault beneath the library, they recognized your symptoms."

"The other Knights of Rosewood?" Robbie asked.

The doctor nodded. "We responded to William's distress call, but not in time to save him."

Asher's easygoing confidence seemed to falter at the admission, and his warm presence grew more solemn. He continued after a short pause.

"I arrived in Bethel after the others and confirmed their assessment of your condition."

Something in the doctor's words struck Robbie as significant. Where had Dr. Asher arrived from? The question made him think of the other man he encountered beneath the library that night. The one who appeared seemingly out of nowhere.

What was his name? Hamza, I think.

The doctor's retelling of the night's events continued.

"The gas leak, the explosion in the atrium, and the broken glass table were cover for your injuries and William's death."

Robbie shook his head. "Cover for what?"

"To preserve our secret." The doctor looked embarrassed at his own explanation. "The library's true purpose and why William Breton has lived in this town for the last ten years."

"He wasn't really a librarian, was he?" Robbie's heart fell as he asked the question, already knowing the answer.

"The people of Bethel only knew William as the librarian who moved here to run the Feist Reference Library. But no, William wasn't a librarian."

"Well, I guess that's pretty obvious now," Robbie said, not without anger. "Secret door to an underground lair, magic sword, and all that."

"The sword isn't magic," Dr. Asher replied emphatically. "And those parts of William's life are something else entirely. Before he moved to this town, William was CEO and chairman of one of the largest holding companies in the world."

Why would Mr. Breton keep that from us?

"Look, Robbie. We don't have much time. The nurses are distracting your mother with some paperwork, but she'll be back any second. I know you have questions, and I wish I could answer them, but—"

Robbie interrupted Dr. Asher. "What stops me from telling people—my parents, the police, the news—about what really happened that night?"

The doctor shook his head. "While it might complicate things a little, in the end, it wouldn't truly matter if you did. Imagine the headline, Robbie. 'Fifteen-year-old gas leak victim wakes from coma and accuses dead billionaire of membership in a secret society.'"

Robbie's eyes narrowed as he contemplated Dr. Asher's words. "So, you'd make me out to be some kind of crazy person? Mentally unfit or whatever."

Dr. Asher looked regretful, and he sounded it, too: "We would rather not go down that path. Truth be told, we've done much worse."

Robbie closed his eyes and laid his head back atop his

pillow. He didn't know what to think. Then he remembered something the doctor had said about taking longer to reach Bethel.

"You're not from around here, are you?" Robbie finally asked.

Dr. Asher shook his head. "I practice medicine in Los Angeles."

"So, why come all this way to treat me yourself?"

"Not even the most sophisticated radiological devices known to the world's top scientists can detect the type of radiation Demeter's sword emits. They could neither diagnose nor treat you. You would've died."

The revelation struck him suddenly.

"Why not let me die? It would've been so much easier."

Before Dr. Asher could respond, Robbie formulated his own answer.

"It's because you need me for something. That's why that woman grilled me about the scroll and Mr. Breton's phone and the notebook."

To his surprise, Dr. Asher actually nodded.

"Yes, we need your help, but I'm not here to threaten or coerce. The Rosewood is not your enemy, and I'm happy that we were able to save your life."

Robbie frowned at the admission. "You need my help with what?"

Dr. Asher shook his head. "Not now. Your mom will be back at any moment. Someone will be in touch soon."

The room remained silent for a brief moment.

"Please don't think ill of William Breton. He was a good man and, from what I understand, quite fond of you and your family."

Robbie thought about his time with Mr. Breton. Not just the charismatic librarian behind the reference desk but also the kind and funny man who came for Sunday dinners and played chess with Robbie's mom. "He was like family."

The doctor reached into his lab coat and pulled out a thick, worn leather wallet. The moment almost made Robbie smile. There was something strangely masculine and old-fashioned about a folding leather wallet full of cards, cash, and other trappings. His father carried such a wallet. The librarian had too, he remembered. Dr. Asher handed Robbie a folded photograph of William Breton and a young girl smiling at a stage show of some kind.

"Who is she?"

"My daughter, Alice." Dr. Asher smiled broadly, with genuine, unrestrained joy. "William was Alice's godfather. He was like family. He believed in the Knights of Rosewood. Dedicated his life to it."

The door swung open, and his mom entered the room. "Look who I found wandering the hallway like a lost puppy dog."

Robbie's dad peeked his head around the corner. His ear-to-ear grin brought Robbie immediate comfort. "I like to think it was more like a swagger than a wander, Lauren."

Robbie's dad practically charged the last few steps to his son's bedside and hugged him. His eyes looked on the verge of tears as he pulled Robbie's head tightly against his chest.

"Hi, Dad," Robbie said, voice muffled against his dad's sternum.

"I'm sorry I wasn't here when you woke up, but I drove as fast as the laws of man and physics would allow when your mom called me."

"I'm glad you're here," Robbie whispered.

Dr. Asher moved toward the door. "Robbie, Mr. and Ms. Noble, please excuse me. I'll let you catch up."

Robbie's dad offered his hand to Dr. Asher, who

responded in kind. "Thank you so much for taking care of our son, Doctor. And for coming to Bethel so often. We can never repay you."

"I am happy that Robbie will make a full recovery, Mr. Noble. Get a few meals into him, and he can go home the day after tomorrow."

7

TATTERED AND TORN

Robbie returned from the hospital to a welcome home party that included most of his friends from school. They greeted him with cheers, hugs, and a few tears.

Robbie learned that Artie had taken his absence from school particularly hard. He visited the hospital several days a week, sitting at Robbie's bedside, watching their favorite movies on his tablet. He'd made the trek to the hospital even when his parents or Robbie's parents couldn't drive him, which meant riding the city bus for an hour each way. Instead of inundating Robbie with everything he had missed, Artie acted as though nothing had happened and no time had passed. That suited Robbie perfectly.

Artie described his summer break, which involved helping his movie reviewer dad with a new social media campaign and going to Quebec for a month. The annual Rutherford family vacation took place at a lakefront cottage in Saint Hippolyte.

His months-long coma had affected Blake, too. She embraced him so tightly that it hurt before they sat down to talk. Blake surprised him when she explained that she and Gallant had pulled out of the main performance of *Eurydice and Orpheus*. Instead, their understudies performed in their places, thus costing Blake the coveted distinction of being the first sophomore to star in the annual school production.

"I couldn't speak three words without crying, Robbie. We didn't know if you were going to live or—"

Guilt cut through him once he realized she had missed the performance because of him.

"I'm sorry, Blake. I know the play meant a lot to you. Won't it affect your college applications?"

She laughed, her voice strong yet melodic and full of life. "Robbie, you don't need to be sorry. I have another year to pad my college applications with irrelevant and arbitrary criteria. I'm not worried. I promise. I'm just so happy you're okay."

"Blake, why didn't Gallant perform that night?"

She had shrugged at the question, clearly looking uncomfortable.

"He's been— I don't know. Off, maybe? Since your accident. He disappears, sometimes for hours at a time. I don't know where he goes or what he's doing."

A small part of him had wondered if Blake knew about her boyfriend's membership in the secret organization. Her comment set his mind at ease. Robbie wanted to tell Blake about Gallant and the Knights of Rosewood. His loyalty was to her, not Gallant.

What about my loyalty and the oath I gave to Mr. Breton? The one that involves my death if I break it.

He needed more time to think it all through.

Blake told him about her summer break. She planned to split her time working reception at the veterinary clinic and as an assistant to Ms. Versteepen, helping the St. Boniface principal prepare for the new school year.

Robbie's physical and emotional exhaustion by the time the party ended left him in a haze. He fell asleep rather quickly that first night back in his bed. The next day, Robbie learned that Ms. Versteepen would allow him to finish grade ten through an accelerated summer program. Grateful and relieved that he wouldn't have to repeat the previous academic year, Robbie tried not to let his disappointment at the prospect of summer school get the better of him.

Robbie took a deep breath and prepared to exit the car. His mom smiled reassuringly.

"Have a good day at school, kiddo. Call me if you need anything."

Robbie tried to match his mom's good cheer. "Thanks, Mom."

"I know summer school is less than ideal." She held out her fist for him to bump.

He frowned at her cringy awkwardness but obliged her.

"Yeah." He nodded. This conversation was not their first on the topic.

"Your dad and I are always here for you if you want to talk. And if you'd rather speak to someone else, we've found someone who specializes in counseling kids your age who have experienced trauma."

Trauma. The word echoed inside his head.

What had been my trauma? Was it watching Mr. Breton die? Almost dying myself? Being chased through a pitch-black tomb by a robot predator cat? Not being able to tell anyone about what happened to me? Losing three months of my life?

"I'll be fine, Mom," he said, forcing a smile.

"Robbie. Look at me. There is no shame in talking about how you feel."

He nodded. "I don't want to be late for my first day back."

"I love you," his mom said as he exited the car.

"I love you, too. I'll see you after school."

As he walked to class, Robbie thought about the last two weeks. Dr. Asher had been right. He felt much better, at least physically. The day after being discharged from the hospital, his appetite returned—with a vengeance. Once he started eating again, his strength came back, and his atrophied muscles began to recover from the months of inertia. His clothes were still a little loose, but with the amount of food he consumed since leaving the hospital, that problem would resolve quickly.

The quiet, empty halls of St. Boniface Catholic High School were surreal. He'd never seen it so lifeless in his two years at the school. Even during class time, when all the students were behind the heavy fire doors of their respective classrooms, the building buzzed with boundless energy that must be common to all high schools.

He didn't realize how much he missed Artie's unending commentary about the teenage condition. His witty quips and humorous observations accompanied their trips together through these hallways. The silence that now accompanied Robbie reinforced his sense of isolation.

He opened the door to room 212B. The eleven students sitting at their desks turned to look at him. Robbie knew them from his sophomore year but didn't hang out with any of them. Some smiled and waved, and others said hi. They all knew about his coma. St. Boniface wasn't large enough for a situation like his to go unnoticed. His eyes traveled the curious faces to the front of the classroom until he locked eyes with Valeria Anaya. He looked down immediately and groaned quietly to himself.

Don't look at her. Don't look at her. Don't look at her.

He glanced up and made eye contact with Valeria once again.

Damn it!

But the expression on her face wasn't one he was expecting. She didn't look triumphant or gleeful or disgusted by his presence. Her dark-brown eyes concealed a different emotion, one he couldn't figure out.

"Robbie."

The sharp, though not unfriendly voice broke him out of his musing. He turned to see the only adult in the room walking toward him. He recognized her immediately, though not as a teacher. The shock of seeing her flooded his body with an uncomfortable heat, like the feeling he got when riding his bike too far and too fast on a hot, humid day. She smiled as she approached without any indication that she recognized him. Her unlined hazel eyes and smooth skin bespoke a youthfulness that contrasted fiercely with her maturity and the self-assured way she carried herself.

"Welcome back to school. My name is Ms. Pirhadi, and I'll be teaching this class for the summer. Please, take one of the empty desks."

Ms. Pirhadi returned to the chalkboard. As Robbie moved between the desks to an empty seat, he heard Jace and Grayson whisper 'coma boy' and then snicker to themselves.

"Enough!"

The teacher's rebuke split the relative silence like a whip, causing everyone in the room to jump. She glared at the two boys until they mumbled embarrassed apologies, and then she continued with the lesson.

Robbie's attention drew inward as he struggled to understand how the postgraduate student who frequented the library and whom he last saw on the night of the incident had become his summer school teacher. Seeing her reminded him of the catastrophic night that led to his coma. The memory twisted his stomach in knots.

His thoughts drifted to the librarian. Two days after arriving home from the hospital, Robbie's father showed him the obituary. He didn't know what bothered him most about the dead man's tribute, which had been reprinted in newspapers worldwide. Dr. Asher hadn't lied when he said that Mr. Breton was no small-town librarian. The obituary honored a man well-known and highly respected in the realms of international finance and business. William Breton, cofounder and former chief executive officer at Worcester Norwich, one of the world's largest and most profitable global holding companies. William Breton, the man with a personal fortune estimated at nearly one hundred billion dollars. William Breton, world-famous philanthropist, who donated vast sums of his wealth to worthy charities on six continents. A man whose scholarships, endowments, grants, and fellowships were awarded to legions of financially disadvantaged students the world over so that they could study at the best academic institutions. William Breton, father to Elizabeth and grandfather to Charlotte.

Perhaps it was the last of these revelations that caused Robbie the greatest confusion. The man had never mentioned his family.

Except for the night of the attack. I remember he said the name Elizabeth.

As far as the Nobles knew, he was a childless widower—a man they invited over for dinners and holidays because he had no family. Something else bothered Robbie about the obituary. The lack of any reference to a clandestine life that included glowing swords and old scrolls seemed a glaring omission, though he didn't expect it to be there, of course. What had Dr. Asher said? Something about the library's true purpose and why William Breton came to Bethel.

Robbie still didn't know the answer to those mysteries. When he slept, he slept fitfully, and nightmares plagued his nights. Those awful dreams often took him to a strange place underwater, surrounded by white light and ominous, shadowy figures floating in the dark spaces between. Those inscrutable forms watched him intently, like predators waiting for their prey. He'd wake from those nightmares gasping for breath, as though he'd been drowning.

It dawned on him that he hadn't paid much attention in his first class back at school when his classmates began gathering their belongings to prepare for the next period. Robbie looked around, and the staring faces made him realize that he'd be an object of curiosity for a while. The thought made him uncomfortable. He hoped they'd grow bored of 'coma boy' sooner rather than later. He risked a glance at Valeria, but she stared in the opposite direction as if purposefully avoiding his very existence.

Fine! Two can play that game.

The bell rang, and the students made their way to their second-period classrooms. Ms. Pirhadi stopped him before he left the room.

"Robbie."

"Yes?"

"I just wanted to say that I'm sorry about what happened to you."

"It's fine. I doubt 'coma boy' will follow me beyond high school."

The quizzical look on her face meant he had incorrectly guessed the intent of her words. He corrected himself immediately.

"Oh. Ah, yeah. It's okay."

Ms. Pirhadi continued. "I was at the library that night, doing some research."

"Yeah, I remember," he stated simply.

"I am available to talk about what happened, okay? We can reminisce about William."

He nodded. "Thanks, Ms. Pirhadi. I may take you up on that offer."

Robbie exited the classroom, turned the corner, and stopped at a wall that shouldn't have been there. Robbie looked up to see that the wall was actually Drake Gallant, who stared down at him without expression. The two boys stood alone in the hallway. Robbie didn't know what to say.

Hey, man. How about that secret society?

"Meet me in the school parking lot at twelve-thirty," Gallant said in his deep, rumbling voice, then turned to walk away.

"I can't. I have class."

Gallant didn't stop but replied loudly enough for Robbie to hear him. "No, you don't."

Robbie watched Gallant disappear down the stairs. He unfolded his timetable and confirmed that he had English class with Ms. McKenna at twelve-thirty. He shook his head and went to his second-period classroom.

The remaining morning periods unfolded much the same way as his first class. He'd walk into a classroom. The students stared and whispered, the teacher expressed a sympathetic word, taught the day's lesson, and then the class ended. After lunch, Robbie entered Ms. McKenna's classroom and was surprised to find the lights off and the room empty. Again, he consulted his timetable to ensure he had the correct time and place, which he did. Confused, he reentered the sparsely populated hallway and walked toward the school office. He wasn't paying much attention and almost collided with an open locker door.

"Oh, I'm sor—" The person at the locker closed the door. His apology sputtered and died. Valeria.

"Ah. Hi," he said instead, somewhat awkwardly. He was not in the mood to renew their war of words. He had taken two steps down the hallway when Robbie heard her say something. He looked back and saw that her eyes were watery and red. She took a deep breath.

"I'm happy that you're doing okay."

"Oh. Thanks."

And then Valeria hugged him. It happened so quickly that he didn't have time to be surprised. His back stiffened, and he kept his hands by his sides. She stepped back.

"Without you around, who else can I match wits with?"

His face grew hot, and he felt his anger boiling up, but then it subsided when he realized she wasn't being mean. Her shy, almost embarrassed smile and the slight twinkle in her eyes contained no hostility. She was being playful.

"Gotta go, Robbie. I'm finished with classes for the day."

She walked past him. He noticed her perfume.

Or is it her shampoo?

Usually, he hated that scent, as it always reminded him of Valeria. Today, it smelled sort of good.

He started toward the office. He looked up at one of the clocks in the hallway, then groaned. He was going to be late again.

"Hey! Do you know which room Ms. McKenna is in?"

Valeria turned around to respond. "She's not teaching the summer semester. Her family went to Scotland for two months."

"Oh," came his confused reply.

"See you tomorrow?" Valeria asked.

"Yeah." He scratched his head and watched her walk away. Several seconds later, Gallant's gargantuan form sauntered into view from the direction Valeria had gone.

"You're late, Noble."

"Late for what?" Robbie asked.

"Look, do you want answers or not?"

Though Gallant didn't say the rest, Robbie understood the unspoken part of his question.

Do you want to know about the Knights of Rosewood?

Robbie nodded. "Yeah, I do."

Gallant left the way he came in, not even checking to see if Robbie followed. They emerged into a mostly empty school parking lot. The sun shone brightly overhead. Gallant stopped beside his motorcycle.

Robbie had to admit that the machine was a work of art —dark red, gray, and black with the name *Aprilia* emblazoned on its sides. Gallant handed Robbie a white helmet, placed a black helmet atop his own head, and then sat on the bike.

Robbie tried to figure out how to climb aboard in the least awkward way possible.

"Not much room back here." His voice was muffled by the helmet, which didn't matter because he was speaking to himself. He still hadn't figured out where to put his hands when the motorcycle's engine revved to life. Robbie gripped Gallant's waist to secure himself, afraid he'd fall off the bike. A moment later, Gallant forcefully removed his hands.

"Hold the strap."

"What strap?"

Either Gallant didn't hear him or ignored his question because the motorcycle started moving. Robbie spotted a thin leather strap on the seat between his thighs. It looked flimsy, and he was skeptical that it was strong enough to hold him. He gripped it as tightly as he could. After a few turns, they sped down the streets of Bethel.

8

LOUD THE WAVES ROAR

Exhilaration turned to fear when Gallant maneuvered the motorcycle onto the expressway. The quarterback switched gears rapidly, and the engine whined progressively louder. Two seconds of acceleration sent the bike whipping down the road, passing slower vehicles as if they were stopped. Robbie closed his eyes and took refuge behind Gallant's frame. With every turn and each gut-wrenching burst of speed, Robbie feared that he would fly off the motorcycle.

Abruptly, Gallant slowed the bike. They had pulled off the expressway and were moving at a more reasonable speed up to a sprawling building that Robbie recognized through the helmet visor.

The abandoned mall.

Kids in elementary school would tell each other stories about how the old mall was haunted, so his dad had brought him here to prove that the stories weren't true. The plan backfired. Nightmares about people chasing him through the mall beset Robbie for weeks after their visit.

The two-story shopping complex was run down, the

windows boarded up, and the paint faded and chipped away from years of rain, snow, sunshine, and neglect. Parts of the brick structure had crumbled into disarray. The mall sign, towering above the torn-up pavement of the parking lot, was missing entire sections. The S in the word *Starlight* had disappeared long ago. Nature in the form of overgrown grass from the nearby forest slowly reasserted its dominion over the land nearest the mall.

Gallant drove the motorcycle around a bend and stopped at one of the large department store entrances that bookended the mall on the north and south sides. He flipped up his visor.

"We're here."

Robbie climbed off the bike. He removed the helmet and looked around, unconsciously flexing his hands, which were sore from hanging on to the strap. Gallant secured the helmet behind him, flipped his visor back down, and prepared to go.

"Head inside. Someone's waiting for you."

Before Robbie could respond, Gallant opened the throttle and shot back toward the expressway.

"C'mon, man! Don't leave me here." Robbie's shout mixed with the fading rev of the motorcycle's engine, but no one was around to hear it. He stared at the row of six doors leading into the department store of the abandoned shopping mall. The steel had rusted, while the glass panes were shattered or missing. They were covered with tape, newspapers, and cardboard.

Robbie weighed his options.

I can stay and maybe learn more about this Rosewood stuff, or I can walk home, which I might have to do anyway.

The prospect of crossing the expressway on foot didn't

appeal to him. Besides, he was curious about what, if anything, awaited him inside the building.

He attempted the first three doors but found them locked. The fourth one, however, yielded with a loud creak, and he proceeded into the complex. Though dark, he could see well enough to navigate through the old department store on his way to the mall. Vacant-eyed mannequins, broken and dismembered, like the victims of some violent catastrophe, were arrayed haphazardly in various stages of undress. Tables and shelves had been tossed around, and the glass cases that typically house all manner of fashion accessories from watches to jewelry were smashed, their metal frames twisted by vandals or something else. The floor was littered with detritus, and each step resounded with the crunch of broken glass. A mustiness hung in the air, its scent exactly what he had always imagined this mall would smell like.

He made his way into the mall proper from the department store. He saw a similar state of vandalism and disrepair wherever he looked. Although not superstitious, Robbie felt uneasy in the quiet emptiness of the place. It reminded him of the dark, silent vault under the library, but unlike the vault, the mall was intended for human use. This distinction made the empty mall more unsettling.

The building's layout was straight from north to south, so he didn't need signs or a map to know he was walking toward the mall's center. He emerged into an open space that looked like an atrium, empty except for a pair of long tables and a shadowy figure standing between them.

"Hello?"

His voice echoed loudly, startling him as the architecture or the building materials amplified the sound. He approached the figure, and a light blazed from somewhere to his left, then another from his right. It took a moment for his eyes to adjust. Inexplicably, he stood on a cobblestone street beneath a beautiful clear blue sky. The avenue was vast and expansive. Columned buildings ran up and down either side of the road. Everything around him appeared incomplete, a little fuzzy around the edges, like he was staring through a haze of fog. Sounds filled his ears. Bleating goats, creaking wooden carts, and human voices talking and shouting and singing.

Another voice, somehow different from the others, broke through the growing din, though Robbie wasn't sure of its exact location.

"This is where it began. Not just where but when, too. The city of Alexandria in Egypt. Not as it is now, but as it was more than two thousand years ago."

A third light flared to life, and the scene became solid, clearing the haze, and it was as if he actually stood in that ancient place. People appeared out of nowhere, bustling here and there, dressed in loose-fitting fabrics. They walked around him, unaware of his presence, like a ghost from the future.

Robbie looked up again and had to shield his eyes from the bright intensity of the heatless sun, which sat almost directly above his head. Various noises soon reached his ears, building slowly out of the silence into the sounds of a vibrant metropolis from long ago. The people spoke in a language unknown to him, the horses pulled carts full of food or other goods, and he heard the sounds of a quayside nearby. His eyes and ears told him he had traveled to another time and place, but the dank air and musty odor assured him that he remained inside the deserted shopping mall. To confirm what his nose told him, he reached out to touch one of the nearby carts, and his hand passed through it without making contact. Men, women, and children slipped by him, and again, he reached out to touch what his sight told him was there, with the same result.

A girl walked down the street toward him. As she drew nearer, he saw she was a little older than he had first surmised. Maybe in her late twenties. She, too, seemed out of place. Not the light bronze of her skin, long dark hair, or almost-black eyes, which seemed native to this strange place where he now stood. Her trendy eyeglasses, dark jeans with white sneakers, and white blouse set her apart from the residents of this city. She also carried a computer tablet.

"Thanks for coming, Robbie. Please follow me."

Robbie gestured around them, indicating the incredible sights and sounds. Something unmistakable had blossomed in his chest and spread warmth through his body.

Wonder.

"What is this?" he asked in amazement.

The woman waved for him to follow and then began walking down the street. Robbie followed, and they weaved through the crowds and between the buildings without speaking. They passed through a market and cut through a lush garden. He gawked at several buildings that looked like temples, with beautiful statues that honored one god or another. They emerged along the quay, and Robbie marveled at the sights and sounds of a magnificent harbor that ran along the coastal side of the city.

How is this possible?

Robbie was sure they had walked for at least a mile, turning down this street and that, but the mall atrium was certainly not that large.

Ships large and small were moored along the wooden docks. Hundreds of men, many stripped to their waists in the brilliant sunshine, carried cargo to carts or the warehouses lining the harbor. Merchants, or perhaps city officials, patrolled the docks, checking shipping manifests, accepting fees, arguing, greeting, and bartering with ship captains and other sailors.

Incoming and outgoing ships filled the bay. The vessels varied in more ways than Robbie thought possible. Large ships with enormous sails, some vibrantly colored and adorned with strange symbols, some with sails so faded and worn, it was apparent they had sailed for years under the scorching sun. He could also make out smaller ships, some without sails, but instead with wooden oars moving in time that propelled the sleek crafts through the water. His breath caught as he saw a wondrous white building rising to the heavens from an island at the far edge of the bay. It dominated the living tableau like a beacon of light in the darkness.

The stunning vista, with all its attendant details, caused him to lose sight of the woman. He spotted her a moment later, walking up a huge pier that extended into the sea. Robbie navigated the jetty, avoiding obstacles and people as if they were real, though he knew they were not.

The woman stood at the edge of the empty dock, staring out across the water. She was looking for something on the horizon. Before Robbie could speak, she pointed to an object so far away that Robbie didn't recognize it at first. But after several moments, the object resolved into a ship, and then more ships appeared just above the point where sea and sky met. Steadily, the vessels sailed closer to the harbor.

"Caesar sailed the Roman navy to Alexandria," the woman said.

The scene around them changed. The sky shifted from clear, perfect blue to a nightmare of thick, black smoke. The moored ships, cargo, and buildings of the harbor were ablaze. A thousand fires burned, and screams and shouts echoed all around them.

"A devastating fire broke out in the harbor, engulfing the ships and burning parts of the wondrous city."

The scene changed again. The wooden dock beneath his feet, the blackened sky overhead, the ships, and even the sea dissolved, reforming into the interior of a building engulfed in flames. Robbie and the woman stood at the center of an inferno that burned everything around them, scorching even the ground and the stone. Scraps of paper, black and burned around the edges, drifted before Robbie's eyes. Mesmerized, he knelt to pick a piece off the floor, only for his fingers to pluck at empty air. It was an illusion, like everything else around them, though the rampaging fire burned so bright, he squinted and turned away to protect his eyes. The shelves and wooden support beams cracked, shifted, and collapsed, creating a roar that caused him to flinch. And yet, Robbie felt no heat nor smelled the smoke that would have surely killed him.

"The Royal Library was a repository for all the knowledge in the known world. Science, mathematics, navigation, philosophy, history, and literature. As a port city of vast importance, scrolls and scholars passed through every day. A city law allowed officials to seize any scroll from docked ships. The scrolls were taken to the Royal Library, where they were copied and studied. Most of the library's collection burned in the great fire. The collected knowledge of an age burnt to ashes."

The scene shifted again.

They were outside, and it was nighttime. They stood with a tall stone wall to their backs, just beyond a wooden gate. A steady stream of people accompanying horse-drawn carts walked toward the distant horizon. The young woman watched the carts depart and then focused on Robbie. She gestured at the caravan, which slowly disappeared into the light of a new day.

"But not everything was lost to the fire."

The scene faded around them slowly until the ancient world was gone, and they stood once again in the darkness of the forgotten mall.

"What— what was that?"

The woman spoke matter-of-factly, as if he hadn't just experienced something miraculous. "A computer graphic representation of history, rendered in three dimensions. What do you think?"

"Ah, I'm sorry?" Her question caught him off guard. This woman had shown him something remarkable, and now she was asking his opinion like she had made him a peanut butter and jelly sandwich. She smiled expectantly at him.

"My hologram. What do you think of it?"

"Incredible. I have never seen anything like it. But what do you mean by *your* hologram? Did you make that?"

She nodded. "It's sort of a side project of mine. I think it's my best one yet. Alexandria is my hometown, so I spent more time on the details." She paused. "Well, I was born in modern Alexandria, not the 50 BCE version of it."

A side project?

Robbie's most ambitious side projects usually involved household chores, like figuring out how to do his laundry.

"The hologram was phenomenal, but your entrance could use some work. Maybe say hello first or tell me your name or what I'm doing here."

"I'm sorry. Didn't Drake mention that I would be meeting you here?"

He shook his head. "Gallant was rather vague."

"Oh! That's too bad. It must be odd coming to a deserted

building in the middle of nowhere to meet a stranger. Very creepy. My name is Yasmin Elsayed. I understand that you've already met my brother, Hamza. The night Demeter attacked you and William."

The events following his encounter with Andars Demeter were forgotten in a haze of sickness and fear. Still, he vaguely remembered glimpsing a man in Gallant's company. The man with the ponytail who had emerged from the darkness.

"Why am I here?" he asked, looking around the space. "Come to think of it, why are you here?"

"Well, we need your help, and we can't meet at the library since it's still closed. Officially, at least. It'd definitely raise some questions."

Yasmin motioned for him to follow her. They moved toward the center of the atrium, which was dark except for the ambient light streaming through the cracked skylight above their heads.

"Do you always work in the dark?"

It took Yasmin a moment to respond to the comment. "Lights! Right."

She began to swipe and tap on the tablet in her hands. Three objects, each slightly smaller than a kid's soccer ball, came floating from behind them a moment later. They resembled spheres, though it was hard to tell their exact shapes from his vantage.

"Meet the stars of my hologram show: Ultra, X, and Gamma."

The spheres beeped and spun in the air around Yasmin.

"Increase the light in this space to five hundred lux, please."

The objects moved to different positions and slowly

increased their brightness until the atrium was filled with warm light.

"Do they understand you?" Robbie asked.

She tilted her head to the side. "No, they're not sentient like Isa, if that's what you're asking. I programmed them to respond to various inputs, including natural voice commands."

Sentient? Robbie wondered at the word. Was this woman suggesting that the voice in Mr. Breton's phone was — alive?

Something on one of the tables caught his eye. Matte-black metal, hard edges, and sleek curves shaped like a large animal. His veins turned to ice when he realized what it was.

"Hellcat."

9

—————

THE MOON SHINES AS BRIGHT AS DAY

Robbie's tongue tripped over the word, and his heart thundered in his chest. He gasped for air and took a step back.

"Oh! No, no, it's okay," Yasmin assured him. "It's incapacitated. We found it in the vault, cut in half with several blown-out CPU cores. It can only cause harm if it falls on you."

He closed his eyes and tried to catch his breath. Looking at the hellcat again, he saw that Yasmin was right. Its front and back halves were placed in proper alignment but severed. His breathing slowed. Yasmin retrieved something from the workbench.

"Mr. Breton's smartphone," Robbie said.

"Only an authorized user can access the phone. That's you, apparently."

He took the device, and the screen came to life. Yasmin's eyes widened.

"Expected, but surprising nonetheless. I need to see the device logs from the night William died."

Robbie tried to return the phone to her, but she shook her head. "It won't work for anyone but you."

"How is that possible? I've never heard of a phone that stops working when someone other than the owner touches it."

A slight smile appeared on Yasmin's face. "Advanced biometrics."

"Like, it scans my face or my fingerprints or something?"

"Those are two data points. The device is also tuned to the owner's sclera, heartbeat, vascular system, and a few other unique biomarkers. The authentication system locks or unlocks the phone so quickly that it seems instantaneous."

"That's pretty cool," he acknowledged.

"You'll need to navigate to the log and send it to me. I'm sure you don't want me reading over your shoulder."

Yasmin relayed instructions for accessing the log, which Robbie followed. When he finally reached a time-stamped document dated the night of the attack, she asked him to make a swiping gesture toward her, which he did. A moment later, her attention shifted to the tablet and the information on its screen. She seemed to forget that he was there. After locating a stool under the workbench, he sat and waited.

Yasmin's shoulders slumped forward, and she closed her eyes, letting out a long breath. She swiped up on her tablet, and a clear projection of the document materialized in midair above their heads.

"The log recorded significant gaps between the times when William had the phone in his possession. Morning, very briefly around noon, and then not again until shortly before he died."

Robbie nodded. "Mr. Breton complained about mobile

phones all the time. You know, people at the library on their phones instead of reading or learning. Typical old-fashioned stuff. He used to joke that he gave me the job at the library because my parents wouldn't let me have a phone. I dunno. Maybe he wasn't joking."

The information from Yasmin's tablet remained mirrored above their heads, but she was scrolling through it so quickly Robbie could barely decipher a word. His curiosity got the better of him, and he looked around the immediate area, searching for the light source that projected the image from Yasmin's tablet. It didn't take long to find it. A small sphere floated in place about ten feet in the air. He walked under it, trying to get a closer look. The floating device resembled one of the hologram spheres he saw earlier, but smaller. Upon closer inspection, he realized the baseball-sized silver object wasn't round at all. Instead, it was many-sided. Each side was the shape of a pentagon.

What is this called? A polyhedron?

He hated geometry. Robbie quickly forgot about his least favorite subject as he admired the levitating device. The image it produced was unlike anything he had seen before. The projectors at school were weak and required a screen and absolute darkness to look mediocre. The image this device projected looked solid enough to touch. Unsurprising, perhaps, given the hologram from earlier, but still impressive. Yasmin's barely audible lament drew him back to her analysis of the mobile device log.

"Oh, William."

Robbie caught the phrases 'critical blood loss' and 'death imminent' in the words above their heads before she began scrolling again.

She spoke a few moments later. "It's true, then." She made the pronouncement to herself. The log must've confirmed a truth that the young woman had been desperate to avoid or deny.

"You swore the oath. You are Breton's heir."

Robbie remained silent. He didn't even know what it meant to be William Breton's heir. According to the news reports he'd seen, the librarian's vast fortune went to his daughter and granddaughter.

"Unprecedented," Yasmin whispered before closing the document and opening a new one.

Several more minutes passed until she found what she sought. She clapped her hands together and spoke excitedly. "Here we go!"

Robbie tried to make sense of the words overhead, but they looked like computer code, which he could barely read despite his A grade in computer science class during the first semester.

"Look here." Yasmin highlighted one section that was as indecipherable as all the rest.

"Ah, I can't read that," he admitted.

"Isa attempted to breach the drone's firewall but failed."

"Drone?" he asked.

"What did you call it? A hellcat?" she asked.

He shrugged. "Yeah."

Yasmin continued.

"She tried to infiltrate the hellcat repeatedly, using different techniques."

Robbie frowned in confusion at the woman's excitement. "Is that good or bad?"

Yasmin scrolled through thousands of lines of code.

"Here, Isa tried something new. It disguised its cyber-attack as an update patch to the hellcat's firmware, but the hellcat's firewall rejected the packet because it was too small. Isa needed a lot of immediately available data to mimic an authorized firmware update, so it transmitted itself over the hellcat's own network. I can see in the code that Isa left behind enough of itself to ensure your kit still functioned."

Robbie shook his head. "I don't know what you're talking about, but that doesn't seem right. Isa was talking to me one second and was gone the next."

"Isa processed all of that in less than half a second. It would have required more time to execute its plan once it transmitted over to the drone, but that is speculation since I have no log for that. Isa's problem-solving skills are awe-inspiring. It learned from previous attempts, adapted to adversity, and attempted new solutions, exceeding my explicit programming."

Robbie thought back to the moment in time they were discussing, then asked a question. "Why didn't it replicate itself instead of transferring to the hellcat? A copy and paste instead of a cut and paste. It seems— I don't know. More efficient?"

"That's a good thought, Robbie. But no. Part of Isa's source code forbids her from replicating herself. One of our safeguards to keep it in check."

"'Herself?'" he asked.

"Oh, did I say that?"

He nodded. "Yes. Is Isa an AI?"

Yasmin laughed in response and rolled her eyes. Her reaction made her seem younger than she probably was.

"The term 'artificial intelligence' doesn't mean much anymore. It gets thrown around and applied to vacuums, lawnmowers, and air fresheners. No, Isa is the cornerstone of my inorganic self-awareness project."

Inorganic self-awareness. ISA.

"What makes Isa different from AI?" he asked.

Yasmin beamed, apparently excited to discuss this topic, and she launched into an impassioned explanation. "AIs are glorified chatbots. Programmers combine natural language recognition and statistical probability models with rudimentary machine learning to create the illusion of sentience. My ISA project meets the Cartesian threshold of *cogito, ergo sum*, and it gets smarter over time without my intervention."

Robbie nodded as though he understood, but some of what Yasmin said was lost on him. "So, what happened to it — or *her*?"

Yasmin pointed at the hellcat lying on the table. "I think *it*'s in there somewhere." She overemphasized the pronoun. "I'm trying to get it back out."

"Why not use the source code to make a new one?"

She shook her head. "No, Isa was one of a kind, tied exclusively to William's smartphone, helping him with his work in Bethel."

"Work? As in, pretending to be a librarian?"

Yasmin stared up at the computer code. "I built Isa to help William translate the scrolls. The more time they worked together, the more Isa evolved."

"How is that possible?"

"Robbie, do you know the location of William's notebook?"

Yasmin's abrupt change of subject surprised him. "That lady asked me the same thing at the hospital. I saw Mr. Breton with tons of books. He worked in a library, remember?"

"He likely treated this book differently. He would not have wanted others to see it."

"I remember he carried a brown leather notebook sometimes. It had a leather strap that wrapped around it."

Yasmin's eyes were intense now and locked firmly onto his own. "Can you tell me anything else?"

"That's it. I only ever saw it when he was alone in his office."

The words she spoke next seemed more for herself than for Robbie. "We checked his office. It's not there."

"What's so important about the notebook?"

She returned her attention to her tablet. The screen above their heads disappeared, and the three objects she used for her holograms converged on their location. "Let me show you something."

The light flashed, and when his vision adjusted, the atrium was gone. Once again, he stood in a city, but this one differed from ancient Alexandria. People walked the streets here, too, but they wore turbans and desert robes. The architecture reminded Robbie of a mosque.

"This is Baghdad during the Golden Age. It was an era of incredible scientific discovery."

Yasmin pointed to a large, spired building in the distance. "That is called Bayt Ul-Hikma, the House of Wisdom. It was also known as the Grand Library of Baghdad. Much of the advancements of that era come from Bayt Ul-Hikma."

Robbie let the sights and sounds wash over him. His open mouth and stunned silence were proof of the effectiveness of the illusion. History class would be much more interesting if lessons could be taught inside a hologram. Yasmin spoke, and her voice was more solemn. "The House of Wisdom was destroyed in the thirteenth century when the Mongols turned sword and spear against the city."

The scene shifted so suddenly that it made Robbie dizzy. They stood not far from a ruined building where fires burned down to embers, and the men who looked to have recently fought a battle lay dead or dying. Robbie surveyed the scene, recognizing it as the same place where he had just stood, but at a different moment in time. His attention was drawn to the carnage. He knew it wasn't real. Nevertheless, it disturbed him. Trying to ignore the scene, he asked a question. "Why did they destroy it?"

His question made her smile, though he did not know why.

"Like the Royal Library, the details surrounding the destruction of Bayt Ul-Hikma and the fate of certain works in its magnificent collection are not as historians and scholars believe."

Again, the people, surroundings, and sound shifted and rematerialized into another place and time. They stood on an empty cobbled road between two rows of tall buildings. The pale light suggested dawn or nightfall, though Robbie couldn't see the sun and had lost all sense of direction. A loud wind blew between the buildings, whipping the falling snow into a frenzied dance. The wintery scene that his eyes beheld and the warm, humid air on his skin and in his lungs created a strange juxtaposition. His brain warred with itself. He saw and heard one reality while his remaining senses experienced another. Yasmin began walking up the narrow street, which angled steeply toward a building at the top of the hill. Robbie again marveled at the sophistication of the illusion. His eyes perceived the road sloping upward with each step, though he didn't think the ground was any less flat than it had been elsewhere. He held out his hand and watched as a snowflake fell toward his skin and passed through on its way to the ground.

"This is Buda in Hungary during the fifteenth century." Yasmin's voice recaptured his attention.

"Let me guess." Robbie had to speak louder because of

the violent whistling of the wind. "We're here to see another library?"

She regarded him a moment. "No. The same library."

Robbie furrowed his brow in confusion.

"I don't understand. You've shown me three cities spanning more than what ... fifteen hundred years. How can they be the same library?"

"Let me show you." Yasmin continued walking until they rounded a corner where a walled castle with tall battlements and towers dominated the entire vista. Robbie had only a moment to digest the scene before it shifted again, and they were inside a large hall lined with hundreds of books. Two men in what Robbie thought must be Renaissance garb sat hunched over broad wooden desks, their quill pens moving from ink bottle to page and back at a steady pace.

"This castle was the home of Europe's philosopher king, and the books you see here are part of the library collection he commissioned—the Bibliotheca Corviniana."

A moment later, the scene flashed again. The colors, light, walls, floor, and decor reformed into a dark, windowless room. Yasmin walked from the room and into a dark hallway. Light, originating from a different room at the end of the hall, diffused dimly through the darkness. There wasn't much to this illusion other than the stone floor and walls with no ornamentation. As they neared the end of the hallway, Robbie could make out an arched doorway and a room lit with numerous torches on the other side.

Beyond the doorway, elaborate tapestries hung from the stone walls, and a rich carpet was spread across the floor. A large hearth blazed with a fire he could not feel. Robbie immediately ignored the intricate details of the room, his attention drawn to the people assembled within. All were bearded, though some beards were short and trim, while others were long and uneven. The men ranged in age from their mid-twenties to their forties. Some had black, red, or yellow hair, while others were bald or had hair and beards streaked with gray and white. Almost everyone seemed at ease. Mugs were scattered around the room, wherever a man rested against a wall or conversed with another.

Robbie moved between the men. He counted twelve. Some stood out from the others. One, positioned off to the side, conveyed obvious discomfort and distrust. The largest man in the room wore a dark expression. His mug remained untouched, and his body language suggested he wanted to be left alone. Another man stood out by his gregarious nature. He wore a wide grin and spoke in a loud, booming voice, though Robbie could not understand the language. He was obviously likable, surrounded by three others who watched, listened, and laughed. Robbie smiled at his easy nature. The solitary man scowled at the gregarious man.

A lean figure strode into the room from the arched doorway where Robbie and Yasmin had entered a few moments before. The men turned or stood up from their chairs upon seeing the figure and kneeled before him in deference, all of them bowing their heads to look at the ground. The man's demeanor was regal. Yasmin had mentioned Europe's philosopher king. This must be him.

The king began to speak in an unfamiliar language, and the men around the room rose and walked to meet him. He clasped each of their right arms and embraced them.

"Pause Corvinus commission simulation."

Yasmin spoke the words, and the men around them froze in place. She gestured to the young man. "This is Matthias Corvinus, king of Hungary. He chose the men in this room from across Europe, regardless of their country of origin, religion, or political affiliation, for a very important task. The philosopher king knighted them, gave them commissions, and swore them and their children and their children's children to duty without end: to protect something and defend it with their lives. All of this was done in complete secret. They were bannerless. As time passed, they adopted a name: the Knights of Rosewood."

The scene flickered and resolved into yet another fire. The inferno licked the ceiling high above their heads and consumed the bookshelves. The sounds of a battle raged somewhere outside the room. The maelstrom continued for a time, and Robbie walked in its midst, allowing the heatless flame and wail of collapsing support beams to wash over him until, finally, the illusion winked out.

"The Bibliotheca Corviniana, the House of Wisdom, and the Royal Library of Alexandria were all destroyed by fire."

"Wait. Are you trying to tell me that these fires were related somehow?"

"The fires weren't accidents, Robbie. Each was an effort to capture the scrolls."

His mind immediately flashed to the scroll on the desk below the library.

"Think back to the first hologram I showed you. A cart departing the city of Alexandria under cover of night. That cart carried twenty-seven scrolls out of Egypt."

"You're saying that the scroll Mr. Breton told me to protect came from Alexandria? From the time of Julius Caesar?"

"Well, papyrus and vellum aren't the most durable materials, so the scrolls were painstakingly copied from one decaying medium to another over the years. However, many of the wooden spindles are that old, yes."

Robbie rubbed his brow, trying to process all this information. "What's so important about the scrolls?"

Yasmin turned her attention back to her tablet for a moment, and an image of an unrolled scroll appeared above their heads. She zoomed into the black ink to reveal strange characters.

"They contain advanced forms of mathematics, physics, biology, chemistry, cosmology, and other topics."

Robbie shook his head, not believing what Yasmin was saying. "Yeah, but no. What do you mean by advanced?"

"Robbie, all of the extraordinary things you've seen since that night at the library: Isa, the barrier that protected you, the weapon that pierced your shoulder, even the things here like the dodecahedrons, were created based on the knowledge the Rosewood translated from the scrolls."

He began to walk alongside the workbench, looking at the levitating geometric devices, remembering those glowing indigo swords. Yasmin looked at him as if weighing what to say next. Finally, she spoke. "Corvinus established the Knights of Rosewood to protect the secrets of the scrolls. You swore a five-hundred-year-old oath to a dying man to preserve that secret."

Robbie sat back down and rubbed his forehead. His mind churned with questions and uncertainties. He finally gave voice to one of those questions. "Are you saying that someone in ancient Rome or Greece or wherever was walking around with cellphones that make swords appear from thin air? I don't remember reading about that in a textbook."

Yasmin laughed. "Not quite. The scrolls contain advanced knowledge but don't necessarily show us how to bridge the technology gap to use or even understand that knowledge."

Yasmin correctly interpreted Robbie's frown as confusion and tried a different tack. "What do you think would happen if people from the first or second centuries discovered blueprints for a modern internal combustion engine?"

Robbie shrugged. "Not much. They probably wouldn't know what they had."

"Exactly! But what if they looked at those blueprints after the first combustion engines were invented and recognized that they possessed plans for a more advanced version of machines that already existed?"

He thought about it briefly. "I guess it depends on whether or not they could copy what they saw in the blueprints. It's unlikely the same manufacturing techniques we use today were available to the inventors of the first engine."

Yasmin nodded. "Very true, but parts of those plans might result in some immediate advancements. Over time, through new manufacturing or metallurgic methods or new fuels, and so on, the gap between their technology and the technology in the blueprints would become smaller, and thus, easier to bridge."

He thought he understood. "So, where or when did the scrolls come from?"

"The scrolls themselves are a human invention, but the knowledge contained within the scrolls? That's more complicated."

He shook his head. "You're not going to tell me?"

"We'll have a chance to discuss that over the days and weeks to come."

"Um, excuse me?" he asked, confused.

Yasmin smiled. "Your training begins tomorrow."

10

A WATCH I'LL KEEP

H501U9993948

Robbie frowned at the mix of numbers and letters staring back at him from the screen of what was once Mr. Breton's smartphone. The sequence first appeared shortly after he left the mall with the device. Upon waking the following day, the screen displayed the same message. He sent a screenshot to Yasmin, who seemed just as perplexed by its appearance. She offered to help him run a diagnostic on the smartphone when he came back to the mall after school was finished.

Robbie was thrilled when Yasmin allowed him to keep the device, as he seemed to be the only fifteen-year-old in Bethel without one. The biggest obstacle to enjoying his new gadget was his parents. However, after the 'gas leak' and his three-month coma, they seemed more receptive to the idea that he was ready to enter the modern era of humanity instead of living in the Dark Ages. Even if they agreed that he could own a smartphone, he'd need a plausible explanation for where this device came from.

Yasmin surprised him when she revealed that he'd never

need to pay a cellphone bill or charge the phone. She promised to explain how it worked when they had more time. She said that a lot, it seemed.

Dinner with his parents following his first meeting with Yasmin had been awkward. Normally, he felt comfortable talking to his mom and dad about almost everything that troubled him. This time, he couldn't tell them anything. His new clandestine schedule meant he'd spend his afternoon at the mall when he should have been in school. The deception left him with a sour feeling in the pit of his stomach.

Despite his best efforts, his parents could clearly sense his despondency. And in turn, he sensed their worry. They probed gently about how he was feeling and what he thought of summer school. Robbie answered that things were fine without much elaboration. His unenthusiastic answers sounded inadequate to him as well.

He couldn't figure out how Yasmin managed to trick his parents and the school's administrators regarding his timetable. According to the school's version of Robbie's class schedule, he was at home in the afternoon for remote learning, while his parents believed he was physically in class. What he would be doing at the mall remained a mystery, but after Yasmin's impressive history lesson, he was curious to learn more about the Rosewood.

He enlisted Artie's help in his pursuit of more time at the mall. Robbie informed his parents that he'd be riding his bike to Artie's house after school every day that week so the two friends could hang out. Worried that this particular lie was enough to bring down his house of cards, Robbie told his friend about the deception. Artie made it clear that he was unhappy with the arrangement, primarily because Robbie refused to tell him where he was really going. In the end, Artie agreed, but only if Robbie promised to actually hang out before he left for his family vacation to Quebec.

As he walked through the hallways of St. Boniface on his way to Ms. Pirhadi's math class, he finally felt like a normal kid, thanks, in large part, to the smartphone in his hand. He was so distracted, excitedly typing messages to Artie about the device, that Robbie collided with Valeria outside her locker for the second time in two days.

"I don't know, Robbie. You're either trying to kill me or aggressively flirt with me."

Sputtering and red-faced, he barely managed to squeak out an apology before she laughed at his discomfort. She nodded in the direction of homeroom.

"We should go. After yesterday's beat-down of Jrayson, I'd prefer to avoid Ms. Piranha's wrath."

"Jrayson?" He articulated the word into a question.

"You know, Jace and Grayson. They're attached at the hip, so they become a single entity, like a celebrity couple."

Robbie smiled despite knowing very little about celebrity couples. Then his eyes widened when he realized something. "Do you have a name for me and Artie?"

Valeria looked down at the floor without speaking for a minute as if deciding what to say. "Arbie," she practically whispered.

He stopped walking. "What!"

"Ugh. I know! It's stupid. I'm sorry."

She looked up at him with wide, repentant eyes and gently touched his arm, waiting to see how he would respond. Indeed, "Arbie" annoyed him, but at the same time, he had to admit that he had been an equal participant in their conflict over the years.

He shrugged. "Just not very clever. I'm sort of surprised, actually."

She scanned his face, likely trying to gauge his feelings. Eventually, she smiled and nodded. "You're right. Not my best work."

They continued toward the classroom.

"Speaking of nicknames, what's with 'Ms. Piranha?'" he asked.

Valeria let out a breath. "She's intense. Very and always."

Robbie stared straight ahead. "She was at the library that night."

He knew Valeria was looking at him, though she remained silent. Thankfully, he didn't have to clarify what he meant by 'that night.'

"Mr. Copeland was supposed to teach the class. Well, he did, for about a week, actually," Valeria clarified.

"The music teacher?"

"Yes. Mr. Copeland told us he was 'very eager to demonstrate that math and music are not so different, after all.'" Valeria imitated the music teacher's distinctive high-pitched voice.

"What happened?"

Valeria shrugged. "Ms. Versteepen showed up last week, introduced Ms. Pirhadi as our new math teacher, and then announced you were attending summer school with us."

As they entered the classroom, they noticed that most other students were already seated. Ms. Pirhadi was writing the day's lesson on the chalkboard. They went to their desks on opposite sides of the room and sat almost simultaneously.

Valeria's nickname for their math teacher seemed more justified as the period progressed. Ms. Pirhadi glared and was anything but patient when she asked someone a question. The awkwardness that followed each interrogation was worsened by how ineffectual she was at teaching them math. Robbie remembered snippets of conversations he had overheard between her and Mr. Breton, wherein the two adults spoke eloquently on a variety of subjects. He figured that she was pretty clever. Yet, in math class, she lacked the ability to impart the principles they were trying to learn.

After sitting anxiously through half the class, hopeful that she didn't ask him a question he couldn't possibly answer, Robbie noticed that Ms. Pirhadi was picking on everyone except him and Valeria. He assumed the teacher was going easy on 'coma boy,' and Valeria was the only student in class who seemed to know the answers, which didn't surprise Robbie at all. She was known as one of the smartest students in the whole school.

Then why is she taking summer school?

The bell rang, which resulted in a collective sigh of relief from his classmates. He prepared to leave, but Ms. Pirhadi asked him to stay behind for the second time in as many days. Everyone exited the classroom, including Valeria. He felt an odd pang when she left without so much as a glance.

"How are you feeling today?" the teacher asked.

Surprisingly disappointed, if I'm being honest.

"Good."

That was the best response he could manage, though he sensed that she didn't care how he answered the question.

"Robbie, did you know about Mr. Breton's secret life?"

His eyes widened, and he croaked out an uncomfortable reply. "Ah, what secret life?"

Ms. Pirhadi studied his face before smiling—not a warm smile. He had almost asked, *which secret life?* But checked himself at the last moment. Still, his response seemed to satisfy his teacher in a way he didn't understand.

She shook her head as if admonishing the dead librarian. "He was less than honest with the good people of this town. Hiding so much of who he was."

Robbie said nothing else. She stared at him, and the silence stretched for what felt like several minutes, though likely only a few seconds had passed.

"Can I go, Ms. Pirhadi?"

Her eyes narrowed in a flash of momentary anger, and then she smiled and nodded. "Of course."

The change from pleasant to angry back to pleasant happened so quickly that Robbie wondered if he had imagined it.

"Ah, thanks." He exited the classroom.

Robbie was running toward his next class when a familiar voice called out to him. He turned to see Blake coming toward him. A moment later, she hugged him tightly. She immediately relaxed her embrace and suddenly looked apologetic.

"Too rough?"

He shook his head. "I'm fine, Blake."

She laughed warmly.

"Why are you at school?" he asked.

"I'm working with Ms. Versteepen in the office today. It's not as interesting as working at the veterinary clinic. Dr. Dacre lets me observe the animal surgeries, which beats all the filing I do here."

"That's great! I've never met anyone who loves animals as much as you."

"Trust me. My parents are less than thrilled about the clinic. They swore that if I bring home another recovering stray, they will disown me."

Robbie had known Mr. and Ms. Brooks since he and Blake were kids. He doubted she could ever disappoint them.

"How are your classes?" she asked. "You have the new math teacher, right?"

"Ms. Piranha," he confirmed.

Blake covered her mouth to stifle a laugh. "That's terrible! I'm sure she isn't that bad."

Robbie shrugged. "Valeria thinks so. She came up with the nickname."

Blake clapped her hands excitedly. "Wait, are you and Valeria *talking*? With civility?"

"Yeah, I guess so." Robbie nodded. "She's been—different since I came back to school."

Blake looked around conspiratorially. "Valeria would kill me if she knew I told you this, but Robbie, she was distraught when she heard about what happened to you."

The bell rang.

How distraught?

"Oh my gosh. You gotta go! Ms. Versteepen will not be happy if she finds out you were late because of me."

Robbie turned and ran toward the science lab.

Blake's voice followed him down the hallway. "We need to figure out a time to catch up."

"For sure," he yelled back.

Before entering his next classroom, he checked the phone for messages. He wasn't comfortable keeping it in his pocket since the school strictly enforced policies governing the use of electronic devices, and he didn't want to lose the phone, especially on his first day of owning it. Artie had sent him a few messages, mostly memes and videos, which he'd view after class. The phone also indicated he had four messages from an unknown source. All the messages were the same alphanumeric sequence he had received since yesterday. He dismissed the notifications and slipped the device into his backpack.

He was four minutes late for science class, but Mr. Cohen casually waved him to his seat and continued his lecture on the states of matter. Robbie tried to pay attention but couldn't focus on the lesson. His world had become much more complicated since the night of the attack, and seeing Blake had created another kind of dissonance.

Robbie and Blake had been constant companions from grade one until their first year in high school. Along with Valeria, they had played on the same soccer and baseball teams, taken swim lessons together, and hung out at each other's homes. Somewhere along the way, Robbie's feelings for Blake shifted from friendship to something more.

He remembered biking through the sunflower field near Mr. Philips's farm when they were eleven or twelve. The wind caught Blake's hair just so, and the dappled sunlight filtered onto her face when she turned to look at him. That look had been a spark that ignited a fire in his heart, and the fire had blazed since that day.

His fondness for Blake was immeasurably complex, and no one else could understand it. Certainly not Artie, who teased him about his occasional moods of wistful melancholy. Those moods increased in frequency and duration when Blake first told him that she and Gallant were seeing each other. Blake was an incredible person. Smart and kind and generous. But also undeniably beautiful. Robbie reduced Gallant's interest in Blake to nothing but a physical infatuation, while his own feelings were far more noble.

Something had changed since waking from the coma, however. Knowing how his prolonged illness affected her made him realize that their relationship transcended their childhood friendship, as well as whatever unrequited feelings he had harbored. He loved her still, but the longing he once felt was gone, and in its place was a renewed sense of loyalty, admiration, respect, and trust.

Robbie rode his mountain bike to the abandoned Starlight Mall after his last class ended. His unofficial class schedule, the one Yasmin created unbeknownst to his parents or the school, ended at lunch. Combined with the lie he concocted with Artie's help, he had about two uninterrupted hours at the mall. He took a drink of water and then set the bottle back into the cage on his bike. His first long ride since the incident left him tired, sore, and slick with sweat. He scratched vigorously at the myriad bug bites all over his body. The forests that grew behind the St. Boniface football field, through part of Bethel, and up to the west side of the expressway were dense, humid, and filled with insects of all shapes, sizes, and appetites. Yasmin had told him he'd need to find his own way to the mall and then mentioned the trails. Gallant was busy doing other things, and while Yasmin could send a car for him, it was important that no one suspected he was involved with anything unusual.

The most harrowing part of the journey was crossing the four-lane expressway while carrying his bike on his back. Fortunately, traffic was fairly light in the early afternoon. The final leg of the journey was a steep hill that led the rest of the way to the mall.

He stowed his bike inside the department store doors behind a rack of dusty, moth-eaten clothes. He went to the atrium, where Yasmin sat at the table with the hellcat. She swiped and typed rapidly on her tablet. The dissected monster remained inert, but its eyes glowed menacingly once again. The sight made him uneasy, and he tried to hide his shaking hands. Without looking up from her screen, Yasmin spoke as if he had been standing there for hours.

"I found the source of the strange message you're

receiving on your phone. I connected an external power supply to the hellcat yesterday after you left. Our killer robot friend here is broadcasting an encrypted message using conventional cellular signals, which is odd for many reasons."

"Why is that odd?"

"Well, I can't even locate anything resembling a cellular modem in all this mangled hardware and circuitry."

Robbie's eyes widened as comprehension blossomed. "Broadcasting? Aren't you worried that it will give Demeter this location?"

She nodded absently for a moment, then began shaking her head. "Yes. No. Well, normally, yes, it would be a concern. But you see, it only broadcasts a single message to a single device. The device is your phone. And the message is 'QH50IU9993948.'"

"How do you know? Didn't you say the message was encrypted?"

Yasmin looked at him for the first time. She smiled and pointed at him as if he was in on the secret.

"I did. The hellcat is using my encryption protocols to send you that message."

He shook his head. "I don't understand. Why would it use your encryption?"

"Here. Look at this," she responded.

One of the dodecahedrons flew toward them and then projected a computer screen above their heads. Once again, he recognized the lines of seemingly random words and characters as computer code.

"I checked the hellcat's code because we need to know what type of threat actors we are dealing with. How sophisticated is the programming, you know? The hellcat, or something else in its system architecture, is rewriting its own code."

Robbie stared at the robot. "You think it's Isa?"

"Yes!" she answered enthusiastically. "And it's communicating with your phone."

"Why? What does the message mean?"

Yasmin frowned at the question. "I haven't figured that out yet. So far, my search queries haven't netted any plausible results. The likeliest explanation is also the simplest. It's probably an error."

"Sister." The deep baritone that came from behind him made Robbie jump. He turned to see a man stride into the atrium, Drake Gallant following a step behind.

11

HALF A CROWN

Robbie immediately noticed the man's physical similarities to Yasmin. Both had long, black hair, though the man wore his in a ponytail, while Yasmin's was loose around her face and shoulders. Both had brown skin and almond-shaped eyes somewhere between dark brown and black. Yet, despite the uncanny resemblance, they differed in other aspects. Yasmin was shorter and slender, while her brother stood tall and wiry, with lean muscle mass filling out his upper body and legs.

Gallant was taller and broader across the chest and shoulders than Hamza. They wore loose-fitting workout attire, and each carried a towel, which they used to wipe sweat from their faces.

"They were sparring," Yasmin offered helpfully.

"I gotta go, guys," Gallant said. "Thanks for the practice, Hamza."

The man bowed. "Remember, my friend, beware of over-committing on the riposte. You are fast—faster than anyone your size has a right to be, but your speed can compromise control."

Gallant nodded, then walked into the darkness a moment later. Yasmin's brother moved to stand before Robbie.

"My name is Hamza Elsayed of House Hargrave. I am happy that you are feeling better."

Robbie lifted his hand in greeting. "Hi."

"Let's begin," Hamza declared.

Robbie raised an eyebrow. "Begin what?"

"Your training," the man answered, then addressed his sister again. "Flavian's Amphitheatre at dawn."

Yasmin typed on her tablet, and the dodecahedrons began to move. A moment later, Robbie and Hamza stood at the center of a colossal elliptical stone structure with towering walls that rose 150 feet on all sides. The sky directly overhead was dark blue, with a hint of yellow sunlight peeking over the edge of the wall to his right. A series of large stone arches encircled the lower level of the four-story structure. Thousands of seats populated the two lowest stories. Robbie squinted to see the rows of benches that marked the third and fourth levels.

"Wow," he whispered. "I'm standing in a gladiator movie."

He looked around to congratulate Yasmin on another incredible illusion, but she had disappeared.

"The Knights of Rosewood is a martial order, existing for more than five centuries," Hamza explained from beside him. "Long before King Corvinus commissioned the twelve bannerless knights, others protected the scrolls."

Hamza strode forward several steps along the flat, sandy floor of the arena, then spun around to face Robbie. Both arms hung down by his sides, perfectly at ease. He casually reached across his body, and when he drew his arm back, he held a sword. Black, azure, and violet light swirled and smoked from the blade, which was long and straight. The hilt was primarily black, dissipating into smoke along the edges like the blade. Though not the first time he'd seen the sword appear from nothing, it left Robbie awestruck.

"Wait. Do you expect me to learn how to fight? That didn't go so well the last time."

Hamza opened his palm, and the sword dissolved to nothingness.

"Robbie, we hide to protect the secret from the world as much as to protect the world from the secret. When the world comes too close, we must act. Sometimes, those actions involve violence."

Robbie shook his head emphatically. "I came here to get some answers about what happened that night at the library. I never agreed to be a part of your secret club, especially if it involves putting my life in danger again."

"You are to become a knight, though the circumstances of your induction into the bannerless are unprecedented."

"What if I don't want that?" Robbie replied, uncertain.

Hamza furrowed his brow while he looked at him. "I don't understand. You've stumbled upon a great honor."

Robbie shut his eyes, and the terror from the night of the attack washed over him once again. He relived each moment in flashes. The rattle in Mr. Breton's chest as his lungs pushed out his last breath, the red eyes of the hellcats stalking him through the darkness, and of course, Demeter's grotesque face as he drove his weapon into Robbie's shoulder.

"I don't want this honor, Hamza," he said quietly. "And I certainly didn't earn it."

The tall man returned to stand beside him. Gently, he gripped Robbie's shoulder. "I will teach you how to protect yourself. In time, you will come to understand our sacred duty."

"Mr. Breton said something similar before he died," Robbie recalled, staring out at the empty coliseum. The sky was a much lighter shade of blue now. Maybe this stuff makes more sense to you because you were born into it."

Hamza grunted. "You make an incorrect assumption. Yasmin and I were once strangers to this world as well."

Robbie frowned at the man, then remembered his introduction.

"Oh," he uttered quietly, somewhat embarrassed. "How did you come to be part of House Hargrave?"

"A story for another time, perhaps," Hamza said, the slight smile on his face at odds with his downcast eyes. "We grew to think of Augusta as a second mother figure. We came to respect her and William deeply and recognized that the Rosewood's cause was just."

Robbie searched the man's eyes for signs of insincerity. He found none.

Hamza exhaled, then began speaking as a teacher might address a student. "Let us begin with your kit. You must understand what it can do and what it cannot. To use your kit, you must always have physical contact with your phone. You can use your kit as long as your phone is on your person —in your hand, in your pocket. Your kit will deactivate when you break contact with your phone."

Hamza pulled out a phone identical to Robbie's and continued. "Press the icon on your phone to activate your kit."

Robbie removed the phone from his pocket and swiped from one screen to the next. "Which icon?"

"The knight."

He stopped when he saw it. The horse-head chess piece

glowed a reddish-brown. Chess made him think of Mr. Breton. The librarian loved chess. He even kept a chessboard set up in the room where the old card catalog cabinet was stored.

"I don't get it. What's with the chess icon?"

"Corvinus didn't name his secret order of knights. They were bannerless. No name. No heraldry. Why name something that can never be discussed? After the Battle of Mohács, the knights traveled across Europe, North Africa, and West Asia with the scrolls in their care. When not fighting, sparring, or building their wealth, they played chess. Those early knights preferred chess sets made of rosewood. The knight piece became our symbol."

Robbie turned his attention back to the phone and pressed the icon. Nothing happened. "Um, I don't think it worked, Hamza."

The tall man gave a half-smile. "Press it again to deactivate your kit. Good. Now, this time, close your eyes. Take a deep breath and deliberately focus on how you feel."

"How I feel is really stupid, like you're going to hit me in the face with a pie or stick a rat down my shirt and then post the video on the internet."

Hamza laughed and then shook his head. "I love those prank videos, but no. Unfortunately, we have no time for that. Close your eyes."

Robbie complied reluctantly.

"I ask only that you pay attention to your immediate physical senses other than your sight. What do you hear? My voice, yes. But what of your breath? Perhaps your heart beats to a rhythm unique to you alone. Can you feel the humid air on the surface of your skin and the heady moisture that mixes with the oxygen molecules as they journey through your nose, into your lungs, and out again?"

Hamza stopped talking and allowed Robbie to focus for several seconds. Then he spoke again. "Now, open your eyes and press the icon."

Robbie did so and heard a faint hum behind his ears. He nodded. "The hum?"

Hamza smiled. "Just so. Draw your weapon."

His entire experience handling weapons consisted of playing with toy swords and water pistols.

"Reach across your body with your dominant hand toward your hip, close your fingers as if to grip an object, and then draw your arm back across your body."

Robbie followed the man's instructions, wondering how foolish he must look. His reticence vanished immediately as the sword materialized in his hand. The sudden physical heft startled him, and he opened his hand almost immediately. The sword disappeared.

"Whoa."

"Again. Do not let go this time."

He repeated the gesture, and the sword appeared. Speechless, he drew the weapon level with his eyes to inspect the spectral object more closely. The long, dark blade was sharp along one edge and blunt along the other. The hilt was solid and slightly warm in his hand. Robbie noticed a subtle pulsing sensation that beat in time to the hum behind his ears. From pommel to blade, the sword shone with its own dark glow instead of reflecting the ambient light in the room. He exhaled.

"You sure this isn't magic?"

"I understand why it appears so," Hamza answered. "Humans commonly attribute supernatural explanations to phenomena that exist beyond our current ability to comprehend. What you see is not magic, however. The scrolls taught us how to harness nature to power a nearly limitless energy source. We can instantly shift that energy into matter, shaping it into predefined objects."

After ensuring that he had enough space around him, Robbie set about swinging the sword. The sound of the blade cutting through the air proved strangely satisfying, though it didn't take long for his arm to grow tired. "It's heavier than I expected."

Before Robbie could ask another of the questions consuming his mind, something caught his attention. A blue light appeared in the lower-left corner of his peripheral vision. He turned his head to see what it was, but the light moved with each turn. "Where is that light coming from?"

Hamza tilted his head a moment, then chuckled. "Ah, your phone has received a new notification. Focus your eyes on the circle without moving your head."

Robbie drew his eyes down to the left and focused on the small blue circle of light. A second later, crisp white text sprang into his view.

QH501U9993948

"Oh. It's the weird error message I keep getting," Robbie clarified.

Hamza nodded. "My sister mentioned it."

"Can you see it?"

"No," Hamza replied. "The phone projects the message directly onto your retina."

Robbie turned his head in different directions, and the message overlaid everything he looked at, including Hamza.

"Cool. How do I get rid of it?"

"You can control the system using your eyes, voice, and even hand gestures. Locate the *X* icon next to the message and focus on it. This action will select it. Then say 'close' or perform a prolonged blink."

He blinked at the X, and when he opened his eyes, the

message and the blue dot were gone. "I don't think I'll ever get used to that."

"You can use your phone instead, but never during combat. Too much risk of losing contact with the device, which may prove fatal."

"Who checks their text messages in the middle of a fight?" Robbie couldn't help but ask.

"Excellent point. Now, let us turn our attention to the defensive system of your kit."

Hamza's sword reappeared. "Once activated, the system is completely automated. Machine learning responds to any physical threats to your body. Your phone instantaneously converts energy into matter, which manifests as a glowing lattice over the part of your body that is threatened. Your kit makes you invulnerable to most conventional threats."

"What do you mean by 'conventional threats?'"

"The usual. Firearms, bladed and blunt weapons. But you mustn't become overconfident. You remain susceptible to other dangers, such as asphyxiation, smoke inhalation, drowning, and so on. Your kit is a remarkable piece of technology, but the laws of science will only bend so far before they push back."

Without warning, Hamza thrust the sword at Robbie's chest in a barely perceptible blur. Light flared, and intersecting lines of darkly glowing indigo appeared at the point of contact, protecting him from the killing stroke. The impact forced him back a step. Robbie stared, startled by Hamza's demonstration. He remembered how those lines of light protected him from the hellcat's attack.

Reflexively, Robbie's left hand reached up to rub his right shoulder. While the flesh had healed, the memory of the wound remained fresh.

Robbie's brow furrowed in confusion. "But Demeter's weapon cut through my kit."

"The kit protects you from conventional attacks. Demeter's glaive is a technology similar to ours, though several generations older. Sustained attacks from such weapons can overload parts of your kit or shut the whole system down."

Hamza paused for several heartbeats before speaking again. "Without your kit, Demeter's glaive would have cut through your shoulder effortlessly, which was likely his intention."

Robbie closed his eyes and rubbed his forehead, overwhelmed by the number of things to consider. Every question seemed to lead to even more questions. He struggled to decide which line of inquiry to take, but eventually, one question stood out above the others.

"Hamza, Yasmin seemed pretty upset when she learned that Mr. Breton didn't have his phone the night he died. Do you think Mr. Breton would be alive if he had been carrying his phone when Demeter attacked?"

The man appeared troubled as his eyebrows furrowed and his mouth formed a straight line. "It's impossible to know for sure," he replied, his tone grave. "We certainly would have arrived sooner if William had notified us of the attack earlier. He was also a great fighter in his own right, and duty to the Rosewood was a cornerstone of his life. But he was old-fashioned. He preferred newspapers and fountain pens to smartphones. William didn't have his phone. He let his guard down. As did we all."

Robbie gave voice to a question that was bothering him. "Do you think Demeter knew Mr. Breton didn't have his phone that night?"

Hamza's expression darkened. "We've wondered the same thing but do not have an answer."

Robbie thought of another question that had troubled him since waking from his coma. "When I first saw Demeter with Mr. Breton, he talked about his father and mentioned a truce. He isn't just some random guy chasing the scrolls, is he? Demeter, I mean."

Hamza shook his head. "No, House Demeter was part of a group called the Writhen. They have warred with the Rosewood for centuries. William, Augusta, and the other Rosewood knights of that generation defeated the Writhen many years ago at a place called Son Doong. Andars Demeter was a child then. He and his mother were absent from the final battle. The Rosewood established a truce with the Demeter matriarch to spare their lives."

Before Robbie could pose another question, the illusion disappeared. He looked around, somewhat surprised to find himself in the mall, having almost forgotten the amphitheater was a hologram.

Yasmin sat at one of the long workbenches. "Time to go home, Robbie. We don't want your parents to get suspicious."

The next few days unfolded in a similar fashion. He went to school in the mornings and crossed the expressway to reach the derelict mall in the afternoon. Hamza took him through different drills with the sword. Each practice was interspersed with discussions about the Knights of Rosewood, usually during much-needed water breaks.

"The Writhen used knowledge from the scrolls to transform themselves," Hamza explained during one such discussion. "They discovered a process that allowed them to graft a specially treated metal directly to their bones."

Robbie involuntarily touched his hand to his forehead as he pictured Demeter's face from the night of the attack. "Did Demeter do that, too?"

Hamza nodded gravely. "His physical appearance suggests that he has."

"But why?" Robbie asked.

"It provided the Writhen with a distinct advantage over the Rosewood. The grafting protects them much the same way that our defensive kits protect us, but without the need for an external device. The Rosewood had no answer to the Writhen's grafting for many years."

"Why not just copy the grafting process?"

Hamza's eyes narrowed at the suggestion. "It's an abomination, Robbie. Not only does it alter their bodies, but also their minds, making them prone to fits of rage and violence."

"Oh. So, how did the Rosewood defeat them at, ah, Son —" The name escaped him.

"Son Doong," Hamza finished. "The Rosewood emerged victorious through strategy and will, not technology. The knights who defeated the Writhen, William Breton among them, used large, heavy canes like Demeter's walking stick until my sister discovered how to incorporate the energy-to-matter projection system into our smartphones."

Robbie shook his head upon hearing the explanation. "I guess Yasmin is some kind of genius or something?"

"Yasmin is uncommonly smart. A characteristic she inherited from my father," Hamza declared proudly. Robbie noticed that the man actually stood a little straighter whenever he discussed his sister.

Robbie completed his training that day and returned home exhausted and famished after a combination of school, bike riding in the summer heat, and Hamza's sword drills. Several days passed in a similar fashion. He wanted to hang out with Artie, Blake, or his parents, but he usually went to sleep after dinner and homework. His parents' questions suggested they were worried he was becoming more withdrawn, though he tried his best to reassure them that he was fine. He had difficulty maintaining eye contact with them, and his frequently incoherent answers to even their basic questions were evidence that the guilt from his incessant lying was beginning to take a toll.

"Hamza, of all the places in the world, why did Mr. Breton choose Bethel?" Robbie asked one afternoon.

The man opened his hand to dismiss his sword before answering. "Well, the reference library, for one. Gerhardt Feist was a Knight of Rosewood."

Though surprised by the revelation, Robbie didn't know why that was relevant. "How is that important?"

Hamza considered the question. "The library is more than it seems, Robbie."

He steered the conversation down a different tangent. "After the Rosewood defeated the Writhen, the knights focused on their regular lives. William ran a successful company for many years but grew weary of the business world and all its trappings. He retired here to translate the scrolls and train Drake Gallant."

Robbie shook his head, unnerved by the revelation. Somehow, he hadn't thought about how Gallant fit into the puzzle of the Knights of Rosewood.

"Mr. Breton and Gallant were close?" Everyone in Bethel knew the librarian, but Robbie couldn't think of a moment that might've suggested Gallant was more than just another high school student to the man.

Hamza shook his head. "That is not my tale to tell. You

might ask Drake yourself. My sister and I have noticed that he and you are not friendly. Why is that?"

Robbie thought about the question and discovered he didn't have a decent answer. *Was I just jealous of Gallant's relationship with Blake?* Perhaps. Though Gallant wasn't making the whole friendship thing very easy.

A notification popped up as a blue dot in the corner of his eye. He sighed, ready to dismiss it, but then took a deep breath when he saw what the message contained. Hamza looked at him, concern lining the man's face.

"Are you all right?"

Robbie opened his hand, dismissing the sword. He looked around frantically for his backpack. "Message from Artie. My mom is looking for me. I gotta go! "

12

SWALLOW THE SPIDER TO CATCH THE FLY

Robbie finished securing his helmet when he was already halfway down the hillside. White-knuckled and soaked in sweat, he barely had the spare brain power to recall his hasty exit from the mall. The only thing he cared about was getting home.

Why is Mom looking for me? I need to call Artie.

He completed the descent in a fraction of the time it took him to climb the steep hill. He slowed his bike as he reached the first guardrail of the expressway.

"Uh, phone. Call Artie."

His eyes widened when a blue dot appeared in his peripheral vision. He focused on the dot long enough for the text to appear.

'Calling Artie.'

He heard the digital dial and the subsequent ringing behind his ears and wondered if the sounds were audible only to him.

So much I still don't know.

While waiting for his friend to answer, he began to lift his bike over the guardrail. Cars, trucks, and more than a few big rigs drove past his position with barely a break in the flow of vehicles.

"Hello?"

Robbie looked behind him when he heard Artie's voice. "Hey."

"Robbie! Where are you? It sounds like you're at a racetrack."

"Long story. How do you know my mom is looking for me?"

"She called. She wants you to go home right away."

"Did she say why?"

"She said something about a guest."

"You didn't tell her about my new cell, did you?

"Obviously not! I'm hurt you'd even ask."

"Sure, you are. Can you text her for me? Tell her you gave me the message and that I'm coming home."

"No problem."

There was a pause several heartbeats long. For a moment, Robbie wondered if he had lost the connection. When Artie next spoke, his tone was more serious than usual. "Are you okay, Roberto?"

"I'm good, Art."

"All right. Text me later."

"Sure thing."

The text in his peripheral vision indicated that the call was disconnected.

Guest? Who could that be?

He didn't have time to worry about it now. The expressway was visible for a few miles in either direction. He focused on the lanes closest to his position, rested the down tube of his mountain bike on his shoulder, and then sprinted to the median when the road was clear. He felt the cars disperse the air and heard the engine noise around him. A few drivers honked their horns, likely surprised at the sight of a person standing at the median. Robbie set his bike down and took a few breaths before attempting the second leg of this incredibly dumb crossing. He wondered if his kit would protect him from the high-speed impact of a two-ton automobile. He shook his head.

I never want to find out.

Again, he waited for a break in the traffic coming from the other direction. He saw his opportunity and bolted across the lanes, hopping over the guardrail on the other side. A blue dot appeared in his peripheral vision as he rode the remainder of the way home. He flicked his eyes toward it and saw the message.

QH501U9993948.

He returned his attention to the trail. Yasmin told him that Isa was sending him, or more accurately, his phone, the strange message. But why? Was Isa malfunctioning? It had transferred itself to the hellcat, and then Demeter destroyed it.

About thirty minutes later, Robbie cruised onto his street. A black SUV blocked the end of his driveway. A faint silhouette behind the dark-tinted windows meant someone was sitting in the driver's seat. Ignoring the vehicle, Robbie leaned his bike against the garage and removed his helmet. His hair and shirt were drenched in sweat. He looked around to make sure that no one was watching, then deactivated his kit before hiding the phone in his bag.

Robbie opened his front door and shouted, "Mom?"

She emerged from around the corner, which led to the living room.

"Hi, kiddo! I'm glad you're home. Someone is here to see you." She hugged her son and then stepped back a moment later. "Whoa! Sweat much?" She smiled at him. "Why don't you head upstairs and get changed? Mr. Demeter is waiting in the living room."

The name hit him like a baseball bat. "What did you say?"

Before his mom could respond, a towering figure moved into the foyer. Black dress shoes, black suit, dark-gray tie, and lacquered tree stump of a cane. Just like that night at the library. Andars Demeter grinned.

"It's so nice to see you again, Robbie."

Involuntarily, Robbie took a step back and stumbled against the doorframe. His mom grabbed him to prevent him from falling. The world around him reeled. This man, this murderer, was in his house. He wanted to yell. Wanted to grab his mom's hand and run. He thought about his kit.

"Oh, my goodness, Robbie. Are you all right?"

His heart pounded so hard he barely heard Demeter respond.

"He's okay, Ms. Noble. Likely just light-headed from such a strenuous bike ride. Isn't that right, Robbie?"

His mom led him to the living room couch and guided him to sit. She wrapped the throw blanket around him. He shivered from the adrenaline. She sat beside him and placed her arm around his shoulders. She lowered her voice and spoke so that only he could hear her. "Do you know this man?" Her eyes were narrow and fierce.

Robbie sat unmoving, unspeaking for a time. His stomach churned with bile. His right hand twitched toward his left hip, wondering if he could take the intruder unawares with the weapon of the Rosewood, but he remembered the phone was in his bag. Even if he could summon the weapon, he doubted his own willingness to strike Demeter down in cold blood.

He forced himself to look up at the murderous tyrant

standing in his living room. Demeter remained smiling, his scarred and pitted face like a mask of terror.

"I'm glad you are well after the accident at the library. No doubt you are curious to know why I am here. I promise not to overstay, of course. I was in town and thought it would be beneficial to reminisce about our good friend William. Your mother was kind enough to share some memories while we waited for you to arrive."

Robbie locked eyes with Demeter and received the unspoken message loud and clear.

Play along, or else.

Robbie did not trust him, but did he have a choice? He needed to make sure his mom was safe. So, he took a deep breath and then nodded. "I'm okay, Mom. I know Mr. Demeter from the library. He and Mr. Breton were, ah, friends."

Lauren smiled and stood. She squeezed Robbie's shoulder reassuringly. "I will be right back with your tea, Mr. Demeter. I'll get you some water, Robbie." His mom left for the kitchen.

Demeter sat down in the armchair. His colossal form made the furniture look comically small. He placed the cane between his feet and steepled his fingers over the dark metal pommel. It seemed as though his scarred hands were large enough to crush Robbie's head.

"We will need more privacy for this discussion than your mother is likely to provide us."

Demeter removed a cell phone from inside his suit jacket. He typed something on the device and then returned it to his pocket.

Robbie's mom walked back into the room holding a tray, which she placed on the coffee table. She handed a cup of tea to Demeter, which he accepted graciously. She gave

Robbie the glass of water and held up a small plate with some plain cookies.

He shook his head. She frowned slightly but didn't insist.

"Mr. Demeter, while making tea, I realized that I know who you are."

Robbie tensed, and his eyes grew wide.

Demeter simply smiled again. "You looked me up?"

She waved her hand in the air, dismissing his comment. "I looked you up to confirm what I already suspected."

"Indeed. And what did you confirm?"

"I remember you from a famous cover story a few years ago. What was the title? *The New Age Robber Barons*. You own Forras Oil and Gas, one of the largest energy companies outside of Saudi Arabia, am I right? It makes sense that you knew William before he traded his billionaire club for a quiet life in small-town Bethel."

While she spoke, Demeter's smile changed. His eyes narrowed a little more, and he looked more predatory. "Alas, that story was inaccurate. Very one-sided."

"Yes, of course. I am so sorry about your oil platform in the news recently. All those workers. What a tragedy."

Demeter bowed his head as if in regret or solemn remembrance. "A tragedy indeed. All hands lost. The platform shall remain unmanned for years while we affect repairs."

Mom's phone began to ring. She removed the device from her pocket, pressed the screen, and laid it face-down on the coffee table.

"My apologies, Mr. Demeter. That was my job. I already let my assistant know I'd be offline for a bit. I guess she forgot."

"May I ask what you do for a living?"

"I work in publishing. I am fortunate enough to work from home most days."

The phone on the coffee table began to vibrate. She blew out a breath but chose to ignore the device.

"Please, don't ignore the necessities of your work on my account." Demeter's tone was polite and helpful. "I have learned from experience that ignoring repeated messages from my assistant can have grave consequences."

His mom pursed her lips. Robbie could tell that she debated violating her own rules of etiquette.

"I'm sorry. My assistant isn't usually this persistent. I will take this call just in case something urgent needs my attention. I'll be right back."

Lauren left the room, and Demeter remained silent. He stared at the hallway, waiting for Robbie's mom to return, which she did a few minutes later. She was pale and flustered. She was typing furiously on her phone and didn't look up at her son or their guest.

"Everything okay, Mom?

"Yeah, no. I need to make some calls. I just learned that someone is trying to acquire the publishing company through a hostile takeover. Robbie, I'll be in my office if you need me. I'm sorry, Mr. Demeter, but I must cut this visit short."

Demeter stood and extended his hand. "It was my pleasure to meet you, Ms. Noble. I will say my farewells to your son and then be on my way."

Robbie's mom stared up at Demeter and then shook his hand. "Robbie, come see me when Mr. Demeter is gone. I'll likely be in meetings most of the night, so we'll need to plan dinner before your dad gets home."

He knew that his mom needed no such help with dinner. She had likely messaged Dad already to bring something home. Her instructions were code for *come see me as soon as the stranger is gone.*

"Okay."

His mom left the living room for her office. He did not hear her close the door. Demeter walked to the window and stared outside. Robbie glared at the man's back.

"Did you do that? The hostile takeover of my mom's company or whatever."

Without turning, the man spoke a single word. "Expedience." After several moments, he spoke again. This time, his tone was almost gentle. "This conflict is not yours, and for that, I am sorry."

He turned to face Robbie. The gruesome smile was gone, and in its place, a furrowed brow and downturned mouth. "William Breton was not the man you think he was."

He's not wrong about that.

"Okay. So, what do you want?" Robbie asked.

"Do you have any notion of what the scroll I took from you contains? Nothing less than the solutions to humankind's greatest problems. Clean, limitless energy for all. Control over the weather, meaning no more droughts, hurricanes, or floods. New medicines and treatments. We could eliminate disease and famine and war."

Robbie admitted to himself that Demeter's words provoked a thought that had troubled him since his first meeting with Yasmin. *Why didn't the Knights of Rosewood share the knowledge of the scrolls to help people?* "Seems crazy," he mumbled when he couldn't think of a response.

"Breton and the others, and those before them, have kept the knowledge hidden for centuries, enriching themselves while the world burns and people die from preventable causes."

Robbie could not look at Demeter. The man seemed to

reiterate Robbie's own doubts and burrowed holes through the fortress of his convictions. He reached down for his glass of water instead. Demeter's onslaught continued. "Do you know how I know all this?"

Robbie shook his head.

"My family once belonged to the same organization as Breton—the Knights of Rosewood."

"What?" Robbie's eyes found Demeter's while his brain tried desperately to reconcile the man's admission with what he had learned about the secretive organization since waking up in the hospital.

That explains why Demeter's glaive is based on the same technology as my kit. The Rosewood and the Writhen were the same.

Demeter seemed to read his mind. "Before you or I were born, a schism split the Rosewood along ideological lines. House Breton and its supporters desired to hoard knowledge, while House Demeter and a few others longed to share the knowledge of the scrolls with the world. Inevitably, the schism led to bloodshed. Of the four houses that dissented, all were destroyed. I am the sole survivor of their terrible pogrom."

Robbie thought about the smartphone in his backpack. Yasmin had told him he'd never have to charge the device. Cell phones that never died were only one tiny benefit. The other applications for this technology seemed without end. Demeter was right, wasn't he? The Rosewood keeping all this incredible knowledge to itself was wrong.

"Why are you here?" Robbie's voice was hoarse and less forceful than he intended. "You tried to kill me, remember?"

Demeter's expression changed, and Robbie wondered if he was attempting to express remorse. He doubted the man could look anything but terrifying.

"That was a regretful misunderstanding. I thought that you were one of Breton's knights."

He inflected the last word with contempt. When Robbie didn't say anything, Demeter continued. "Do you know the location of Breton's notebook?"

He blinked in surprise at the question. *Again, with the notebook.* "No," he replied simply.

The large man crouched down until his cold blue eyes were level with Robbie's dark brown. The deep, red welts and uneven ridges in Demeter's face were more prominent from this distance and angle. Demeter's nose looked broken, and his forehead and cheekbones were raised in some places and sunken in others.

"Breton's notebook will confirm all that I have said. Find it, read it, and decide for yourself if Breton is the man you believed him to be."

Robbie exhaled, more uncertain than ever. Demeter rose to his full height and handed Robbie a business card.

"What's this?" Robbie asked.

"That is my direct number for when you find the notebook," Demeter replied.

"But why do you care if I find it?"

"I believe Breton's notes will reveal much about the scrolls, which will benefit us all."

Demeter left the living room and opened the front door. Outside, Robbie saw the SUV driver move around the car to open the rear door for his employer.

"Goodbye, Robbie."

"Um," Robbie began, "can you stop the hostile takeover thing?"

Demeter nodded. Robbie saw him typing on his phone as he headed down the driveway to the waiting SUV.

Robbie returned to the living room and sat. He didn't

know what to think. He'd need to tell the Elsayed siblings about Demeter's visit. And what about looking for Breton's notebook? Where would he start?

His mom walked into the living room a few minutes later. She looked around and then out the window.

"I asked you to tell me when Mr. Demeter left."

"Ah, oh yeah. Sorry, Mom," he replied weakly.

"What did he say to you?"

"Not much." Robbie tried to sound casual.

Her eyes narrowed suspiciously. "Are you sure? Seems odd that the billionaire owner of an oil company takes time out of his busy schedule to visit out-of-the-way Bethel."

"He was looking for a notebook that belonged to Mr. Breton."

"And he couldn't have one of his people do that?" his mom asked.

Robbie shrugged. "Guess not. He said it's very important."

She tilted her head to the side while she looked at him. He needed to divert this conversation away from Demeter.

"So, what's going on with the takeover?" he asked.

His mom stared at her phone and shook her head. "Adele from the CEO's office messaged me a minute ago. The takeover is off the table. We have a meeting in fifteen minutes to debrief. I guess the mystery buyer got cold feet."

"Yeah," Robbie agreed. "I guess."

"The whole thing is so odd. No one at work has ever heard of a corporate takeover coming together and falling apart in so short a time."

His mom looked thoughtful and then shook her head.

"Anyway, your dad is picking up pizza on his way home from work."

After dinner with his parents, Robbie locked himself in the washroom and messaged Yasmin that he needed to talk. His apprehension increased throughout the evening when she didn't respond.

He lay in his bed and tried to sleep but was restless for most of the night. His mind raced in a thousand directions all at once. New doubts sprang to mind, and other concerns, relegated to his subconscious, worked their way to the surface. He worried about his vow. Had he sworn an oath to serve some ignoble organization? But how could that be? Mr. Breton had been a good man. Except, how much had he known about him before his death?

He ran his hands through his hair and closed his eyes tightly. The uncertainty made him feel as if he stood on a cliff's edge. The wrong choice threatened to plunge him over the brink. He got out of bed and opened his bedroom door.

The house was quiet and dark. Soft snoring emanated from his parents' bedroom. He didn't want to disturb them.

They'll worry even more if they think I can't sleep at night.

He walked silently to the bathroom, carefully avoiding the creakiest parts of the floor. Locking the door behind him, Robbie switched on the light and stared at his face in the mirror. He knew that he couldn't trust Demeter, but Robbie hated the idea of the Rosewood hoarding knowledge that could help so many others.

His heavy sigh turned into a yawn, reminding him how late it was.

"Robbie?" The whisper came from the other side of the door.

"Yeah, Dad?"

"Everything okay?"

"Yeah. I drank too much milk before bed."

"Sure. Happens to us all," his dad replied.

Receding footsteps and the creaking floor suggested that his dad had moved away from the bathroom. Robbie returned to his bedroom and climbed back into bed. A few minutes later, his dad's dark silhouette appeared at his door.

"You awake, kiddo?"

"Yeah."

His dad sat down on the edge of his bed. The glowing digits of his alarm clock lit the room in faint blue light. Robbie preempted his dad's question. "I'm fine."

His dad chuckled at the comment. "I had no intention of asking that, smart guy."

"Oh, yeah? Then what?"

"I was going to tell you about a new drag-reducing polymer we're testing at work."

"Uh-huh. I'm sure, Dad."

"Okay. You got me. What do you expect? We love you and want to make sure you're okay. You went through something—"

"Don't say *traumatic*."

"Well, yes."

"I hate that word. Trauma sounds too much like drama."

His dad chuckled again. "I suppose it does."

They sat in silence for a moment until Robbie spoke again. "Can I ask you something?"

"Only if it's about drag-reducing polymers."

"C'mon, Dad."

His dad held up his hands defensively. "Okay, okay. I'm sorry. What's up?"

"Just wondering about something. Do you think information or knowledge, like new technologies and stuff, should be free for everyone or kept in the hands of a few rich people or elites or whatever?"

Robbie could see his dad's confused expression even in the dimly lit room.

"Wow. What a question for—." His dad looked at the clock. "—two thirty-seven in the morning. Is this for a class assignment?"

"Something like that, yeah."

His dad rubbed his hands over his face as if trying to wake himself up to tackle the question.

"Well, in the most simplistic terms, maximizing utility for the greatest number of people is generally a metric for measuring whether a choice is ethical, moral, or good. But human nature is rarely so simple. Imagine if the sole outcome of splitting the atom was clean energy. What would the world look like if nuclear fission hadn't also given us atomic bombs?"

"So, you're saying they should have kept the nuclear stuff secret because the knowledge can be used to make bombs?"

"Not necessarily. I'm saying that choices have consequences, and many of them are difficult, if not impossible, to predict. Splitting the atom gave us weapons of mass destruction *and* relatively clean, cheap energy. Clean, cheap energy is a net good for the world, while atomic bombs are the opposite. However, atomic bombs helped end the Second World War, while nuclear reactors created a dangerous waste problem, not to mention disasters like Chornobyl and Fukushima. To complicate matters more, even the idea that some outcomes are objectively good, such as the end of World War Two, likely didn't seem positive to the Japanese who survived the bombs."

Robbie sighed.

"I'm sorry, kiddo. I don't think I helped at all, did I?"

"It's okay. I'll just ask Mom next time."

"Hey!"

His father tucked him into bed like he was a kid again, and the gesture eased his disquiet just a little.

"Get back to sleep. Hopefully, the great philosophical questions you're contemplating will seem less daunting in the morning."

"I love you, Dad."

"I love you, too, kiddo. Good night."

"Good night."

Robbie lay awake for another hour. After much deliberation, he finally decided he would find Mr. Breton's notebook.

13

THEY'VE ALL GONE AWAY

The next morning, Ms. Versteepen greeted Robbie and Valeria as they entered homeroom together.

"Ms. Pirhadi is away today. Please use this period as study time."

The two students exchanged smiles and thanked the principal before leaving for the school library. A few minutes later, they had cloistered themselves in a private study room.

For some reason, Robbie was lightheaded at the prospect of spending time alone with Valeria. His heart beat a little faster, and he couldn't help but notice the pleasant scent of her shampoo or perfume again, how she twirled her hair when she read from her textbook, and how her dark-brown eyes lit up when she laughed. He was surprised at his own disappointment when they heard the knock on the door, thus ending their brief seclusion. Artie poked his head inside, a broad grin on his face that quickly flipped into a frown.

"Hi, Artie," Robbie said, smiling.

"Hi, Artie." Valeria smiled as well, but it was more reserved and uncertain.

The tension between Artie and Valeria had always been more of a proxy conflict than full-blown aggression. Artie had Robbie's back, so he came to his defense whenever Valeria attacked.

Artie recovered quickly from his surprise at seeing them together, sat down at the far end of the table, and pretended that nothing was out of the ordinary.

"I dropped by your first class to see you, Robbie, but the room was empty. I figured you might come here. I guess you both have a free period this morning?"

Robbie nodded. "Ms. Piranha isn't here today."

"Piranha, eh? She's the mean one?" Artie inquired.

Valeria and Robbie responded in the affirmative at the same time.

"What are you doing at school?" Robbie asked his friend.

Artie glared. "My God, man. I'm leaving for Quebec this afternoon, remember? You promised that we'd hang out before I left."

Robbie groaned and smacked his own forehead. Artie had messaged him for two days, asking if they could hang out before the Rutherfords went away on their family vacation. Robbie was so consumed with the Rosewood that he had forgotten about it.

"I'm really sorry, Artie. I'm a terrible friend."

"You *are* terrible, and you should be sorry." Artie's smirk let Robbie know that he wasn't upset. He continued in a more serious tone. "I'm just happy you're out of that damn hospital bed." He looked around at the study room and shook his head. "I can't believe I came to school in the summer to say goodbye!"

Valeria snorted. "How do you think we feel?"

Artie stared at her. "Why are you even taking summer school? If you tell me you're trying to upgrade your A in math to an A-plus, I will absolutely lose it."

Her face grew flush before answering. "Close. It was an A-minus."

Now it was Robbie's turn to stare. "You're stuck in summer school because of an A-minus?"

"Yeah." She frowned and rolled her eyes simultaneously. "My parents revoked access to all my social media accounts when they saw my report card."

Artie pounded a fist on the table. "Outrageous! How are you handling the withdrawal?"

"Terrible, obviously! I'm in here hanging out with coma boy." Valeria smiled coyly.

Artie's eyes widened in disbelief at the remark. He looked at Robbie, clearly expecting an unkind response. Instead, Robbie smiled and nodded toward Artie.

"I'm coma boy. Pleased to meet you."

Valeria and Robbie burst out laughing, which seemed only to confuse Artie further.

She continued. "You know, not having social media hasn't been that bad. I can still text message my friends, and I've enjoyed not feeling like Pavlov's dog constantly."

A look of sudden realization spread across Artie's face. "Ohhh, wait. Is this—" Artie pointed back and forth between his friend and Valeria "—a thing?"

Robbie's eyes widened at the insinuation. "No! No. Not that."

Valeria's mouth hung open in shock, and she laughed when she saw Robbie's face. "Wow, Robbie. I don't think I've seen that shade of red on a human before."

The door opened again, and Blake walked in, her eyes scanning until they fixed on Artie.

"I'm sorry, Artie, but you can't be here. Ms. Versteepen saw you enter the building from her office. I told her I'd get you to leave."

"What do you mean? I go here!" he protested.

"You aren't enrolled in summer school, so technically, you can't be here. It's a liability issue with the school board."

Artie opened his mouth to respond, but Valeria spoke first. "Artie's here because he's sad that his best friend doesn't want to hang out before the Rutherfords leave for their vacation."

Artie looked like he might object to Valeria's summation but nodded instead. "Pretty much, yeah."

Blake looked pointedly at Robbie a moment later.

"And you!" she said, her voice accusatory and eyes narrowed.

Robbie pointed at himself and mouthed the word 'me.'"

"Yes, you."

Blake lowered her voice to just above a whisper despite the closed door. "The soup kitchen downtown is having a food drive."

He frowned in confusion at the non sequitur. "Okay?"

Blake kept going. "I thought that you might want to volunteer. Your timetable said you were home for remote learning, but when I called your house to ask for your help, your mom answered and said you were at school."

An icy chill crept up Robbie's spine. He knew that the deception around his schedule was about to unravel.

"Did you— tell my mom or Ms. Versteepen?" Robbie asked, his voice cracking.

Blake raised her eyebrows in disbelief and put her hands on her hips.

"Of course not! I'm worried about you, and your parents are worried about you. You're ditching your friends, tampering with your schedule, skipping school, and going to bed early every night. Yes, your mom told me that part, too. What's going on with you, Robbie?"

His friends stared at him, waiting for his response. He didn't know what to tell them. He could go on lying to everyone, but the cost of the constant deception had begun to weigh on him. He realized that the secrets he kept since waking up from the coma had isolated him from the people he loved most.

I can't tell them what really happened to me, can I?

He didn't think they'd believe him. The truth was just too fantastical. Reality had become less believable than the fiction the Rosewood had created. As if in response to this last thought, Mr. Breton's phone seemed to gain mass in his pocket, pulling at him with an inscrutable heaviness, beckoning him to take it up.

The Rosewood took their oaths seriously. He knew that for certain. And he had made his oath to Mr. Breton while the man's life bled out in the underground vault. Except, Robbie reasoned, his vow was not freely given but compelled in a desperate moment of terror.

His friends neither moved nor spoke. He looked at each of them, and they waited like they knew he was deliberating some profound decision. If he did this— if he told them— he could never take it back. When he finally made his decision, he knew that he did so because the alternative had grown too burdensome to bear.

Robbie let out a long breath and rubbed his forehead. "Okay. I need to tell you something."

Artie spoke reassuringly. "Bro, I'm here for you."

Valeria stood up and grabbed her bag off the table. "I'll give you guys some privacy. Have a good trip, Artie."

"I want you to stay," Robbie blurted. "If that's okay."

Valeria paused and looked at him, an unreadable expression on her face. "Are you sure?"

He nodded.

She gave him a supportive smile and sat back down in her chair. "Well, okay."

Robbie pulled sheets of paper from his binder, then walked to the study room's transparent glass door, which looked into the library and allowed those outside to see in. He used the paper and some sticky notes to cover the glass. Robbie faced his friends.

"There was no gas leak."

The silence that permeated the room after his pronouncement spoke volumes.

"What are you talking about?" Blake asked before sitting down in an empty chair beside Valeria.

"That night. At the library. There was no gas leak."

Whether real or imagined, Robbie immediately felt their skepticism. Artie started laughing.

"C'mon, man. Stop messing with us."

"I'm not joking, Artie. I know what you're thinking. My brain got all scrambled, right? I was in a coma for three months."

Blake opened her mouth to speak, but Robbie held up a hand. "It's okay. If I were you, I wouldn't believe me either."

"So, if it wasn't a gas leak, tell us what happened." Blake made her statement with a calmness that seemed at odds with the torrent of emotions inside Robbie.

"Mr. Breton was murdered."

Three pairs of eyes stared up at him. His friends wore expressions that were equal parts supportive and disbelieving. Robbie pulled the phone from his pocket and pressed the horse head icon. Blake pointed to the device.

"Hey! Your parents let you have a phone?"

He ignored the question. Instead, he reached across his body, grasped the air, and drew his arm back. The coruscating indigo sword sprang into existence. His friends gasped.

Artie was the first one to speak. "What the hell is that?"

Robbie told them the story—the library, the hellcats, waking up at the hospital under the care of Dr. Asher. Mr. Breton and the underground vault. Meeting Yasmin and Hamza at the abandoned mall and about Demeter. Finally, he told them about the librarian's missing notebook. He saw the disbelief creep back into their expressions and then flee again each time they looked at the sword.

Artie was the first one to speak once Robbie finished. "The Knights of what?"

"Rosewood."

"Never heard of it."

Valeria snorted. "Imagine that. The secret society is secret."

Artie slapped the table. "There's the Valeria I know and love."

She tilted her head and flashed him a saccharine smile, which lacked the usual malice.

Blake sat thoughtfully for a time before speaking. "Robbie, why would you believe the man who murdered Mr. Breton and almost killed you?"

"I don't," Robbie admitted. "Not really, anyway, but he said some things that make sense to me. I need to find Mr. Breton's notebook. It might help me figure this out."

"Did you tell the brother and sister about a murderer

showing up in your house?" Artie asked, much louder than necessary.

"I tried," Robbie answered. "I saw them yesterday but haven't heard from them since."

Artie scratched his head. "Is that normal?"

Robbie shrugged. "I have no idea what's normal, Artie. I just met them."

Blake's pensive tone gave way to one of conviction. "I agree about the importance of giving this knowledge to everyone. Robbie, if the technology in the scroll is what you claim, it could benefit billions of lives."

"This technology," Valeria interjected, pointing to Robbie's sword, "could also benefit criminals, terrorists, and tyrants."

Valeria's comment made Robbie think about his dad's atomic bomb example. He opened his hand and let the sword vanish, which left his friends open mouthed and wide eyed.

"Dude," Artie began, "I gotta ask. Why a notebook? You're talking about crazy advanced tech here, but then you're looking for a notebook? Really?"

Robbie shrugged. "I agree. It doesn't make sense."

Artie shook his head and exhaled. "So, where is it?"

Robbie shrugged again. "Yasmin hoped I knew where it was. Same with Demeter."

"It's somewhere in the library." Valeria's matter-of-fact response made them all turn to look at her.

Blake was the first to ask the question on everyone's mind. "How can you be so sure?"

"Where does a mechanic fix his car? In his shop. Where does a banker keep her money? In her bank. The librarian keeps his super-secret book in his library."

Artie groaned. "But now we're talking needle in a

haystack, right? How do you find one book in a building full of books? We gotta assume that the Rosewood would've checked the most obvious places. Breton's office, the front desk—"

"The weird underground place where he died," Robbie finished.

Artie gave him a sympathetic look.

Valeria shook her head. "You said needle in a haystack, but the analogy doesn't hold up. In this case, the 'haystack' is a methodically organized library, not random bits of hay in a barn."

As the meaning of Valeria's words registered in Robbie's mind, a warm flush overwhelmed his entire body. His heart began to race.

Artie must've noticed something in his friend's demeanor because he asked, "What's up, Robbie? You feel okay?"

Robbie barely heard the questions. "Valeria is a genius, and I'm an idiot."

"Only sometimes," Artie said with a grin.

Robbie approached the door, declaring, "I need to get to the reference library."

"Now?" Artie asked.

"It's closed for repairs," Blake insisted.

"What about class?" Valeria asked half a second later.

The door swung open, and everyone inside the study room froze.

Ms. Versteepen glared at each student in turn, lingered on the seated Blake with a look of blatant disappointment, and then settled on Artie.

"Arthur Rutherford, if you don't leave my school immediately, I will give you a full month of detention."

Defiantly, Artie stood up to meet the challenge. "You can't give me detention. I'm not enrolled in summer school."

The deep shade of red rising from Ms. Versteepen's neck and spreading over her entire face indicated that Artie had challenged the wrong authority.

"Remove yourself from school premises now, Arthur."

"But Ms. V, I'm off to *La belle province* in an hour!" Artie persisted.

The principal was unmoved. "And you'll see your friends when you return." She cut him off before he dared voice another objection. "If you don't leave this instant, your month of detention begins the first day of school."

Artie's defiance quickly turned to contrition. He dropped his eyes to look at the floor, moved past the principal, and out the door.

"Text me later, Robbie."

"And by later, he means after school," the principal stated emphatically.

Ms. Versteepen moved on to the room's other occupants. "Blake, remember that stack of files I asked you to sort later?"

"Yes, Ms. Versteepen." Unlike Artie, Blake's reply was respectful.

"Later is now. Get to it, please."

"Yes, Ms. Versteepen." Blake left without turning to look at her friends.

Before the principal could say anything to Valeria, she packed her bag and excused herself.

"I don't want to be late for my next class. See you later, Ms. V."

That earned a pleased nod from Ms. Versteepen.

Robbie started packing his things, then remembered the paper sheets stuck to the door. He moved past his principal and hoped she wouldn't ask him about the impromptu window coverings.

Instead, her expression softened, and she asked a question he was sick of hearing. "How are you doing, Robbie?"

"Ah, I'm not feeling well today. Do you think I can leave early?"

Valeria's right. The notebook is at the library, and I think I can find it.

The principal's eyes grew wide with concern. She gently gripped his shoulder as if he might fall over. "Do you have a headache? Is your vision blurry?"

"Nothing like that," Robbie reassured her. "Just a stomachache. Probably too much milk this morning."

"You can rest in the nurse's office," the principal offered.

If I go to the nurse, Ms. V will call my mom, and I'll be stuck at home.

"The, ah, nurse's office? No, no. It's okay. I'll just go home."

"Absolutely not, Robbie!" Ms. Versteepen's response sounded worried and skeptical at the same time. "That would be a violation of board policy. Come, let's get you over to the nurse."

"Oh, shoot! I just remembered something. My mom is out of town," he lied. "And my dad is super busy testing a new polymer prototype. I don't want to bother him. I'd rather tough it out."

"Are you certain?" she asked apprehensively. Ms. Versteepen's genuine concern made him feel good but also guilty. He hated lying.

"I'll be fine, Ms. V."

"Come see me or go to the nurse's office immediately if you start to feel worse."

"I will."

As Robbie walked the empty hallways to his first class of the day, a glowing blue dot appeared in his peripheral vision. He flicked his eyes to the dot long enough for the message to appear in the air before him. The top of the message identified Artie as the sender and included Blake and an unknown number, which Robbie guessed was Valeria.

Artie: What's your great epiphany, man?

Robbie deactivated his kit and answered the group chat from his smartphone.

Robbie: Valeria is right. Libraries are organized using a system. The message I keep getting from Mr. B's AI—I think it's a call number.

Artie: Call number?

Unknown: (eye roll emoji)

Blake: (rolling on the floor laughing emoji)

Robbie: That number on book spines in libraries. It's like an address for a book. It tells you where to find it.

Artie: (angry face emoji) I know that! Just didn't remember what it was called (ironically).

Blake: When are we heading to the library?

Artie: Guys! Can't it wait till I'm back? I'm heading out of town!!

Unknown: You're going for a month, A!

Robbie: WE aren't heading anywhere!
No way.

Blake: (angry face emoji) Why not?

He put his phone away instead of replying. The rest of the morning seemed unusually long, and each tick of the classroom wall clock moved at a glacial pace. He couldn't concentrate on his lessons. Part of him wished he hadn't deactivated his kit so he could see his friends' messages without falling afoul of St. Boniface's strict no cellphones in classrooms policy. Another part of him didn't want to see the conversation. The more he thought about his decision to tell his friends, the more he realized he had made a terrible mistake.

Seeing Demeter yesterday reminded him that he didn't belong in the world of the Rosewood and the Writhen. Robbie worried that he had put his friends at risk. He knew that he had to visit the library alone.

Anticipating that Blake and Valeria would meet him at his locker after classes, Robbie ran straight for his bike when the lunch bell rang. He rode to the library with only the rain to keep him company. He ignored the phone vibrating in his pocket.

14

A CERTAIN SLANT OF LIGHT

Alice ran the thumb of her right hand along the bandage covering her left wrist. Unable to stem her curiosity, she lifted the covering to look at the black ink now permanently marking her skin. The artist's instructions were clear—keep it covered for twenty-four hours. Her mom and dad were going to kill her when they saw it. Then they would ask her where she had it done, with the express purpose of shutting the parlor down for inking a minor. She sighed at the thought. She wouldn't tell them, of course.

The memory of the pain slowly faded. She had almost called off the procedure, convinced she'd rather live with a partial tattoo than endure another moment of the needle's excruciating assault. The artist, Talia, had offered to pause the process for a few minutes so Alice could recover. Forcing a smile through gritted teeth, she declined the offer.

Talia's online reviews were full of praise. Her clients insisted she was the best artist in the city, and in a city like New York, being the best at anything meant quite a lot. In particular, the artist was renowned for her flowing script, which attracted Alice in the first place. Not to mention that the tattoo shop had a perfect health record.

Talia had checked Alice's identification twice before starting, but whether the artist had known the driver's license was counterfeit was unclear. On more than one occasion, the suspicious look in Talia's eyes suggested she was not fooled, though she completed the tattoo anyway.

The subway car came to a stop, the doors opened, people shuffled on and off, the doors closed, and the car began moving again. Alice's conscious mind took no notice. The song played through her headphones, and she touched the bandage until her thoughts drifted away from the tattoo.

Someone kicked her foot. Not hard, but enough to get her attention. She looked up and saw two familiar faces smiling down at her, one tall and wispy thin with long hair that belonged in a shampoo commercial, and the other looked like a young male pop star. She groaned inwardly and removed her headphones.

"Oh my God, Alice! It is you."

"Hi, Aspen."

Alice looked past Aspen to the figure behind her.

"Tom. It's nice to see you."

It wasn't, really.

"Come on, Alice. You know it's Thom. Not Tom."

"I swear there was a boy named Tom in our class."

"You mean Tom, son of the fourth biggest real estate mogul in Manhattan, Tom? Yes, he was in our class last year, and no, he is not me."

"Right, right. Sorry, Thom." She made sure to overemphasize the t-h sound.

Aspen took back control of the conversation.

"What are you doing back in New York? We thought you moved to Missouri or something."

"Los Angeles," Alice corrected in a flat voice.

Aspen didn't seem to hear or care.

"Did you run away? Is that why you're back? Are you a street kid now? I mean, who could blame you? From Park Avenue penthouse and the best private school in the world to the trailer park and public school in a blink."

"No, I didn't run away. And I live in a nice house on a quiet cul-de-sac in Brentwood. Not everyone wants to live in outrageously overpriced Soho."

Aspen's expression reflected contrition. Alice thought it looked genuine, but it was hard to tell.

"I'm sorry, Alice. Didn't mean to offend. I forgot that your family has dragged you all over the world on some life-affirming hippie adventure or something. Was it you who lived in grass huts and pooped and peed in holes in the ground, or was that Sophia?"

Thom wrinkled his nose and gently slapped his friend's arm.

"Ewww, Asp. Stop it. You're so gross!"

Alice took a deep breath before speaking and reminded herself that she didn't care what Aspen thought of her life.

"Not quite."

The hippie adventure part was wrong, but the rest was reasonably accurate. Her physician parents had taken her to some very remote places over the years on one humanitarian mission or another. Many of those places lacked the conveniences that people here took for granted, like running water and, well, toilets. Alice cursed herself for the presentation she gave last year that revealed this information to Aspen, Thom, and the other kids in her class.

A feeling of uneasiness crept into her stomach, unrelated to this unfortunate reunion with the biggest gossip from her old school. She felt like someone was watching her. A man wearing a baseball cap and sunglasses a few seats down seemed to be staring at her, but his tinted glasses made it impossible to tell for sure. Alice shook off the feeling. She was not the first girl on the subway unsettled by a strange man looking at her, and she would not be the last. No doubt she was just on edge. Her godfather had been murdered, and his murderer remained on the loose. Alice returned her focus to the conversation.

"I chose to go to public school this year. The kids there are pretty cool."

She didn't use the word *friends* because they weren't really. She didn't seem to fit in. Here or there. Thom gasped suddenly. He tapped Aspen on the shoulder and pointed at Alice's left wrist.

"Oh my God, Alice. Are you okay? You're not—"

Confused, Alice looked around until her eyes fell on the bandage. Realization hit her suddenly, and her eyes went wide.

"No! It's not what you think. It's a tattoo." She blurted it out before thinking and immediately regretted it.

"Shut up. You didn't! Let me see it."

"Ah, it's fresh! I have to keep it covered."

Alice pulled away, causing Aspen to narrow her eyes slightly. The public address system announced the next stop, and the subway car began to slow down. Thom said something to Aspen, who seemed to forget about Alice's tattoo.

"Our stop."

The two friends began moving closer to the nearest set of doors. Aspen turned her head toward Alice as the train came to a stop and the doors opened.

"Come for a visit next time you're in Soho!"

Thom waved. "See ya, Alice."

"Bye, Thom. Bye, Aspen."

The crowd exited the subway car. The doors closed, and the train began moving again. Alice sighed, relieved that the mentally exhausting exchange was over. They weren't bad people. Mostly, they were just out of touch with reality. Aspen, Thom, and all the other kids at their school came from excessively wealthy families. Alice did, too, of course. Her grandfather's steel mills were responsible for a third of the world's skyscrapers. Her parents, however, had always sought to balance penthouses and concierges with shanty villages and anti-malaria drugs in a genuine effort to make the world a better place and their daughter a better person.

A man leaned against the post next to where Alice sat, practically looming over her. She hadn't noticed him before. He must have boarded at the last station. Her heart thumped faster as she saw his baseball hat and dark sunglasses. Glancing at the subway map above the door, she confirmed that her destination was three stops away. Alice looked for an employee in a transit authority uniform but didn't see anyone. What would she say, anyway?

Excuse me, these two men are creeping me out.

Once again, her unease made her feel foolish. Whether it was justified or not, she decided it was better to get as far away from the situation as possible instead of causing an unnecessary scene. A loud chime in her ears caused her to jump in her seat. Just her phone, notifying her of a new message. Alice didn't recognize the number, but her eyes widened when she read the two words glowing brightly on the screen.

Alice, run!

Panic began to rise in her chest, though she willed herself to remain calm. She looked around the subway car. Everyone else seemed at ease, except for the two men with baseball caps, who were definitely watching her through their glasses.

The train stopped at the next station. This time, when the doors opened, no one boarded from the platform or disembarked from the train. Alice's mind pushed down these insignificant details, focusing instead on the need to escape from possible danger. As the doors began to close, Alice stood and slipped past the man leaning against the post. She squeezed through the doors just as they closed behind her. The train began to move again, and in a moment, it was gone.

No one had followed her off the train.

Her relief was short-lived, however. Looking around, Alice realized she had made a mistake. Instead of disembarking at a regular subway station, she was alone on what looked like a service platform. The only illumination came from the dimly lit corridor before her. A moment later, she heard the rapid approach of the next train. It sped past the platform without slowing.

The only way is forward.

Alice used the chess knight icon on her smartphone to activate her kit. The soft, subtle hum started immediately just behind her ears.

"I'm such a coward," she said sheepishly to herself, though Hamza would expect her to take the precaution.

She let out a long, calming breath and headed for the corridor just as a figure in a Transit Authority uniform appeared in the doorway.

"Excuse me."

The female voice called to her in a firm but unthreatening tone. Soon, the woman was close enough for Alice to see her face. She was at least half a foot taller than Alice. Broad at the shoulders and smaller at the waist, she reminded Alice of a bodybuilder. Her hair was dark and cut short.

Alice greeted the woman. "Hi?"

"I received a report of a trespasser down on the service platform. I guess that's you."

"Yeah, about that. I got off at the wrong stop." Alice laughed nervously, feeling embarrassed.

The woman barely cracked a polite smile in return.

Yikes. I must be putting her out.

"I'm very sorry for the inconvenience," Alice stated sincerely.

The woman gestured to indicate that Alice should go through the narrow corridor first. "After you."

They advanced, and Alice stowed the phone in her pocket.

The corridor opened into a large, irregularly shaped room with tiled arches and exposed fluorescent lights along the ceiling. The space was empty except for a few benches covered in plastic sheets and a closed door at the far end. Alice took several steps before realizing the transit employee was no longer following her. She turned around to see the woman staring at her from a few feet away. Alice spun the other way when she heard footsteps behind her. Two imposing figures emerged from the recessed shadow of an arch, both wearing caps and sunglasses.

The woman and two men moved toward Alice in what looked like a practiced maneuver. Alice's breath came rapid and shallow. Her heart pounded forcefully in her chest, and a small part of her brain wondered if she might have a heart attack. Her eyes darted around the room, looking for a way to reach the closed door.

Alice detected movement in her peripheral vision. She whirled in time to see the transit employee step in close with a small device in her hand. An electric arc crackled between two silver electrodes—a shock weapon meant to incapacitate her. The woman's arm shot out, aimed squarely at Alice's chest. She tried to dodge, but the strike was too fast. A panoply of dark blue and purplish light flashed at the point of contact between the shock weapon and the protective lattice that appeared suddenly. The device in the transit employee's hand began to smoke and spark. The woman tossed it aside and reached behind her back.

Alice counter-attacked before the woman could recover. She made a fist and struck the woman hard. Dark light flashed around her hand, and Alice heard her opponent's collarbone crack from the impact. The woman screamed as the momentum of the punch spun her around and sent her crashing into the concrete floor, where she lay whimpering.

Now it was Alice's turn to be shocked. In her panic, she had forgotten Hamza's lessons. The master-at-arms had warned her about the potential dangers of the kit's defensive system. The barrier, which used a sophisticated real-time algorithm to detect anything that would harm the person holding the smartphone, had triggered around her hand to protect the bones from breaking. The system somehow altered the second law of motion, amplifying the mass and acceleration of her strike many times over, thus generating much more force than normal.

Alice's attention was now drawn to the two men standing behind her.

Are they arguing?

"What the hell did she just do?" shouted the man on her right. His eyes were wide and frantic. He took a step backward.

"I don't know, man," said the man on her left. "Our contact said we need to take her phone. Just grab her."

"Nah. I ain't getting my face broke," his partner declared. He reached into his jacket and withdrew a black handgun, pointing it directly at Alice. She raised her hands above her head.

"What are you doing?" screamed the man on her left. "We nab the granddaughter unharmed! No money if we kill her."

A desperate grin appeared on the gunman's face.

"Come on, girl. You heard the man. The three of us can walk out of here. No one else gets hurt."

Alice eyed the gun warily. The blood pounded loudly in her ears. Hamza once demonstrated that her kit was impervious to projectile weapons, but standing in front of someone pointing a loaded gun at her significantly diminished her confidence in the technology she barely understood.

Alice tried to appear calm despite her shaking hands. She nodded toward the woman still writhing on the ground. "Just the three of us. What about her?"

The man with the gun shrugged. "Collateral damage."

Alice snorted. "Some friend you are. How do you treat your enemies?"

"You're not my enemy, sweetheart. You're a paycheck," the gunman replied.

The man on her left rushed forward, grabbed her around the waist, and lifted her into the air. Her kit didn't activate. His too-slow movements failed to meet the algorithm's threat threshold. Instinct and adrenaline took over. She pulled an arm free of the man's bear hug and drove her elbow into the top of her assailant's head. Dark light flared, and the man collapsed, sending her sprawling to the floor. Alice scrambled to her feet, sparing a glance at her attacker. The man looked still as a stone.

Three loud cracks echoed in quick succession around the room. Indigo light sprang to life along her back, and she felt the slightest impact from the metal slugs hit her shield. It happened so quickly that she flinched after the shooting stopped. Upon turning, she saw the gunman's jaw slacken in shock. She didn't think about her next action. Alice reached behind her back and drew the impermanent daggers. The man took aim again, but Alice spun into him, simultaneously whirling the weapons in her hands. She sliced through the gun with the blade of one knife, then spun the other knife and thrust its pommel into his face. The resultant crack of broken bones and sunglasses preceded the spray of blood by a half second. He dropped to the floor.

Alice's breath came in gasps as she looked around at the carnage she had caused. The gunman clutched his shattered face in blood-soaked hands. He fell each time he tried to stand. The woman continued writhing around and sobbing. Blood pooled around the man who had grabbed her. He had yet to move.

Oh my God! Did I kill him?

Then she ran.

She tried the nearby door, which led to a set of dusty concrete stairs. Alice took each step cautiously and exited through a rusty steel door into the dark alley of a nondescript Transit Authority maintenance building. As she emerged, she saw a figure crouched against the wall and lowered her hands to draw her blades. The bedraggled man looked at her before holding out an empty hat and offering a weak smile.

"Oh," she said aloud and forced herself to take a breath. "Ah, I'm so sorry. I don't have any cash."

The homeless man looked about to respond, but his

eyes focused on her clothing. He quickly turned away from her and shuffled further down the alley.

Confused, Alice looked at her clothing and realized they were covered in blood stains. She considered tossing her sweater, which had taken the brunt of the carnage. Instead, she turned it inside out and then tied it around her waist.

I've seen too many crime dramas to leave bloody clothing in a New York City alley.

She moved to the mouth of the lane and looked out at the busy street beyond. Realizing she didn't know where along the subway line she had emerged, Alice took out her phone to check her location.

Wrong side of Central Park.

Next, she tried to call her mom. Nothing happened. She tried again. Same result. Next, she tried her dad. Nothing. She stepped onto the sidewalk and headed toward the penthouse. Calls and texts to her grandfather, Hamza, and Yasmin also failed.

What is happening?

She split her attention between navigating the sidewalk and trying to contact her family. After several more failed attempts to reach her parents and grandfather directly, she took a different tack. Alice found the number for the hospital where her dad worked and eventually connected to someone in his office.

"Cedars-Sinai Medical, General Surgery. Can I help you?" answered the flustered female voice.

Surprised that the phone had connected, Alice stammered an awkward reply. "Ah. Hi, Dominique. It's Alice Asher."

"Hi, Alice!"

"I'm looking for my dad."

"I guess he hasn't reached you yet. Dr. Asher and your

mom left the hospital about thirty minutes ago. They're heading to Spain."

"What?"

"Yeah, emergency surgery. They're flying out right away. Your dad said he would call you from the car. Ah, just a second, Alice."

She heard muffled voices in the background before Dominique addressed her again.

"Sorry, Alice. I have to go. We have a situation."

"Okay."

The line disconnected.

Her parents hadn't messaged or called since the morning. That was unusual. She tried to keep her thoughts straight, replaying the facts in her head as she hurried through Central Park. Her phone worked, but she couldn't contact her family or the other members of the Rosewood. And what had happened on the subway? She had received a message on her phone that told her to run just as the train stopped unexpectedly at the maintenance platform. It seemed someone was targeting her, but why? She needed to reach her grandfather's penthouse. He'd know what to do.

As Alice hurried along the path behind the Met, she realized the bandage had fallen off her wrist. She traced the flowing black script across the inside of her wrist and read the words imprinted into her skin, almost surprised to see them.

She rose to her requirement.

15

IN A SHOWER OF RAIN

Robbie could barely see through the sleeting rain. The distant cracks of thunder made him wonder if his kit would save him from an errant lightning strike. Although he didn't think it would, he stopped long enough to press the chess icon on his phone. He had left his helmet in his locker and wanted to avoid breaking his head open if he fell off his bike. It wasn't just the rain that made the trek to the library so treacherous. Buffeted by the wind, he struggled to retain control of his bike as he rode across town, navigating around cars whose drivers couldn't see out their windshields.

Little by little, the dark, blurry shapes obscured by distance and deluge resolved into the Feist Reference Library. He dismounted when he reached the stairs leading up to the central hexagon. Robbie didn't notice the two figures standing beneath the jutting arch of the large doorway until he reached the top of the stairs. Blake and Valeria huddled against the door, much dryer than him.

"What are you two doing here?" Robbie demanded.

"We took a cab," Valeria replied. She dropped her gaze to the ground as if embarrassed.

Blake folded her arms, either consciously or subconsciously. "We're going to help you find that book, and no, we're not changing our minds."

Robbie struggled with how much he should try to make them leave.

Keeping this secret and lying to the people he loved was harder than he thought, but he could never live with himself if something happened to his friends because of his decision.

The choice was taken from him a moment later. The three of them turned toward the bright headlights and low hum of a small but powerful engine that heralded the arrival of a performance motorcycle. The rider parked beside Robbie's bike, removed his helmet, and walked up the stairs to meet them. Robbie groaned as Drake Gallant approached the group of friends. Unmindful of the rain, he stopped beside Robbie and looked between him and Blake. His expression was unreadable, but his basso voice held an edge, making Robbie feel deeply uneasy.

"What's going on?"

Blake answered, though it was unclear who Gallant expected to respond. "Hey, Drake. Like I wrote in my text message, Val and I are helping Robbie find a book."

"The library is closed for repairs." As Gallant spoke, he fixed his gaze on Robbie in what seemed like a warning.

"I told them," Robbie said, trying to sound confident.

"You told them what?" Gallant's unblinking gaze focused on Robbie to the exclusion of all else.

Robbie didn't flinch. "About what happened here the night Mr. Breton died and about the Knights of Rosewood."

Gallant's eyes grew wider, and the muscles in his jaw tightened. He took a step toward Robbie. Blake was shaking her head. Clearly confused, she interposed herself between them.

"Robbie, why are you talking to Drake like he knows what happened? I thought we were the only ones you told."

Gallant grunted. He removed a keychain from his pocket and approached the entrance. Bewildered, Blake and Valeria parted to give him space. A moment later, he opened the door to the central hex, and the four of them went inside. The library was dark, except for the wan gray light that spilled through the windows from the gloomy sky outside.

Someone must have fixed whatever damage the hellcats had caused because the library interior looked the way it had before the attack. Blake broke the silence first. "Drake, why do you have a key to the library?"

Ignoring Blake, Gallant gave Robbie a hard look.

"You have your kit on?" he asked, an edge to his voice.

"What?" Robbie asked in turn.

"Is your kit active?" Gallant tried again with obvious frustration.

"Yeah. I was riding through traffic and—"

Robbie's mind barely registered Gallant's blazingly quick strike until both of their kits flashed from the impact. Robbie staggered backward. Before he could even respond, Gallant grabbed his shirt and lifted him off the ground. He slammed Robbie's back against the reference desk, causing his kit to flash again. One end of the large desk splintered and then collapsed. Rage contorted Gallant's face. He drew Robbie up and slammed him down again and again onto the remnants of the desk.

Blake yelled at him to stop. She and Valeria each

grabbed one of Gallant's arms and tried to prevent the ruthless onslaught from continuing. Robbie watched all of this as though it was happening to someone else. He felt the impact, not as pain but as a vibration. The assault continued until Blake laid a hand on the side of Gallant's face, much like a caress, and spoke to him in a voice slightly more than a whisper.

"Please, Drake. Stop."

Gallant let Robbie's prone form drop to the floor. He took several steps, then looked back toward Blake. The rage on his face was gone, and in its place was something much worse—fear. He sank to his knees and buried his head in his shaking hands. Blake and Valeria moved to check on Robbie, who was mostly unscathed. Both girls expressed shock when they discovered he wasn't hurt. He had told them about the kit at the school library, but seeing it work was an entirely different experience.

Gallant lifted his head and stared at Robbie. When he spoke, his voice was low. "You don't know what you've done."

Blake rounded on him angrily. "What he's done? You could have killed him!"

"Not likely," Gallant said, obviously struggling to control his emotions. "But I sure want to."

Blake moved to stand over Gallant and peppered him with questions. "You know about all this? What really happened to Robbie? These Knights of whatevers?"

Gallant shook his head. "You don't understand, Blake. I couldn't tell you."

"How do you keep a secret for over five hundred years?" Valeria asked no one in particular.

Slowly, the quarterback rose until he towered over Blake

once again. He reached out as if to touch her arm but decided against it.

"Blake, I planned to tell you. When they permitted it, I would have. I swear. Valeria is right, and she has way more sense than you, Noble. Do you know how they keep a secret this long?"

The question hung in the air until Gallant answered it himself. "By doing whatever is necessary."

The words visibly startled them all, but again, Blake broke the silence. "What does that mean? Are your knights going to kill us now?

Frustrated, Robbie began to stand.

"Maybe Demeter was right," Robbie declared angrily. "The Knights of Rosewood are only interested in hoarding knowledge."

Anger flared behind the bigger boy's eyes again, and he tried to step forward, but Blake remained firmly in his path. Gallant resorted to shouting instead. "Demeter? What the hell are you talking about?"

"I saw him yesterday!" Robbie shouted back. "He told me that if I find Breton's notebook, I'd learn the truth about the Rosewood."

Gallant stopped and forced himself to take a breath. "Demeter is here in Bethel?"

"Yes!" Robbie's voice began to crack. "He came to my house. He sat on my couch. My mom—" He trailed off and quickly turned away so they couldn't see him bite back his tears.

The library went eerily quiet for several seconds, except for the sound of the rain against the windowpanes.

"Have you told Hamza or Yasmin?" Gallant asked him.

Robbie shook his head. "I messaged Yasmin, but she hasn't responded."

Gallant exhaled. "They left Bethel last night and asked me to keep an eye on you while they were gone. I haven't heard from them or anyone else since then." He walked toward the nearest bookshelf, sat down, and rested the back of his head against the stacks.

Concern seemed to override Blake's anger. "What's wrong, Drake?"

Gallant shook his head. "The less you know, the better. I swore an oath. So did he."

Valeria scoffed loudly at Gallant's rebuke. "An oath? Not even old enough to vote, and he's expected to keep an oath to some weird secret society?"

"He should never have involved you or Blake in this," Gallant growled. "He's put your lives in danger."

The three friends shared a look, which Gallant noticed immediately. "What is it?"

Robbie debated remaining silent, but his anger and embarrassment at the thrashing he took from Gallant made him defiant. "I told Artie, too."

Gallant cursed loudly. "You don't get it, do you? The Rosewood will do whatever it takes to keep its secret, but it isn't just the Rosewood that we need to worry about. You said it yourself. Demeter is in Bethel. Anyone who knows about the Rosewood is in danger."

Robbie stared absently at the wreckage of the reference desk.

Gallant is right. I put my friends in danger.

He looked at Blake and Valeria. "I'm sorry. We need to leave."

Blake didn't seem to share his urgency. "What about Mr. Breton's notebook?"

"Wait!" Gallant scrambled to his feet and moved toward

Robbie. "Do you know where to find it?" The anticipation in his voice was palpable.

"Sort of. Somewhere in the library, I think."

Gallant scowled and then waved Robbie away dismissively. "We searched. It isn't here. Unless Breton hid it on a random shelf deep in the stacks, and why would he do that?"

"I have a call number," Robbie stated flatly.

Gallant turned to glare at him. "Why would Breton's notebook have a call number? It isn't a library book."

Robbie took the phone from his pocket and showed him the repeating alphanumeric message.

"Yasmin thinks Isa sent it." He chose not to mention that Yasmin didn't know about his call number theory.

Gallant's eyes narrowed skeptically when he looked at the screen. "I thought Isa was stuck inside that hellcat Demeter cut in half."

Robbie shrugged.

Gallant pointed to the computer at the unbroken end of the reference desk. "Should be easy enough to check."

Robbie walked toward the device, turned it on, and logged in with his employee password. The others crowded around the screen as the computer loaded the user interface for the library database. Robbie typed the alphanumeric combination into the search field and held his breath. The computer found a match—a book authored by somebody named Lawrence Canon. Robbie felt his stomach drop, and his face grew red from the shame and embarrassment. While he didn't know what to expect, he knew it wasn't this.

"It's just some stupid book," he whispered aloud. He had been wrong. He had involved his friends and endangered their lives for no reason.

Blake's tone was soft and encouraging. "It's okay, Robbie. It was worth a try."

He closed his eyes and waited for the inevitable admonishment from Valeria or Gallant, or perhaps both. He knew he deserved it. When it didn't come, Robbie turned to look at the others.

Gallant was staring at the screen thoughtfully. He put his hand to his head as if trying to extract information from his brain. "I've heard that name before but can't remember where or why."

Gallant's response prompted Valeria to take out her cell phone and start tapping. Her eyes widened a minute later.

"What did you find, Val?" Blake asked.

"Maybe nothing," Valeria replied while looking at the screen of her smartphone. "It's an online encyclopedia entry. 'Dr. Lawrence D. Canon, disgraced academic and *conspiracy theorist*.'" Valeria emphasized the last words.

Gallant perked up immediately. "Yes! Canon. My father mentioned him. This guy wrote some stuff on the Knights of Rosewood a hundred years ago, so they completely ruined his life."

Valeria began to read the entry. "'Renowned historian Lawrence Donald Canon earned a doctorate from Trinity College, University of Dublin. He published many nonfiction books throughout the nineteenth and early twentieth centuries. Canon eventually developed an obsession with secret societies that possessed some connection to the paranormal and began to write about them frequently, damaging his credibility in the academic world. Canon's reputation was completely obliterated with the publication of *Esoteric Secrets and the Societies that Protect Them*. Other academics, historians, and scholars decried Canon's loss of sense and sanity. The book received near-universal scorn, which led to the demonization of Canon's entire body of work, including the books that had won him acclaim in decades past. By the 1930s, Canon had lost his post as emeritus professor at Cambridge University in England. He died a few years later—alone, destitute, and disgraced.'"

Valeria looked at her friends. "We're looking for Mr. Breton's notebook," she reasoned. "Mr. Breton was in a secret society. This Canon guy wrote a book about secret societies. That can't be a coincidence, right?"

Blake turned to face her boyfriend, her eyes filled with comprehension. "Oh my God. Your father. He's one of these knights, isn't he?"

Gallant looked away.

Blake pressed him. "Does your mom know you're part of all this?"

He remained silent but shook his head slightly.

According to talk around the school, Gallant lived alone with his mom and was estranged from his father. The man had never attended a single football game, despite Gallant's preeminent position as one of the best starting high school quarterbacks in the state.

Valeria moved to stand very close to Robbie and stared down at the computer display. Her body touched his, and her heat spread warmth to every part of him despite his cold, wet clothing.

"I see two entries for Canon's book," she remarked, seemingly unaware of the effect that her proximity had on him.

Robbie coughed to clear his throat and then looked at the screen himself. "One is in the nonfiction book stacks, and the other is in special collections."

Blake began moving toward the stairs on the west side of the central hex. "What are we waiting for? Let's go."

Gallant gently grabbed her arm. "No, Blake."

Robbie echoed Gallant's words a moment later. "Yeah, no way."

Blake pulled her hand away, glaring at the two boys. "Why not?"

"You and Valeria need to leave," Robbie said emphatically.

A loud snort from Blake made it clear what she thought of their prohibition. "Oh, not this again, Robert Noble."

He flinched at the use of his full name. His parents called him Robert when they were upset with him.

"If this Demeter guy knows we're here, are we safer if we leave?" Valeria's question stopped the boys short.

Gallant let out a long breath. "I don't know," he grumbled.

"Excellent point, Val." Blake began walking up the stairs to the second floor. "I'll check special collections." She soon disappeared from view down the corridor.

Valeria smiled. "We can always count on Blake to do the right thing."

Gallant swore under his breath and then walked after her. "You two coming?"

Robbie headed for the doorway that led to the northern hex. "I'll check out the nonfiction stacks and meet you back here when I'm done."

Gallant shrugged and kept walking. "Don't do anything else stupid."

Robbie looked at Valeria. She spoke before he could say anything. "I'm coming with you. Those two have a lot to talk about."

Valeria and Robbie walked the corridor that connected the central hex to the northern. Valeria looked at her phone and typed something.

"Your parents wondering where you are?" Robbie guessed.

She shook her head. "No. My mom knows I'm here."

Robbie stopped mid-stride, and his eyes widened with apprehension.

Valeria laughed at his reaction. "Don't worry about my mom. She doesn't even know that the library is still closed. She thinks I'm studying with Blake."

They carried on, walking in silence, until they reached the northern hex. The stacks were dark and dusty from more than three months of disuse, but Robbie's experience working in the library enabled him to move confidently through the shelves.

"What are we looking for?" Valeria asked.

"The call number tells us the general location of Lawrence's book. We're looking for natural history, subclass life, which will be on one of these shelves here."

"How is a book about conspiracy theories and secret societies considered natural history?"

"It isn't."

He moved down one of the shelves, looking at the book spines. The fluorescent light fixtures activated automatically when they detected movement. He stopped near the far end of the shelf and examined a pair of books. Robbie frowned.

"What's wrong?" Valeria asked.

"It should be between these two books here, but it's not."

Valeria removed the book from the shelf that would have preceded Canon's, and a piece of worn, yellowed card stock fell to the floor. When they came together to see what it was, Robbie heard Valeria's breath catch. He looked up, and his eyes met hers, their faces only a few inches apart. Neither of them moved or spoke. He let the moment pass and picked up the card.

"It's, ah, from a card catalog," he said suddenly.

Valeria's brow furrowed in confusion. "What?"

He held up the item that had been sandwiched between the two books on the shelf.

Valeria's eyes lit up with recognition.

"Didn't Mr. Breton teach us about them when we came here for a field trip in grade school?"

Robbie nodded. "Yeah. Libraries used card catalogs to organize books before computers."

"So, what's on the card?"

Robbie read the information on the card, flipped it over, and saw the other side was blank.

"It doesn't make any sense. This card is for Canon's book. See?"

He pointed at the call number on the card.

"Why is it on the shelf where the book should be and not in the catalog?"

They stood silently, uncertain of how to proceed. The northern hex was plunged into darkness a moment later. Valeria gasped and grabbed him.

"All right, tough guy. What's with the lights?"

He began to laugh, then waved his free arm until the light fixture above them reactivated.

"The fixtures are set to power-saving mode. They turn off after a few minutes if they don't detect any movement."

"Forget about the stupid lights," Valeria said excitedly. "Listen, if the card in the catalog references the book on the shelf, what is the card on the shelf a reference to?"

Robbie stared at her like she was speaking an alien language. "The card doesn't belong on the shelf."

Valeria sighed in frustration. "Robbie, where is the catalog?"

"Well, when the catalog was still in use, it was located in the central ..."

She shook her head. "No. Where is it *now*?"

"In the storage room across from the librarian's office in the western hex."

She grinned. "Let's go."

16

SOME THINGS THAT FLY

Alice knew something was wrong when she heard the sirens and saw dozens of emergency vehicles crowding the block. Her heart sank even more when she saw the cordon. Metal barricades were arranged around the entrance to her grandfather's luxury condo tower. Uniformed police officers kept people away, and firefighters ushered confused and angry residents to a special holding area across the street.

Alice spotted one of the building's concierges in the holding area. She ran over to him. "Albert!"

The man's eyes lit up when he saw her. "Alice."

Alice forced herself to smile. "Any idea what's happening?" she asked.

The concierge was physically intimidating at over six and half feet tall and at least three hundred pounds, but Alice knew him to be friendly and likable, with a warm smile and a kind word for all the building's residents and visitors. He shook his head in response to her question. "No idea. Nobody told me anything except to hit the fire alarm and get out."

"Have you seen my grandfather?"

Again, he shook his head. "He called my desk to ask about the fire alarm right before the police kicked me out. I told him we had to leave the building."

"What did he say?"

Albert shrugged. "You know your gramps. He said something about 'over my dead body' then hung up."

Alice looked to the top of the condo tower as if she could see the roof. "Did he take the helicopter?"

"Could be. I saw one flying around up there about 10 minutes ago."

Her stomach was leaden, and she tried to catch her breath. First, the attack on the subway, then the Rosewood's private communications network went down, and now this. Something was very wrong here. She needed to get upstairs. Alice's face or her manner must've betrayed her unease because Albert put a comforting hand on her shoulder.

"I'm sure he'll be fine. I heard the cops say they're going through the building floor by floor to make sure everyone is safe."

"Floor by floor! That will take too long."

She approached a police officer who stood behind one of the barricades. "Hi, excuse me."

The large man didn't even look at her. He continued to stare over her head behind a dark pair of sunglasses. She shivered, thinking of the men on the subway.

"Step back, please." His voice was deep and commanding.

"I live here. I need to get inside."

"The building is under an evac notice. No one is allowed inside. Step back."

He still hadn't looked at her.

"Please, officer. I need to find my grandfather. I haven't been able to contact him."

He started to move down the cordon further away from her.

"Hey! Do you know who I am?"

The words almost made her wretch. She couldn't imagine her parents' shame if they heard what she said. They had instilled in her an ethos that reduced the importance of power and wealth while elevating actions that diminished human suffering. Yet here was their daughter, acting like a spoiled rich girl. The police officer swung his gaze around to look at her. She saw his jaw tense and his nostrils flare as he returned to where she was standing.

"I don't care who you are. Step. Back. If you don't leave, I will arrest you."

He straightened to his full height and crossed his arms, staring down at Alice as if challenging her to continue her tantrum. She crossed her arms and glared back at him.

"I own this building. You can't stop me from going inside."

The boast seemed to startle the big man. A broad smile appeared on his face, and he began to laugh. "You don't look like old Calvin Asher to me, ma'am." He infused the last word with false courtesy.

"I'm his granddaughter."

He leaned forward and removed his sunglasses. "I don't care if you're the queen of Moldova."

"Moldova doesn't have a queen!"

The man straightened and called back to one of the female officers behind the cordon. "Take her to the station."

Oh, no.

The female officer stepped forward. Alice suspected she

wouldn't arrest her, but sitting in the back of a squad car for any length of time was counterproductive and embarrassing. Alice didn't wait for introductions. Instead, she ran into the boutique on the first floor of the hotel adjacent to her father's building.

"Excuse me! This entrance is closed," shouted a woman folding clothes at a display table.

Alice slowed to a fast walk as she passed through the store and reached the hotel lobby. She doubted the police officer followed her but couldn't risk another delay. A plan formed in her mind when she saw the elevators.

A no-good, crazy, stupid, moronic, idiotic, insane plan.

She approached the elevator in the bustling lobby once she realized that none of the hotel employees or patrons had noticed her. The elevator doors opened, and she entered the empty car. She pressed the button for the rooftop terrace, which housed a restaurant open to the public. The doors were sliding closed when a hand forced them open. Alice's heart fluttered in her chest, and she expected to see a police officer step into the car.

"I apologize, my dear. It appears we should have waited for the next one."

A man and woman entered the elevator car, each wheeling a piece of luggage behind them. She noticed the Union Jack on a suitcase tag and the man's British accent.

"No, it's okay," Alice replied, quietly relieved to see tourists' accouterments instead of NYPD uniforms.

The man pressed a button on the elevator panel, but nothing happened. He tried again, yet the button refused to light up.

"You need to use your key card or smartphone to access your floor," Alice stated helpfully.

"Yes, of course," the man replied. He tapped his key card

against the card reader. The button lit up, and the doors closed.

"We're staying on the fortieth floor for our fortieth wedding anniversary," the woman said to Alice conversationally.

"How lovely." Alice wasn't feeling particularly talkative. She was too worried about her family.

"Imagine, it took my Bert and me forty years to take our first vacation to the States."

"Leave the girl alone, Bertie. She doesn't want to hear our life story."

Bert and Bertie?

Alice couldn't help but smile.

The elevator stopped at the couple's floor.

"I hope you enjoy New York," Alice said.

"Thank you, dearie."

She held the door open until they exited the car. Alice spent the remainder of her ascent trying to think of an alternative to her current plan, which not only risked exposing the Rosewood but might also result in her death. Other than hiding until someone contacted her, nothing else came to mind.

Upon arriving on the top floor, Alice exited the elevator and entered the restaurant's waiting area. This wasn't her first visit to the popular brunch spot, having previously dined there with her mom. Alice knew where she needed to go. The host greeted her when she entered the restaurant, and she requested to sit outside.

"Are you sure? It's really loud today. Lots of sirens. More than usual. Something's going on in the condo tower next door."

"I don't mind. Do you know what's happening? Next door, I mean?"

The host shook his head. "Fire? Bomb threat? No idea." His smile evaporated as if realizing his joke might offend her, and then he led the way outside. "Take your pick. We're not very busy right now."

She was in luck. The restaurant terrace was empty. Her grandfather's luxury condo tower rose into the sky like an enormous redwood tree competing against the other buildings for sunlight. The hotel was only half as tall at seventy floors. She craned her neck and squinted to get a better look at the top of the condo tower where her grandfather's penthouse was located, but the distance was too great.

I have to go down first before I can go up.

Alice gestured to the side of the terrace closest to her grandfather's building. The host sat her at a table next to the tempered glass railing.

"I'll be your server today. Sparkling or flat water?"

"Sparkling, please," Alice answered. "Take your time. I'm not in a rush."

He went inside, leaving Alice to look over the menu. She glanced around the terrace exterior, searching for any signs of security cameras, but found none.

One less thing to worry about.

Alice rose from her seat and walked over to the railing. The buildings were in close proximity, typical of New York City high-rises. The fiftieth-floor recreational terrace of her grandfather's building was almost directly below the hotel restaurant where she now stood. Looking down, Alice could see the trees, lounge chairs, and large swimming pool that decorated the recreational terrace. Normally, the pool attracted dozens of residents, but the evacuation notice had cleared the building. She took a deep breath and began to climb over the railing.

"Hello again, dearie."

Alice spun to face whoever had spoken. Her server led the British couple from the elevator to a nearby table. Their luggage was nowhere in sight. Bertie smiled at Alice as though the teenager was her favorite granddaughter, while Bert looked more than a little embarrassed.

"You didn't tell me others were joining you," her server stated enthusiastically.

Alice sat down and clenched her fist under the table. She needed a new plan or a way to make the couple leave.

"We'd appreciate some tea, young man," Bertie told the server.

"Coming right up."

The server returned to the restaurant interior, leaving Alice alone with the celebratory husband and wife.

"What's your name, dearie?"

Alice's eyes narrowed at the question. Were these seemingly lovely septuagenarians working with the people from the subway who attacked her?

No way. I'm definitely paranoid.

"Wind your neck in, Bertie. The girl surely doesn't want to talk to a pair of coffin dodgers."

"Rubbish. I'm just making conversation. Do you live here, or are you just visiting like us?"

"I live here," she lied.

"Oh, lovely. You must not even bother with all the sights, then."

"Sights?"

"Oh, you know. The Statue of Liberty, Brooklyn Bridge, Times Square. We're planning to see them all."

Alice had a thought. "The south side of the terrace offers a stunning view of the Empire State Building, especially at this time of day," she said in her most tour guide–like voice.

"Oh! Splendid. Come, Bert. Let's have a look while we wait for our tea."

Bert removed a camera from his jacket, and the couple walked toward the distant end of the terrace. Alice glanced at the doors leading to the restaurant's interior while Bert and Bertie vanished behind some hedges. Despite not spotting any sign of her server or other customers, Alice knew she had to act fast.

After checking that her kit was active for the tenth or eleventh time, Alice climbed over the railing. She held to it fast as the wind almost knocked her off the small ledge. Twenty stories below, the unoccupied recreational terrace beckoned to her. Her heart hammered inside her chest, and she wondered again if she shouldn't just wait for someone from the Rosewood to contact her. Alice heard voices from the restaurant behind her. She knew it was too late to turn back without being seen.

I'm dead if my kit doesn't work.

Shaking her head to rid herself of doubt, Alice focused on the center of the pool below, willing the wind to die down. Missing the pool and landing on the terrace was one thing, but missing the entire terrace and plummeting seventy stories to the crowded streets of Manhattan would be a catastrophe. Even if she survived the fall, people would definitely notice.

And what if I land on somebody?

She pushed the horrible thought out of her mind and jumped.

Time sped up and slowed down simultaneously. The hotel windows rushed past. The wind gusted into her face and blasted through her hair and pushed against her body. The air felt solid enough to carry her from one current to another, and for the briefest instant, Alice wondered if she flew instead of fell. But the cobalt blue tablecloths and teal umbrellas of the pool deck and the tranquil sapphire surface of the water, shimmering in the light of a golden sun, rose up to meet her, tearing away all such delusions.

She hit the surface of the pool across the length of her body. Her kit pulsed into existence, and she passed through the water like a bullet, striking the bottom of the pool with enough force to crack the liner and the concrete. Her kit had protected her from the fall, but now she was on her own.

She thrashed around, disoriented and panicking. She had forgotten to take a breath before her leap. Her lungs had used up all their available oxygen. An eternity of breathlessness seemed to pass until her brain recognized that one part of the pool was several shades lighter than the rest. Her nervous system sprang into action, and muscle memory from years of swimming lessons moved her arms and legs upward until her head emerged from the water. Alice gulped lungful after lungful of air and pulled herself onto the pool deck. As she stood up, her legs trembled.

She spared a glance at the hotel restaurant terrace and thought she spotted figures standing near the railing from where she jumped. She didn't have time to worry about what they might have seen, never mind the countless guests behind the rows of hotel room windows that looked down upon the pool deck. She walked unsteadily toward the doors of the condo tower interior.

The noise inside was obnoxiously loud. The fire alarm blared and only stopped briefly for an automated evacuation announcement broadcast through the public address system. The alarm resumed immediately after the announcement ended. Alice grabbed some folded guest towels and attempted to dry herself off. Feeling steadier now, she walked through the fitness center and the floor's other amenities until she arrived at the elevators. Uncertainty about what to expect plagued her thoughts. Were emergency services personnel wandering around the building responding to— something? Why did the NYPD evacuate the condo building in the first place? None of it mattered. Alice needed to locate her grandfather.

The penthouse was directly accessible from a private elevator in the lobby, but going down to the lobby increased her risk of running into emergency responders. Alice boarded the elevator and hit the button for the highest reachable floor, one below her grandfather's penthouse.

She sighed with relief when the doors closed, and the car sped upward.

I'm glad I don't have to walk it.

The fire alarm welcomed her to the 136th floor. She walked cautiously through the hallway separating the two large condo suites that composed the entire floor, one of which she had lived in with her parents for three years. Alice reached the stairwell without incident and climbed to the first floor of her grandfather's penthouse. The lock that secured the door clicked open when the proximity sensor recognized her smartphone.

She emerged into a small hallway that connected to the fitness room where she trained alone or with Hamza. The bright afternoon sun painted the space gold and amber. Though quiet and devoid of people, voices drifted down the stairway from the main floor above.

"—at the subway."

An angry grunt.

"Chopper is loaded with the comms room equipment. Leave everything else. We are airborne in T-minus twenty."

"Are you kiddin' me? You're makin' us leave behind a lot

of prime loot, Lieutenant. I could buy a professional sports team with the old man's watch collection."

A pause.

"Do you see stars and stripes on my uniform, Reynolds?"

"I do not."

"Don't call me that again."

"You got it, Kemper. What's the plan for the old man?"

"Two behind the ear when the hacker is done with him. Then we exfil. The boss'll be pissed if we end up in a fire-fight with the NYPD."

Alice covered her mouth with her hands, suppressing a cry of despair. The men's voices trailed off abruptly when the elevator door closed behind them. With a sinking feeling, she realized that the 'old man' was her grandfather, and these people were planning to kill him.

She needed to find him first, but she was wary. As a younger man, her grandfather had been a skilled fighter for the Rosewood. Brave and fearless, according to the stories William Breton told her. Calvin Asher remained in excellent health and fenced regularly with Hamza and Edward Kerrich. How had these men defeated him? Taking a few deep breaths to steady herself, Alice summoned the daggers from behind her back and crept up the stairs.

17

WHEN THE LIGHTS ARE LOW

They made their way from the northern hex to the western hex through the connecting first-floor corridor. The library remained quiet and dark. Robbie's heart jumped into his throat when he thought he saw a flash of red eyes in the darkness until he realized it was just his mind playing tricks with the lights of an exit sign. He shook his head to clear it and tried to ask Valeria something that had been on his mind.

"In the nonfiction stacks—"

"Yes?"

Valeria answered more quickly than he expected and thought he knew why.

I wanted to kiss her. Why didn't I?

He felt the flush on his cheeks return but moved on with his original question. "When the lights turned off—"

"Robbie Noble, if you're going to call me out for being scared of the dark, I will return to calling you Arbie!"

He held up his hands in a sign of surrender and laughed. "No, no! That's just it. After everything I've told you, aren't you scared about being here? You and Blake act like it's a picnic at the park."

"So, you want to know if we're brave or dumb?"

"Wait. What? No!"

Her ensuing laughter indicated she found his stuttered response and horrified expression most amusing.

"I don't know," she answered. "Honestly, it doesn't seem real—secret societies and deadly robot cats. Even though you showed me the sword, and I saw the shield appear from nowhere when you and Drake were fighting, it still seems made up, you know? And this Knights of Rosewood stuff is like something you'd read on the dumbest places of the internet, like the Illuminati or flat earth nonsense."

Valeria used her phone to send a group message. He saw the message in his peripheral vision and heard the notification behind his head.

Valeria: Any luck?

Blake: Still looking (smiling face with smiling eyes emoji)

Valeria: K. We're going to check something out in the room across from the librarian's office. Meet us there?

Blake: (Thumbs-up emoji.) Be there in a few.

"They're going to meet us," Valeria said helpfully.

"I know," he replied.

She looked at him and frowned. "How? Where's your phone?"

"In my pocket, but when my kit is active, my phone projects the messages directly to my eyes."

"That's really cool. Can I try it?"

He removed the phone from his pocket and handed it to

Valeria. When he let it go, he no longer heard the low hum telling him his kit was active.

Valeria took the phone, but the screen remained dark. She pressed and swiped the screen and turned it over repeatedly, but she could not get it to work. She handed it back to Robbie and was amazed when the screen lit up as soon as he gripped the device.

"How?" she asked.

Robbie shrugged. "Advanced biometrics."

She laughed. "You have no idea, do you?"

"No, not really."

He reactivated his kit before stowing the phone back into his pocket.

They arrived in the library's administrative hallway from the central hex. Ignoring the librarian's office with its attendant bad memories, Robbie led Valeria right to the storage room containing the card catalog cabinet. Once again, the door was locked.

"Do you have a key?" Valeria asked.

"No, but I can open it. I'd just like a little more certainty before I break down the door."

She smiled meekly. "I'm definitely not certain, but it's reasonable to assume that Mr. Breton wanted to keep the notebook safe *and* have access to it, right?"

He nodded. "Yep. It wouldn't be much use if it was hidden in some hard-to-reach place."

"Exactly," Valeria acknowledged.

Robbie picked up on her line of reasoning. "The underground vault and his office are the likeliest places, but we know the Rosewood searched them already."

Valeria gestured at the locked door of the storage room. "From Mr. Breton's office, this room affords easy access and security." She took the card from his hand and held it up. "And something else."

"The card catalog," he said pensively. "How do we know the Rosewood didn't search this room, too?"

Valeria simply shrugged. "It's possible, but even if they did, they might have overlooked something."

Robbie's skepticism gave way to the reality that he had no more ideas unless Blake and Gallant found something in special collections.

"It's like I'm Nancy Drew, and you're Frank Hardy!" Valeria mused excitedly. He found her reaction endearing.

"Who?" Robbie scratched his head, confused.

"How do you not know Nancy Drew and the Hardy Boys? Your mom works in publishing!" She shook her head but smiled. "Now, how do we get inside without a key?"

Robbie pushed the door a few times. Nothing happened. Valeria watched him struggle, her expression a mixture of confusion and amusement.

"Stand back."

Using the doorframe to brace his left hand, Robbie slammed the door with his right shoulder. His kit flared to life. Though Robbie felt only a slight jolt from the blow, the door jumped against the frame and settled back into place. He hit the door harder on the second attempt. This time, it broke off its hinges and crashed into the room.

Stepping over the broken door, they entered the room. A small table and two chairs were arranged at the center. A chessboard sat atop the table. A series of large wooden cabinets ran along the far wall from one corner of the room to the other. Each cabinet contained twenty-five small drawers labeled sequentially.

Robbie read through the labels until he found the drawer containing the range matching the card from the nonfiction stacks. Valeria watched intently as he drew open the drawer and peered inside. He saw nothing but more cards, which he scanned quickly. He sighed. "It was worth a shot."

Valeria shouldered past him and looked through the drawer determinedly. A moment later, she slammed the drawer in frustration.

Clink.

The muffled yet distinct sound came from the wooden drawer. They looked at each other wordlessly, and Robbie did something completely unexpected, especially to himself. He kissed her. Shyly and awkwardly. He knew then that he had wanted to kiss her since his first day of summer school. The weight of what he had just done hit him a moment later. Horrified with himself and scared of her reaction, he took a step back and looked at her. She returned his gaze, an unreadable expression on her face.

"That wasn't very good," she said, her voice a little huskier than usual.

His eyes widened at the rebuke, and his face turned a deep shade of red. He began to apologize when she stepped into him and kissed him back. The kiss lasted several seconds. She smiled at him as they parted.

"Much better."

"Definitely," he managed to say.

"Why didn't you do that earlier?"

He shrugged. "I wasn't sure I should."

She leaned into him again. Her dark-brown eyes met his. "Here's a tip. The next time we find ourselves in a dark room together, and I'm looking up at you just like this, you should probably kiss me."

So, he did. Afterward, she giggled.

"Um, let's talk about this later, okay?"

He nodded.

Somewhat shakily, Valeria reached for the drawer handle. She pushed around the cards within, unmindful of their age and deteriorating state. Her eyes went wide as she pulled out a small silver key. She held it up in triumph, which very quickly turned to dismay.

"I have no idea what to do with this key, do you?"

Robbie stared open-mouthed. "No. Way."

"What?"

"It can't be that obvious. They had three months to find it."

Before Valeria could prompt him again for an answer, he led her over to the table in the middle of the room. He pointed at the chessboard. The sixteen white pieces were lined up neatly against the sixteen dark red pieces.

"Look under the board."

Beneath each end of the chessboard was a drawer. Valeria shone her flashlight onto the drawers' facade and discovered a keyhole on both sides.

"I tried to put the pieces back during one of my shifts and noticed the drawers were locked. I remember thinking it was strange because Mr. Breton was always so organized. "'Everything has a place, and every place has a thing,' he used to say."

"Did you ask him about it?"

Robbie nodded. "I did, and he said to let him know if I ever found the key."

Valeria couldn't wait any longer. She unlocked the drawer beneath the white pieces and looked inside. She felt around again. Robbie's heart sank when he saw the disappointment in Valeria's expression.

"Nothing here."

She moved to the other side of the board and opened

the drawer beneath the red pieces. When she withdrew her hand, it held a black leather notebook.

"I *am* Nancy Drew."

"I can't believe we found it!"

She smiled and handed Robbie the item. He set it down on the table beside the chessboard and flipped through its pages. They were filled with sketches, diagrams, math formulae, and written sections ranging in length from foot-notes to longer entries.

"Robbie," Valeria began carefully, "this notebook has a lot of stuff in it, some in different languages. Is this what you were expecting to find?"

The rhythmic tap of metal on marble made him look up. He heard Valeria gasp before he spotted the hellcat stepping gracefully through the door. Its terrifying red eyes seemed to scan the room before locking on to Valeria. The hellcat's segmented metal tail whipped this way and that in time to its movements.

"Robbie!"

Valeria didn't scream, but the panic in her voice was unmistakable. Blood thundered in his head, and part of his brain shouted at him to run. Valeria backed away, keeping the chess table and chairs between her and the mechanical monster. Though Robbie stood closer to the beast, its full attention seemed drawn to the object in Valeria's hands.

"The notebook!" Robbie hissed. "Throw it away."

Instead, Valeria drew the notebook against her body and crouched to dodge the hellcat.

"No!" Robbie shouted.

He had no time to think. Sword now in hand, he moved to intercede, but the machine possessed devastating speed. It planted its hind legs and pounced over the table. He slashed wildly at the hellcat, slicing through the exposed metal tendon that connected the segments of its hind leg. The contact sent it crashing into a cabinet inches from Valeria. It climbed to its feet a moment later. Its head turned toward him, seemingly deciding he should be dealt with first.

As it repositioned itself to attack, it stumbled slightly, favoring the leg Robbie had damaged. Despite the impairment, the hellcat leaped and was on him before he could even raise the sword. He found himself on his back, his right forearm firmly ensconced inside the beast's wicked jaws. His kit blazed brightly at the points of contact. The lattice held the immense pressure of the hellcat's mechanical mouth at bay, preventing his arm from turning into a mess of broken bones, blood, and meat. He fought to move into a better position to use the sword, but the beast would not relent. It shook him violently and snapped its head back and forth, trying to break his arm. Valeria's scream blended with the hum of his kit, which seemed to be getting louder.

Robbie's terror increased a moment later when he noticed the light around his arm shifting through a gradient of pinks and reds, just as when Demeter attacked him with the glaive. Only inches from his face now, Robbie saw that the hellcat's teeth glowed with the same yellow light as Demeter's weapon. His fear turned to desperation. The hellcat would break through the shield if he didn't do something soon. He began punching the flanks of the machine with his free hand. The metal caved inward as his kit flared with each strike, but it wasn't enough. His limited range of motion prevented him from inflicting enough damage to disengage from the beast.

He heard Valeria shout a warning just before the heavy wooden cabinet fell atop the hellcat's hindquarters, causing its back legs to compress downward. Its mouth released

Robbie's arm to snap at the new threat. He rolled away and climbed to his feet. Before it could find its own feet and attack again, Robbie swung the sword down with all the force he could muster. The blow he struck was not elegant or carefully placed. His white-knuckled grip on the hilt and the panicked swing connected with the front third of the hellcat's short snout. The sword sheered through part of its nose and the top half of its jaw. Robbie didn't stop to evaluate his effort. He raised the sword and hacked at the beast again and again. Metal flew, and lubricant sprayed around the room. He continued chopping until his chest threatened to burst, his arms grew exhausted, and he had no choice but to stop. The hellcat whined and jerked until it could no longer continue. The glowing teeth vanished a moment later.

Breathing hard, Robbie looked for Valeria, who stood against the back wall of the room. She rubbed her shoulder.

"Are you okay?" he gasped.

She ran to him, and they embraced. Both of them were shaking now.

"I didn't know what to do!"

"That cabinet was a pretty good idea."

They embraced again, and the shock began to subside slowly. Robbie looked at her. "It wanted the notebook. Why didn't you throw it away?"

"That notebook is important, Robbie!"

He shook his head. "We have no idea what's in that book, Val. You said it yourself!"

"That was before this thing attacked us!" She kicked the immobilized hellcat. "No way it randomly appears right after we find the notebook. And if Demeter sent it because we found the notebook, I don't think it's just a collection of ancient bread recipes, do you? Demeter wanted you to come here and find it, Robbie."

He closed his eyes and ran his hand through his hair. He had been thinking the same thing. Valeria touched his face to return him to the moment.

"We need to find Blake and Drake and get out of here. I'll message them."

Before she could do that, commotion sounded in the hallway. They walked out of a bad dream and into a nightmare.

18

ONE FOR SORROW

Any elation Robbie felt after defeating the hellcat evaporated in an instant. The tableau before them was like a scene from one of the classic Western films Artie liked to watch. Gallant and Blake stood just outside the door. Down the hallway to the right, the sleek, predatory bodies of three hellcats looked poised to pounce as their serpentine tails whipped through the air.

To the left stood two more hellcats, and behind them, Demeter greeted them with a broad, mocking smile. His right hand gripped the huge walking stick. A thought flitted through Robbie's mind as he processed the standoff. These hellcats, and the one he had just fought, were different from those that had attacked him and Mr. Breton. Their mouths possessed the yellow glow of teeth that could pierce their kits.

"I knew you wouldn't disappoint me, Robbie. I will take the notebook now."

When none of them moved, Demeter's smile turned feral. A moment later, the door behind Demeter clicked open, and a new figure appeared. Both Valeria and

Blake gasped. Robbie instinctively shouted a warning but realized how much sense it made and that no warning was necessary. Ms. Pirhadi scanned the hallway, glancing at the students disdainfully before addressing Demeter, whose smile had turned even more grotesque.

"Save your gloating, Demeter."

The large man spread his arms.

"You can't blame the boy for not trusting you, Elaheh. You're as personable as a viper."

The look they exchanged made it clear they did not like each other.

"It was you."

All eyes turned to Robbie, who wasn't even aware that he had spoken out loud. Voice trembling, he continued. "The hours you spent at the library. You watched Mr. Breton, didn't you? Demeter knew Mr. Breton didn't have his phone that night because you told him."

Ignoring Robbie, Ms. Pirhadi turned back to Demeter. "You have your revenge on the Rosewood, Andars. Deliver the notebook and the scroll to me immediately."

Demeter sneered.

"My revenge? Some of them still live."

"For now. They are scattered and isolated. In the meantime, here is another outlet for your retribution."

She gestured at Gallant, who stepped forward to meet the challenge. Blake reached out to pull him back. Demeter waved his hand dismissively.

"Not as compelling a proposition as you think, Elaheh. Edward's bastard by a kitchen maid."

Gallant's face contorted with rage. "My mom's an obstetrician, idiot."

"Deal with them quickly and fulfill your part of the

bargain," Pirhadi demanded before she opened the door and left. Demeter turned back to face the four students.

"A truly dreadful woman. Now, the notebook. Unlike Elaheh, I do not relish the idea of extinguishing your young lives. Give it to me, and the three of you can leave."

He pointed at Robbie, Blake, and Valeria.

"You'll let them go?" Gallant asked.

"Drake, what are you doing?" Blake asked desperately, though his intention was clear.

Demeter smiled magnanimously at Gallant. "They go. You stay."

"No!" Blake shouted.

Demeter ignored her objection. "Despite being only a bastard, you still deserve the same fate that your father can expect, I'm afraid."

Grim-faced, Gallant turned toward the others. Blake's reddening eyes welled with tears. She wrapped her arms around the back of his neck.

"Don't you dare!"

Gallant addressed Robbie in a low voice. "The night that Breton died, do you remember where Hamza came from?"

The unexpected question caught him off guard. "What?"

"Think!"

The answer came quickly enough, as Robbie had often asked himself the same question.

"He came out of the darkness. From the back of the vault, but—"

"You take Blake and Valeria there now! Find the door and—"

Before he could finish, Demeter's voice boomed around the hallway. "Tsk-tsk. I'm disappointed you'd reject my generosity in favor of some childish plot to escape."

"Go, Blake," Gallant insisted. "I'll be right behind you."

Robbie wondered how long Gallant could hold them back. Despite almost matching Demeter in stature, Gallant couldn't win a fight against the older man and five hellcats. Not alone or even with the meager, untrained help that Robbie could offer.

Without warning, Gallant kicked in the door to the librarian's office, shoved the three friends inside, and spun back around to face the threats in the hallway. He planted his feet before the doorway, reached behind his head, and drew his arm upwards. A great sword appeared as though it had been strapped to his back.

Robbie ran to the back of the office, pulling his friends with him until they reached the empty bookshelf that hid the stairs to the vault. The shelf looked newly constructed. The unstained wood did not yet match the other shelves in the room. Books were piled neatly on carts to either side, covered in plastic sheets, presumably to protect them from the repairs.

"Where are the stairs, Robbie?" Valeria almost shouted beside him.

Blake's scream drew Robbie's attention. Her eyes were locked on the scene in the hallway. He turned in time to see two hellcats converge on Gallant from different directions. He deftly slashed one and spun away from another, but a third came in low and unseen, its jaws closing around Gallant's leg. His kit flared defensively. Robbie felt Blake attempt to pull away from him, but he clutched her hand tightly.

"Blake, no!"

"You two go! I'll wait for Drake."

"Robbie! Where are the stairs?" Valeria hissed while frantically pulling at the shelf, trying to reveal the staircase that Robbie had told her existed.

Dread flooded every cell in his body when he realized he didn't know how to open the bookshelf. He cursed and shut his eyes, trying to remember the night of the first attack on the library. Mr. Breton, injured and bleeding, had stopped at the large globe. What had the librarian done to open the shelf?

Blake attempted to pull away again. They needed to reach the underground vault.

"Move!" he shouted and drew his sword.

Valeria saw him and stepped aside. Gripping the hilt with two hands, he hacked the bookshelf. Wood split and splintered with the rise and fall of Robbie's arms. Each cut revealed more of the dark alcove where the stairway was located. Satisfied with the size of the opening, he moved to make room for Valeria and Blake.

"Go!" he shouted.

Valeria climbed through the debris from the ruined bookshelf and disappeared down the dark stone steps. Blake hesitated. He turned at the angry shout from the hall. Demeter loomed outside the doorway. He was about to make his way into the office.

"I'm not chasing you again, boy," he snarled.

Demeter ignited the blade atop his cane. Before he took another step, one-half of a mangled hellcat flew past him into the room. Demeter's eyes turned to regard the debris, and a fist struck him in the side of the head. Gallant's kit flared at the contact. Demeter staggered a step, then responded with a thrust of his glaive that Gallant parried. The small hallway constrained both figures. In seconds, their swings and traded blows laid waste to the walls around them.

Though Robbie was no expert on swordsmanship, his eyes widened at the display of deadly proficiency. Each movement was a skillful, deliberate effort by one to end the other's life. Demeter's glaive slipped past Gallant's guard more than once, causing the defensive kit to light up. After repeated strikes, sections of Gallant's shield shifted from dark blue to purple to red.

Gallant seemed to misstep, and Demeter moved in with a devastating, overhanded blow, but Gallant's stumble was a feint. He dodged the heavy, overconfident swing and, before Demeter could recover, drove his sword straight for his opponent's clavicle. Demeter raised his left hand at the last possible moment. Blood sprayed, and he howled in pain as the sword sank through skin, muscle, and tendons.

The sword struck something and stopped.

Hard enough to cut through a steel engine block, the blow should have sheared off Demeter's hand and cut through his body. Gallant just stared.

Hideous and half-crazed, Demeter smiled despite the injury. "See how it pays to be ugly?"

The word Hamza used to describe the Writhen who transformed themselves echoed in Robbie's mind.

Abomination.

Two hellcats struck Gallant from behind, and he fell. Before Robbie could react, Blake bolted toward the hallway. She picked up a heavy brass telescope that had lain beneath a plastic cover. Blake screamed as Demeter raised his weapon to strike Gallant. She swung the telescope around as hard as possible, using the momentum for maximum impact. The telescope hit Demeter in the side, drawing the Writhen's attention away from Gallant.

Demeter reacted instantly in a terrifying demonstration of strength and speed. He thrust the wooden end of the glaive toward the threat.

CRACK!

Robbie heard the sickening sound before his eyes could process the scene. The blow from the weapon struck Blake in the chest, violently snapped her head forward, and slammed her against the wall.

"Blake!" he cried in desperation.

Demeter turned to face him.

Fight or run?

If he stayed to fight, he'd likely die here. If he ran, Demeter *might* follow, giving Gallant a better chance to defeat the hellcats and help Blake. Would Demeter follow Robbie into the vault as he had once before? The huge man stepped into the office, his disfigured face full of rage.

Robbie descended the dark stairway, dashing around the central spiral. His right hand slid along the rough-cut stone for additional balance. Relief flooded him when he heard the thud of Demeter's walking stick reverberating on the stairs above. Now that Demeter had followed, they still needed to get away. Robbie wondered if the vault had another means of egress. Gallant's urgent question sprang to mind.

'Do you remember where Hamza came from?'

He reached the bottom of the stairs. "Valeria!" he called.

He saw the flashlight from her phone, and then she embraced him.

"I thought you weren't coming." Her voice trembled. "Where's Blake?"

He didn't answer. Instead, he led her away from the stairway. "We have to get out of here. Demeter is coming."

They walked through the archway and out into the vault proper. Mr. Breton's desk area was just as he remembered seeing it, except the librarian's body was no longer slumped in the chair.

"Where's Blake, Robbie?" Valeria's voice was more insistent this time. She began to turn back toward the stairs.

"We're drawing Demeter away from Blake and Gallant."

Valeria frowned. Robbie worried she might argue with him.

"Okay." She nodded slowly. "Where are we going?"

"I think there's an exit at the back. We're going to find it and get out of here."

"What about the others?"

"We'll figure out a way to help them. Call the police. Call the army. I don't care about keeping this stupid secret anymore."

Valeria shut off the flashlight so that Demeter couldn't track them, and they moved beyond the desk area. The plan was simple. Walk quickly and quietly toward the far end of the vault.

"Doesn't that phone have night vision or something?"

Valeria's question seemed ridiculous initially, but then he remembered what his kit could do.

"Night-vision, on," he whispered, but nothing happened.

They continued forward into the void. Robbie couldn't help but reflect on the terrible congruity between this night and the night of the first attack. He squeezed Valeria's hand, and she squeezed back. The comfort of her touch reassured him that he wasn't alone this time.

"I am displeased that you have led me down here again, Robbie. Though, I must admit to some affinity for seeing the place where William took his last breath."

They turned at the sound of Demeter's voice, which echoed around the cavernous vault. The dim yellow light cast by his sword was the opposite of a beacon; it drove them deeper into darkness. Robbie tried to contain his panic.

"No one comes to your rescue this time. Kerrich's bastard and the girl are dead. The Rosewood is naught but ashes."

Robbie stumbled and fell. He shut his eyes and held his hands over his ears to block out the words. Images bombarded his mind. He saw Blake lying against a wall and Gallant falling to an assault of hellcats. Valeria was beside him a second later, whispering in his ear.

"He's lying. Let's keep going, Robbie."

Was he lying? Valeria hadn't seen Demeter strike Blake. She hadn't heard the noise Blake's body made when she hit the wall. But he listened to Valeria. He got up. They kept moving forward, and the faint light of Demeter's sword remained close behind them.

"I can't imagine what poor Lauren and Trevor will go through when their son doesn't come home today, especially after the heartache they endured while you were in the coma. The torment will be unbearable. To get you back, only to lose you again. Every single day of the rest of their lives wondering what happened to their boy while his bones turn to dust in this tomb."

"Stop. Please stop," he whispered. Valeria practically dragged him onward as Demeter's incessant taunting continued. A few moments later, Valeria's hands found a wall.

"We've reached the other side. Which way?"

He tried to remember the moment Hamza had appeared. Robbie had been moving in the same direction that night—toward the far end of the vault when he first saw the light of Hamza's sword.

"If we didn't get turned around in the dark, the exit should be to the right of us."

They kept moving.

"Oh, I have such a plan for that innocent girl you dragged into this. Would you like to hear it? I will lock her down here with those mechanical beasts for some sport. I wonder which of those monstrosities will tear into her flesh first?"

"Shut up!"

In the quiet of the vault, Robbie's voice seemed impossibly loud. He turned to face the dim yellow light. He reached to draw his sword, but Valeria pulled him forward.

"No!"

His outburst had been enough to draw Demeter in their general direction.

"Ah, there you are."

Using the wall to orient themselves, they moved faster in their search for an exit. Valeria's left hand soon found an indentation in the wall that turned out to be a metal hatch. They searched for a handle but found a smooth wheel instead. It was cold to the touch. Robbie turned the mechanism until they heard a loud click and a hiss of air. They were through the hatch a second later. What they found on the other side left them lost for words.

It wasn't a room but a massive cavern that stretched outward in all directions. A faint, greenish light from a source Robbie had yet to identify lit the cavern. The floor was uneven but smooth. He noticed a disorienting shift in the air. His head felt light, and each step moved faster than he expected.

"Robbie? What's happening?" Valeria's reaction suggested she was experiencing a similar sensation.

"I have no idea."

Their voices sounded strange, as if the properties of sound behaved differently in the cavern. He approached the nearest wall and saw delicate threads beyond counting, stretching from the ceiling down to the floor.

Valeria gasped. "The threads. They're glowing."

She was right, Robbie realized. The threads were the source of light. He touched the wall between two filaments, and a cold, clear liquid ran down his arm. He was almost certain that the entire chamber was perfectly polished stone. He peered up at the ceiling, which extended several stories above their heads, to see where the water originated but couldn't locate a source. The luminous threads swayed from side to side ever so slightly in the liquid's gentle flow. Each thread was tipped with an elongated pod. He touched a pod. It dropped to the floor, igniting the thread with intense light and vanishing. The pod began to writhe. Upon closer inspection, Robbie realized that the pod was a glowing caterpillar now inching its way back toward the wall.

"What is that thing?" Valeria asked.

At first, he assumed she was asking about the caterpillars of light, but she was staring at a tall structure in the center of the cavern. It reminded him of an exposed elevator shaft. Four metal rails ran straight down from the ceiling into a pit in the cavern's floor. Some type of vehicle, like an elevator car, was attached to the rails at floor level. He could not see any cables or pulleys to draw the car up and down. Instead, a strange apparatus extended several feet from the top of the car's roof. Thin wires and glass-like tubes wove into and out of the machine.

"That elevator looks like something from a Jules Verne novel," Valeria whispered as she made her way to the unguarded edge of the cavern floor. Robbie joined her but stepped back when he saw that the pit had no discernible bottom. Instead, some sort of fog or mist pulsing with a strange light obfuscated whatever was below. A metal gangway bridged the pit and connected the cavern's floor to the elevator car.

"I don't think that's an elevator," he said. "Elevators have cables."

What could be the purpose of such a contraption, and who had built it?

A few minutes later, the hatch clicked open. Demeter emerged into the cavern, holding his cane in his right hand, blood dripping from his left. He looked around, taking in the sight, and then his face broadened into a huge smile. He began to laugh.

"You have given me such a wonderful gift this day, boy. More than one, it turns out. I knew it was real. None of them believed it. Not even my father. But I knew!"

There was nowhere else to go, so they ran for the gangway, but running in that place was hard. The ground moved in unexpected ways. Or was it their feet or their eyes that behaved unpredictably? Whatever the cause, it affected Demeter as well. He used his cane to balance and followed them to the elevator car.

The gangway was too narrow for them to walk side by side, but unlike the pit's edge, it had a railing that protected them from accidentally falling into the frothy, glowing soup below. Valeria reached the hatch of the elevator car first. She spun open the bronze-hued wheel and ran inside. Robbie followed and pulled the hatch closed behind him. He tightened the wheel with all his strength, then looked for a locking mechanism.

A metal post ran vertically through the center of the car's interior. Six cushioned seats were situated around the post facing out toward the windowless walls. The seats were equipped with safety harnesses and latches, like an amusement park ride. A small control panel on the arm of one seat distinguished it from the rest. The simple device had two buttons at the bottom, two lights at the top, and a small bronze lever in the center. A sign that read 'Buckle up!' was posted on the wall in front of the lead chair.

The gangway groaned, letting them know Demeter was a few seconds from opening the hatch to the elevator car. Robbie looked at Valeria. "Get the harness on. Then, pull that lever."

"What does it do?"

"I don't know," Robbie said, shaking his head.

He moved to the hatch and used every bit of strength and leverage to prevent the wheel from turning. He had to believe that Gallant sent them to the cavern for a reason. This strange contraption had to do—something.

The wheel mechanism began to twist in the opposite direction. He refused to let go, and his kit sparked to life, protecting his hands. He held the wheel still for several seconds, but the force that Demeter exerted on the other side of the door, despite his injured hand, was too great. The inexorable turn of the wheel sent Robbie to his knees. A loud clank resounded through the elevator car, and the hatch swung open.

Robbie spared a glance at Valeria. Her wide eyes were fixed on the hatch.

"The lever!" Robbie shouted.

Demeter was forced to duck through the opening. Once inside, he extended to his full height and gazed around the car's interior with a manic expression. His excitement was palpable.

"That half-mad bastard actually built it," Demeter whispered to himself.

Valeria pulled the lever.

19

MADNESS IS DIVINEST SENSE

As Alice moved through the main floor of the penthouse, the signs of violence were everywhere. The furniture was in disarray, the mirrors and light fixtures were shattered, and pieces of the priceless Steinway grand piano littered the once-pristine living room. Despite her fear, she searched silently, hoping to find her grandfather. Her gut clenched anxiously as she searched each room.

She walked past the elaborate marble-and-glass staircase that led to the penthouse's third floor, where the six large bedrooms were located, and proceeded down another hallway into the more modest area of the expansive suite. This section included the living quarters for the housekeeping staff, even though her grandfather did not employ any. The highly secure room, containing a portion of the Rosewood's sophisticated private communications network, was also housed in this section.

The hallway around the comms room immediately drew her attention. The door and portions of the wall were gone, a gaping hole in their place. The acrid smoke and the smell of sulfur were overwhelming. The light from within the comms room illuminated part of the damaged hallway. She slowly approached the wound in the wall, fearful of who or what she might find.

Three figures inhabited the room. One of them was her grandfather. His upper body was slumped over a table, either unconscious or dead. A man sat next to her grandfather and held up Calvin's hand, making the lifeless fingers grasp a phone that looked just like Alice's. The third man stood at the end of the table, facing the hole in the wall. Much younger but almost as tall and broad as her grandfather, the man watched the two figures at the table intently, a gun holstered at his hip. He wore matte-black body armor over his torso, arms, and legs. Alice watched and listened, wondering what to do next.

"Anything?" asked the standing man.

The sitting man, who looked just a few years older than Alice, shook his head. "No. I can't interface with the phone at all, and the biometric security is next level. Fingerprint, facial, nothing unlocks it."

Her grandfather groaned and tried to pull his hand back. Alice suppressed a sigh of relief.

The standing man pulled the gun from his holster and approached her unconscious grandfather. He addressed the sitting man. "You're out of time. The others are ready to fly."

"Whoa. What are you doing?" asked the sitting man.

"Following orders."

"No one said anything to me about killing the guy."

"Move, Avanish."

"I told you. My name is Avinash."

"And I told you I don't care. Move!"

Just as Alice slipped into the room, a blue dot appeared in the peripheral vision of her left eye, and a ringing started behind her ears. Unintentionally, she flicked her eyes down to the blue dot, and translucent words appeared in the air before her.

'Incoming call: Cedars-Senai Medical Center.'
Not now!

She screamed in her head and blinked to dismiss the call. At the same time, her foot connected accidentally with a small pile of rubble from the blast that took out the door. The standing man's head snapped around at the sound she made, and he trained his gun on her. As her kit intercepted three quickly fired rounds, she launched into the same move she had performed on the subway service platform, spinning into the man while bringing her daggers to bear. This time, however, her first strike was off the mark, and the blade sliced through the man's index finger as it cut the gun in half. The man ducked below her follow-through strike with the second dagger. Her momentum carried her too far. The pommel smashed through a flat-panel monitor and damaged the wall it was mounted on.

She turned to face the room, quickly assessing the information that her eyes conveyed. Calvin Asher remained unconscious; his smartphone lay on the table beside his hand. The sitting man, Avinash, hid beneath the table, his wide eyes darted between Alice and the hole in the wall. The standing man cursed at Alice while he shook and flexed his bloody hand.

"That hurt," he said.

Alice shrugged. "Oops," she replied with a bravado she didn't feel. Her hands shook from fear.

"My turn," the man said through a cruel smile.

He pulled a metallic object from the surface of his thigh armor. The footlong cylindrical handle was topped with a cross-piece. With a flick of his wrist, silvery square segments cascaded from the cross-piece, rapidly clicking into place and tapering toward a point.

Uh-oh.

The man pressed something on the inside of his forearm. A high-pitched whine filled the room, emanating from the man's armor, which was comprised of the same metallic segments as his sword. Alice heard the sound of small pieces of metal striking each other, and the segments appeared to constrict around the man. His suit and sword solidified, and the gaps between the segments disappeared. A strange electric-yellow shimmer coalesced over the armor from his chest to his feet, pulsing with energy. It flowed down his wrist and into the sword.

Alice's mouth went slack, and the man used her surprise to his advantage. He leaped forward with a wild slash that she barely dodged. His sword cut through the metal, glass, and hard plastic of the networking cabinets behind her. He pivoted his body to follow Alice's evasion, tearing his blade up through the equipment and into a diagonal slash that struck her side.

The blow triggered her kit, setting off the protective lattice of dark blue and indigo light. She slammed into the wall. He swung again, but she dipped low enough to avoid the attack. His sword cut the air over her head, and she drove her right dagger at his midsection. The blade struck the armor, flashed brightly, and deflected off to the side, confirming her fear that the man was using a modified version of her kit. The armor at the impact point shifted from gray to charcoal black and began to smoke. He drove his knee into her face, armor striking lattice. The force sent her crashing into another cabinet. She rolled away from his next strike and scrambled to her feet.

The man raised his eyebrows and smiled even more obnoxiously than before.

"Impressed?"

Breathing hard while assuming a defensive stance, she scoffed. "Not at all. Terrible form. Slow and sloppy. You're a toddler pretending at swordplay with a wooden stick. And you're leaking smoke. You should get that checked out."

He glanced down at the place where her blade struck.

"They're still ironing out the wrinkles."

From the corner of her eyes, she saw her grandfather attempt to sit up. Her opponent did not waste the opportunity. He directed a heavy, two-handed cut at her upper body. Instead of dodging, she lifted the dagger to intercept the blow using an underhand grip. She overestimated her strength, however. The man's sword forced her to release the dagger, and his blade continued into the protective lattice at her shoulder. Alice dropped to one knee. He used both hands to apply pressure to his sword, pinning her down. She couldn't raise her right arm. The lattice turned an angry shade of red, and the hum behind her ears was almost deafening. She knew from her training that the shield protecting her shoulder was seconds from failing.

Desperately, Alice stabbed the man with the dagger in her left hand, striking his armor. Each time, another segment turned black and began to smoke. It seemed his armor would soon fail.

Just not soon enough.

Then, she saw something. A three-inch piece of wire connected the inside of the man's wrist to the bottom of his sword's hilt.

A tiny glimmer of maybe.

She slashed upward, the tip of her dagger severing the wire. The yellow light that pulsed along the man's sword vanished, as did the immense pressure that forced down her right shoulder. She drew the dagger in her right hand and struck the sword. It shattered, and the man fell forward into Alice, knocking her over.

He reacted faster than she did. The force from his stumble wasn't hard enough to trigger her kit, allowing him to immobilize her arms with his own. Then he used some sort of judo or mixed martial arts move to climb on top of her. She thrashed wildly, but he was too heavy!

"*Get off me!*" she screamed in his face.

His smirk became a laugh.

She felt a hand grasping at her pockets, and a moment later, he was prying her phone away from her.

"No!" she shouted in outrage.

A heavy arm wrapped around the man's neck and pulled him back. His smirk disappeared, and his mouth opened in shock. He stopped struggling with Alice's phone and grasped the arm of his new attacker. A voice as dead as stone sliced in from behind the man.

"That's my granddaughter."

Then a sword punched through the man's back and out his chest. The armor had lost its light, and the segments were visible once again. She scrambled from under him and backed into the nearest wall. She watched in horror as the man died in front of her. Her grandfather's blade vanished, and the body thumped to the floor of the network room. Blood spilled out from the dead man's wounds.

Alice shut her eyes tightly and felt tears leak down her face. She curled into a ball with her arms around her knees. A shaking hand touched her arm, and she heard her grandfather's voice.

"It's over, Alice."

He sounded strange. Weak or dazed, she couldn't tell.

Alice wiped her face and opened her eyes. Calvin Asher leaned against the wall, then clutched his head.

"What happened, Granddad? What did they do to you?"

"Ambush. They came in from the roof by helicopter. I was expecting my pilots. I think someone hit me." He shook his head. "Likely a concussion. I need an X-ray."

A noise caught their attention. The young man, Avinash, attempted to crawl from the room unnoticed. Calvin said nothing. Instead, he stood unsteadily and then walked toward the crawling figure. When Calvin summoned his sword, it whispered the promise of retribution. Avinash heard Calvin's latticed feet crunch on some broken glass. He turned and witnessed the embodiment of cold fury.

"Stop!" Alice shouted. "No, Granddad!"

Avinash moved onto his knees, his hands covering his face.

"Please! Please don't hurt me! I'm sorry."

Sword gripped casually in his hand, her grandfather stopped a foot from Avinash.

"I'll tell you whatever you want to hear," the young man pleaded.

"You will tell me what you know," her grandfather corrected. "Why did you come here today?"

"We came to take out the comms equipment. And you, apparently, bu-but I didn't know that. Trying to hack into your phone was just cake."

Calvin gripped the hilt tightly and stared as if weighing his next decision. "Who sent you?"

Avinash didn't answer immediately. His eyes darted down the empty hallway, then back at her grandfather with a more resigned expression.

"Please, man," Avinash pleaded. "You've seen these guys.

They mean business. If I squeal, they're gonna kill me in a bad way."

"I am deliberating between two choices," her grandfather stated, and even Alice flinched at the dangerous tone. "Cut your head off or throw you off my balcony. I admit that both options appeal to me equally."

Avinash raised his hands and whimpered. A lump formed in Alice's throat. She wondered if her grandfather would really execute this defenseless man. The body of the dead mercenary who had attacked her answered the question.

Calvin persisted. "Your cooperation may earn you some mercy."

Alice let out a breath. Avinash might save his own life if he revealed what he knew.

"Tell him!" she said, her voice shrill.

"Okay, okay!" the young man almost shouted. "A big, ugly dude named Andars Demeter and a real mean lady boss. Her name is Elaheh Pirhadi."

Her grandfather shook his head. "Demeter is no surprise, but I don't know this Pirhadi woman. Is Demeter here?"

Avinash shook his head.

"Last I heard, he was in a place called Bethel."

Her grandfather groaned suddenly and pushed the heel of his free hand to his temple. He stumbled but caught himself against the wall, causing the sword to vanish from his other hand.

"You need to sit," Alice said urgently.

"After," he managed. "Have you heard from your parents or the others?"

"I can't reach any of them," she answered. "I called the

hospital. Dad's assistant said Mom and Dad were heading to Spain."

Her grandfather turned his attention back to Avinash. "What is the plan for our communications?"

Avinash nodded. "I remotely triggered a vulnerability last night, which killed the relay for a few hours. We came today to hack the network, taking it offline for good, but the encryption was insane, so the other guys ripped it out of the wall. That shut down the whole thing."

Alice frowned. "But my phone still works. I just can't reach the others." She meant the other Knights of Rosewood but didn't volunteer that information in Avinash's presence. Her grandfather seemed to understand.

"Our private network is a closed loop, except when we call out to other numbers."

To Alice's astonishment, Avinash actually smiled. "I scraped together a database of numbers that your little group might call once we shut down the private network." He turned to Alice. "I blocked your number from reaching your dad's assistant. How did you get through?"

"I called the switchboard."

Avinash's face fell. "Damn. I can't believe I missed that."

Her grandfather passed a hand over his brow. "We made no contingency for this. Our carelessness and naivete may result in our undoing." He looked at Avinash again. "How did you learn about the relay?"

The young man shook his head. "Lady boss told me. No idea how she figured it out."

"Granddad," Alice interrupted, "the other attackers are on the roof. I heard them say they were waiting for Avinash and, ah, that one."

Her face paled as she gestured toward the dead man.

"The building was evacuated, and the police are on their way. They're coming up one floor at a time."

"Do you have a radio to talk to your men?" her grandfather asked Avinash.

"I'm not allowed on tac comms," came the reply.

"You're a civilian. The others are military or ex-military?" her grandfather speculated.

"Ex-military," Avinash confirmed.

"Alice," her grandfather addressed her, "take the earpiece off the dead soldier and give it to our prisoner."

She tried not to gag when she moved the corpse. She failed. One side of the dead man's head was pressed against the floor. She struggled to roll him over to reach the earpiece.

"It's not just his body weight," Avinash offered. "The armor is depleted uranium, and he's carrying around sixty pounds of power cells sewn into his jumpsuit."

"The power cells catalyze the armor?" Calvin asked.

"Not just the armor. That retractable sword, too. The armor and sword use a ton of juice and maybe last fifteen minutes or so before the cells need recharging."

Avinash seemed to realize that his audience was paying close attention to his words, so he continued more enthusiastically. "They can't figure out how to cover the power cells with the armor. That's why his back was exposed. And the cells get hot. See those packs on his belt? It's a coolant system. That's what makes that annoying noise. Without the coolant, the cells would toast him up real good."

"You seem to know a great deal about this operation for someone not allowed on tac comms." Calvin's voice was accusatory. "What is your role in this?"

"Just a hacker, man. I'm no field guy."

Alice actually laughed, and the two men looked at her.

"You hacked the people who paid you to hack us, didn't you?"

"Yeah," Avinash confirmed.

Her grandfather's frown deepened even further. Alice knew he didn't countenance disloyalty in any context. This confession was likely to work against the hacker. Avinash's smile faded as he seemed to pick up on her grandfather's disapproval.

"I swear, I got no beef with you. Pirhadi got me out of a jam and said I owed her."

Alice retrieved the earpiece. She helped Avinash to his feet before handing it to him. Her grandfather leveled a dangerous look at the prisoner.

"Tell them you and your companion are coming to the roof now. If you try to warn them, you will not take another breath."

Avinash nodded and inserted the earpiece.

"Ah, hey. We're on our way up."

Alice and her grandfather could not hear the response. They watched Avinash for any sign of treachery.

"No, I can't hack the old man's phone."

Avinash rolled his eyes.

"Yes, I know I'm a useless idiot. Roman's ah, hands are full of stuff he took from Asher. Yep, I'll tell him he's, ah, a dead man when Kemper sees him."

Calvin took the earpiece, dropped it on the floor, and crushed it.

"What's the plan, Granddad? You aren't thinking of stopping those men, are you? You can barely walk straight!"

Her grandfather looked at Avinash and then nodded at the hallway. The three of them began their trek through the penthouse.

"I cannot allow them to leave. They are a direct threat to

the Rosewood. They attacked my granddaughter and invaded my home."

Wait till you hear about the subway.

"Granddad, I thought Demeter wouldn't reveal anything about the Rosewood to outsiders. And how did he know about the relay?"

The question left her grandfather looking even more troubled than before.

"I need to make a call," he replied.

The sudden declaration caused a frown to crease Alice's forehead.

Her grandfather lifted his smartphone to his ear a moment later. "Get me the mayor. Now. Tell her it's Calvin Asher."

Why the mayor?

"Charlene. It's Calvin. Of course, I'm not fine. My building is crawling with NYPD. A credible terror threat? Ridiculous. Probably a troll job by some bored idiot wearing a Guy Fawkes mask in his mother's basement."

Calvin stumbled again. Alice helped steady him. He returned to his phone call while holding his head.

"I don't care how you do it. Just make them leave. Nonsense! I supported your successful mayoral campaign. I assumed I didn't need to remind you. Perhaps the next mayoral campaign I fund will be my own. Of course, you can trust me. No scandals, no proverbial dead bodies."

Alice and Avinash both glanced down the hallway and then at each other. She wondered if they shared the same thought.

Nope. No dead body here.

"Tell the press we had a minor helicopter accident on the roof. No fatalities. And one more thing. Who gave the order to secure the building one floor at a time? Could you? Thank you, Charlene."

Her grandfather tapped the screen of his cell phone and grunted to himself.

"Is that how we handle our problems, Granddad? Threats, intimidation, lies, and extortion to get our way?"

He stopped mid-stride, turning to look at his grand-daughter. He seemed weary but not angry.

"Our family has a duty, a vow to protect the secrets of the Knights of Rosewood. Nothing matters more than that."

She didn't say anything, but the fearful look on Avinash's face made it clear that he had done the arithmetic regarding his survival, and the numbers didn't add up in his favor.

20

HIS TROUBLE BEGINS

The light bulbs on the ceiling of the elevator car blinked red. Demeter stepped toward Valeria. He stopped when the hatch closed behind him and the wheel locked in place, sealing them inside. A pneumatic compressor sounded, and they all reached up to cover their ears simultaneously as the air pressure dropped. The control panel in front of Valeria lit up, preceding a series of loud, abrupt clinks above them.

The car fell straight down, and the occupants were weightless. The mechanism atop the car hissed, and some unfathomable engine propelled them downward at an impossible speed.

An air-shredding boom speared Robbie's eardrums. His kit ignited just as his back slammed into the ceiling. He tried to scream, but he couldn't draw enough oxygen into his lungs. The air suddenly frosted as the temperature dropped, and unrelenting pressure threatened to pop him like a bloody grape. Then the hallucinations began, and all sanity fled from the world. Spectral figures appeared around him. Countless ghostly versions of himself flowed in a line from the hatch to the floor beneath him, then moved in the opposite direction, mixing with a thousand Valerias and just as many Demeters.

The madness crescendoed into a kaleidoscope of light and sound and fury that threaded his perception through a hole no larger than the eye of a micron-sized needle.

And just as quickly as it began, the car lurched to a stop, sending Robbie and Demeter hurtling to the floor.

Seconds later, his brain and eyes synced up again. Stunned, nauseous, and disoriented, he looked around the car. He was relieved to see that the ghost versions of the car's three occupants had disappeared. Valeria, pale but unharmed, struggled with her harness until it finally disengaged from the buckle at her waist.

"What happened?" Valeria's voice wavered weakly.

Demeter lay on the floor near the hatch. Blood pooled around the man's head. His heavy walking stick, blade deactivated, lay strewn next to his body.

Slowly, Robbie climbed to his feet, using the nearest seat for support. Valeria stumbled over to him, her eyes swept over Demeter's prone form. The pigment in her face paled to an even lighter shade.

"Is he dead?" she asked.

As if hearing Valeria's question, Demeter groaned. The sound was guttural and animalistic. Robbie cursed, and Valeria squeezed his arm and pointed to the hatch. "We should go before he wakes up."

"No," Robbie stated in a trembling voice. "I need to end it before he comes for us again."

Valeria's eyes went wide, and she seemed to process his meaning immediately. Robbie shook his head to clear it, drew his darkly glowing blade, and stared at Demeter's motionless form.

"Robbie." Valeria looked at him with grave intensity. He thought he could guess her thoughts, undoubtedly mirrored by his own.

Can I actually end this man's life? Cut him and walk away as he bleeds out and dies?

The memory of Demeter's hand rising up to stop Gallant's vicious sword strike rushed into Robbie's mind. Hamza had said that the Writhen reinforced their bodies through some arcane practice. Robbie wondered if killing Demeter was even possible.

He didn't know how long he remained in that position, poised on the edge of life and death. When he felt Valeria pull him toward the hatch, he allowed his body to follow. Robbie swallowed the bile that had crept from his stomach to his mouth, equally relieved and disgusted at his inability to act.

As they stepped around the huge man to reach the exit, Demeter groaned again and began pushing himself into a seated position. The hand injury Demeter sustained from Gallant's sword seemed not to bother him, though it continued to bleed freely.

"We need to go!" Robbie told Valeria, his panic drowning his other emotions.

He released his sword and stooped to pick up Demeter's cane. He grunted at the effort required to lift it and wondered how the man swung it about so effortlessly.

Valeria opened the elevator hatch and stepped outside. Robbie heard her gasp, and he moved to follow her out as quickly as the heavy cane would allow, glancing back at Demeter just as the man rose inexorably to his feet.

"Um, Robbie," Valeria's voice cracked, full of apprehension and more than a touch of fear.

He didn't know what to expect on the other side of the

hatch. They had spent only a few minutes inside the elevator car. Where could they have gone? Did the library possess another level below the vault?

Robbie's mind reeled at the sight that greeted him. They had emerged onto another elevator platform, but the four vertical rails upon which their car rested rose interminably into a black sky of endless, starless night. Below the platform, a sea of glowing mists roiled and churned, stretching to the four corners of infinity.

Nothing else appeared to exist in this place. No sun. No moon. No land or mountains or buildings or living things that he could see. Just black sky, frothing mists, and four-railed elevator platforms. Not just the one they had arrived on, but dozens or maybe hundreds or even thousands in every direction, stabbing the sky with so much metal and connected by a series of narrow bridges a hundred feet or so above the misty sea. All the illumination in that fell, dark world originated from the metal structures – rails, platforms, and elevator cars – that shimmered with a jade light, muted and dull, and from the coruscating glow beneath the mists.

Something small fluttered onto Robbie's hand. He shook it reflexively and expressed surprise when a butterfly flitted away.

"It looks like the butterflies are the main light source," Valeria whispered incredulously.

She was right. Legions of butterflies, each emitting a tiny radiance from every part of its body—wings, appendages, head, and even antennae—clung to the elevator structures. The insects weren't much brighter than fireflies, but collectively, they suffused the world in a warm, green-hued glow.

Breathless, Valeria asked, "What is this place?"

Good question, but not the only one. I can think of a few more.

Was the Feist Reference Library's true purpose to act as a connection point to this otherworldly transportation hub? Did each set of rails link to a different location?

Valeria seemed to arrive at the same conclusion.

"Where do you think they all go?"

Robbie thought back to the night Demeter attacked the library. Isa said something to Mr. Breton that hadn't made sense until this moment. *'Hamza Elsayed can be here in twenty-six minutes through the Junction.'* Hamza must have traveled to Bethel through this place.

"Astonishing," Demeter said from behind them. "Behold, Feist's grand achievement."

Robbie turned to see the Writhen stagger from the elevator car's hatch.

"Go!" Robbie hissed, hearing the fear in his own voice.

Valeria led them over the nearest bridge, away from the car that had transported them to this world. The same sensation of unsteadiness they experienced in the cavern below the library was present here too, but stronger. Valeria gripped the handrails as she ran, reaching the next platform in seconds. She spun, and her eyes locked onto something behind Robbie.

"He's coming!" Robbie heard Valeria shout, and a small fragment of his mind registered that her voice didn't echo in the strange air.

Demeter started across the bridge, his broad, hideous smile a contrast to the damage his body and face had sustained. His left hand was a mass of congealed blood. Robbie didn't waste any time. He threw the cane over the railing. Demeter watched as his weapon disappeared into the clouds below them. Anger awakened behind his blue eyes.

"I was fond of that cane," he growled. "It belonged to my father."

Robbie reached the next platform, his eyes searching desperately for an escape. The only possibilities were a second bridge leading to another elevator structure or this platform's car. Upon closer inspection, however, he saw a sign on the car's hatch.

Out of Order.

Ah, c'mon!

Under different circumstances, Robbie might find the mundanity of the sign in so extraordinary a place comical. Demeter began to taunt him again as he crossed the bridge.

"I am grateful, Robbie. I already possess the scroll and will have the notebook, thanks to you."

"I'm pretty sure Pirhadi said you can't keep them," Robbie shouted back.

Demeter laughed contemptuously. "No doubt she plans to turn her pack of beasts against me as soon as they are in her possession. You have provided me with an escape from her treachery by leading me here."

With a grotesque smile etched upon his face, he charged across the metal bridge. Each heavy footfall shattered the perfect silence of that place.

The sight of that injured and misshapen goliath rushing toward him sent a spike of cold terror through Robbie's mind. Even without the cane, Robbie could not hope to defeat Demeter. The Writhen's size, experience, and ferocity were far beyond Robbie's rudimentary sword skills, developed over too few hours of training with Hamza.

But the thought of what Demeter had done to Mr. Breton and Gallant and Blake, combined with the profound sense of powerlessness and shame that had gripped him since the night of the attack, produced a new emotion.

Anger.

It formed within his psyche like carbon atoms crystalizing under the intense heat and pressure deep below the surface of the Earth. In spite of the heart-crushing fear that dumped adrenaline into his bloodstream and supercharged his breathing, Robbie would not allow this man to harm Valeria. He knew then that he had only one chance to save her.

He shepherded her onto the bridge that led to the next platform.

"Take the nearest working elevator you can find and get out of here. Don't wait for me."

"Robbie, no! I won't leave you."

Her words stabbed his heart, so much were they like Blake's before Demeter had struck her.

"I'm done running," he said and spun around to face their tormentor.

Demeter reached the end of the first bridge and stumbled onto the platform. The Writhen fell to one knee beside the inoperative elevator car.

Twin suns of unquenchable fire burned in Robbie's heart. Fear and anger. Anger was the catalyst, and fear the fuel. One ignited the other, transforming them at the molecular level into a power he could use.

Robbie drew his sword from the air and swung it at Demeter in a deadly arc. The darkly glowing blade barely sliced the man's coat as he rolled away more quickly than Robbie thought possible.

Demeter launched to his feet, clenched his uninjured hand into a mallet-sized fist, and drove it at Robbie's head. Robbie threw himself backward, and the fist struck the side of the elevator car instead, ringing it like a bell and caving the metal inward.

Robbie tried to find his fighting stance, but his inexperience and Demeter's speed left him greatly outmatched. The Writhen didn't miss a second time. When the punch landed on Robbie's chest, his defensive kit flashed brightly. Though the lattice took the brunt of it, Robbie stumbled backward, and his whole body trembled from the concussive force of the punch. Either Demeter hit harder than Gallant, or Gallant had been pulling his punches when he attacked Robbie at the library.

Demeter charged again, and Robbie fell, his back hitting the platform. He tried to stand, but Demeter was on him a second later, driving his fist like a jackhammer into the lattice at Robbie's face. The protective barrier shifted colors with each successive strike. Indigo to magenta.

"Stop!" A voice screamed from behind them.

The sound didn't carry in the air like it should have, but it had the desired effect. Demeter stopped and looked at Valeria, who held Mr. Breton's notebook over the railing.

"Let him go, or I'll drop it." Her chest rose and fell rapidly, and tears had washed tracks down her face, but she stood defiantly on the bridge to the next platform.

"Valeria, no!" Robbie shouted.

Demeter straightened, nodded, and smiled.

"Well played, girl. Give me the book, and you both walk away."

When Robbie tried to rise, Demeter stepped on his head. The kit came to life before the Writhen could do any physical damage. Robbie's face turned red, burning with renewed shame at his own helplessness.

A moment passed before Demeter lifted his foot and

strode onto the bridge. Robbie sat up, watching intently. He couldn't breathe.

Valeria proffered Demeter the notebook. Grinning, he took it with his good hand and bowed to her.

"My thanks," he said with embellished gallantry.

Faster than Robbie's mind could process, Demeter's bloody hand shot out and grabbed Valeria by her neck. Her eyes widened with terror as the Writhen lifted her off the bridge, her feet desperately kicking the air.

Robbie scrambled to stand.

Then, with shocking nonchalance, Demeter dropped Valeria off the bridge.

Her scream shredded Robbie's mind, and his entire world transformed into a dense singularity of purpose. His breath caught in his throat, and the wail that emerged from his mouth startled the glowing butterflies into frenzied flight. The sword reappeared in his hand, and he charged the larger man, heedless of the danger to himself. He became the purest manifestation of rage.

The indigo blade slashed at Demeter indiscriminately. The narrow bridge limited Demeter's lateral movements, forcing him backward to avoid the first strike. Robbie's wild second swing drove straight for the Writhen's neck, and Demeter could not avoid it. He lifted his injured arm to protect himself. The sword scythed into the underside of his thickly muscled forearm before stopping at the bone. Demeter howled in agony.

Robbie didn't care.

He was insensate. He struck again, cutting through the railing but hitting Demeter's forearm again on the fourth swing. The notebook fell to the floor.

Robbie didn't care.

Demeter unleashed a vicious kick, which drove Robbie back a step and almost knocked him down.

As Robbie moved forward and raised the sword for a fifth time, Demeter's right arm struck him hard in the face. Demeter followed the punch with another kick, which sent Robbie sprawling onto his back in the middle of the platform. Demeter moved quickly until he stood over the now-helpless boy. He trapped the flat of the blade with his foot against the surface of the platform. Robbie tried to raise the sword, but Demeter was too strong. The man grinned in triumph.

"We're finished here, boy."

Robbie opened his right hand and dismissed the sword. Before Demeter could react to the slight shift under his foot, Robbie reached across his hip and drew again. He slashed toward Demeter's abdomen from left to right. Robbie missed his target. The blade cut through Demeter's long coat instead. The sword hit something and stopped instantly.

An ear-shattering sound split the silence like a discordant cathedral bell. The hum from Robbie's kit changed to a painful keening. A split second later, his sword exploded. His kit lit up the air, reflecting off rails, cars, and platforms for a quarter mile in all directions. Pain lanced through his right hand as the defensive lattice failed, and a thousand tiny shards of matter pierced his flesh before dissipating. The air around them was sucked inward and blew out again, driving the oxygen from Robbie's lungs and sending Demeter back into a railing.

Robbie shook his head to clear it, his ears ringing painfully. His right hand and wrist were pinpricked and bleeding. He smelled the fire before he saw it. Demeter thrashed about wildly, struggling to remove his burning long coat. He finally dropped it onto the platform, where it continued to burn. The fire and smoke lit the darkness like a pyre on a moonless night. Thousands of butterflies flew in a vortex around the flames. When a butterfly flew close to the fire, it burst into light before vanishing. Demeter lay on the opposite side of the pyre. The exploding sword had ravaged his face. The front of his body was a mass of blood and burned flesh, his breath loud and labored.

Something in the fire caught Robbie's eye. He watched as yellowed papyrus caught flames before it blackened into carbon atoms, then flitted into the air on unseen currents. He recognized the ancient wooden spindles as they burned to ash in seconds.

Even as the flames subsided, something iridescent shone beneath the ashes. Demeter appeared to notice, too. He crawled toward it as the butterflies were drawn to that place on the platform in their thousands.

Just beyond the incessant tolling in his ears from the explosion, the memory of Valeria's scream continued to sound in his head. He dismissed that haunting cry and stood. He didn't care what lay in the ashes, but if Demeter wanted it, Robbie would make sure he never possessed it. The butterflies scattered as Demeter arrived at the object first. He reached into the ashes with his gnarled hand and lifted the object. Robbie knew it at once, despite having forgotten it until this moment. It had sat on Mr. Breton's desk in the library vault.

Indifferent to the heat generated by the extinguished fire, Robbie snarled at Demeter and leaped forward to wrest the object from the other man's bloody hands. He touched the artifact, the tiny ridges of its uneven surface reminding him of braille.

Then he blinked.

When Robbie opened his eyes, he floated within a lush underwater seascape. The colors above and below him shifted from brilliant aquamarine near the water's surface to impenetrable black at the sea bottom. Beneath him, extending toward the horizon in all directions, were mountains and caves and corals. The sea teemed with life. Schools of fish swam in every direction, their scales a mix of bright hues and complex patterns. A group of large creatures with long heads attached to clusters of tentacles around their mouths swam nearby. Each was larger than a school bus. Below him, a strange invertebrate animal with limbs below its segmented neck moved gracefully through the water. Its shell was a shade of pink Robbie had never seen in nature before.

Amid the sea life and untamed vegetation, one area stood out. An abyssal plain surrounded by towering basalt spires drew his eyes. Columns of light between the spires appeared and disappeared, seemingly at random.

Demeter floated nearby, speaking to himself.

"The artifact. Hidden inside the scroll. Just one or all of them? Do they know? They must!"

The man's voice sounded odd but still identifiable. Despite his grievous wounds, Demeter wore the expression of someone who stared directly at the face of a god. He, too, seemed to have located the plain below. He swam toward it without acknowledging whether he knew Robbie was there. The columns of light were pulsing now, and within the light, Robbie could make out glyphs forming in black ink and dissolving back into the light. He followed Demeter into the depths.

As they approached the plateau, a long, straight line of static shapes became visible. The objects were strangely familiar in such an alien place. Demeter swam directly to the closest shape, and Robbie overheard part of his monologue.

"Statues here? This cannot be."

He was right. Dozens of tall bronze-like statues of individual men and women set atop elaborate pedestals stretched into the distance.

Demeter began to choke. Robbie's eyes snapped toward the commotion as Demeter swam away from the statue he had examined. The fear in the Writhen's eyes obliterated Robbie's courage and froze the blood in his veins. Demeter continued backing away. Now he looked like a man expecting to see the face of a god but was confronted with a devil's visage instead. Apprehensively, Robbie swam to the statue and understood Demeter's distress.

The statue was an unmistakable likeness of William Breton. Before he could even process what he saw, Demeter screamed behind him. Robbie turned just as they were engulfed in a surge of inky blackness. The world around him vanished as the dark, cloying liquid eclipsed the light and bled into his mouth and nostrils. He could no longer breathe. His ears filled with the thunderous percussion of his heart, threatening to burst.

I am a grain of sand against an ocean tide.

Then, everything stopped. He floated in darkness and silence.

Is this death?

A sudden rush of strange sounds intermixed with human voices. The voices mostly spoke a language or languages his brain couldn't understand. The unknowable words crashed into him.

Out of the tumult, three words rang clearly in his head. Three words echoed infinitely and imprinted themselves onto every cell of his body.

Keeper. Creator. Destroyer.

The voices faded, and the blackness began to dissipate. A face appeared before him. At first, Robbie thought it was Demeter, but he was wrong. It was Mr. Breton. The lifeless statue Robbie had seen on the plain had transformed into a man. He wore a dark suit and bore no signs of the injuries that had killed him.

They stood side by side on the empty plain Robbie had seen from above. The basalt pillars and pulsing columns of white light were visible in the distance.

"Mr. Breton?" Robbie spoke the name quietly, afraid that if he opened his mouth, the sea would rush into his lungs and drown him.

The librarian shook his head. "Welcome, Keeper." The voice was assuredly that of the Nobles' family friend.

"Mr. Breton, it's me, Robbie." Somehow, the water didn't impede his ability to talk.

"I am not William Breton. The old Keeper is dead, though you can refer to me by his name. I am a simulation designed to adopt the identity of the last Keeper when a new one enters the entanglement for the first time. Though, this is your second visit. You likely do not remember the first."

Robbie tried to parse through the flood of new information.

"I don't understand," Robbie admitted. "I've never seen this place before."

"You're inside a spatial and temporal entanglement. You activated the cipher, which brought you here."

Robbie shook his head. "Cipher?"

The apparition held up his empty hand, and an artifact like the one hidden inside the scroll appeared.

"I didn't activate anything," Robbie insisted.

The figure smiled knowingly. The subtle mannerisms bore an uncanny resemblance to the librarian. "An organic catalyst is required to activate the cipher."

Robbie thought back to his and Demeter's final moment on the platform, then looked down at his injured hand. "Blood."

The Mr. Breton simulation nodded.

"Wow, that's kinda gross," Robbie stated flatly.

"A necessary security mechanism. We cannot allow the machines direct access to this repository."

"Repository for what?" Robbie asked, more confused than ever.

"For everything."

Blinding light blossomed behind Robbie's eyes, and millions of images, numbers, figures, and faces inundated his mind. He witnessed the birth and death of a star across a great distance. He watched as a blood-red sky resolved into a burning mountain of rock that collided with the atmosphere and set the world on fire. He saw a not-quite-human female give birth to a child that looked slightly more human than she. His breath caught deep in his chest as sheets of ice larger than the biggest waves of a tsunami consumed the land and sea until the planet was a shimmering white sphere. He glimpsed in the blink of an eye an infinitesimally small pinprick of light blossom into an impossibly large black void filled with fire. When the vision stopped, he lay panting on the empty plain. His head throbbed in agony, and the memory of all that he had witnessed began to slip away like a dream upon waking.

Robbie sat up after the pain dissipated. Mr. Breton's simulation remained beside him.

"I apologize. Most human minds are incapable of

receiving so much information at once, but you must understand your responsibility."

"What is my responsibility?"

"You are the Keeper of the repository," Mr. Breton answered matter-of-factly.

"Who created the entanglement or the repository or whatever? It was aliens, right?"

The simulation smiled before it answered. "The last four Keepers asked the same question when they first arrived here. The planet you call Earth is almost five billion years old. You cannot possibly appreciate the sheer hubris required to believe that yours is the only species to achieve advancement, especially given that humans have only existed for 0.00004% of this planet's lifetime."

A dozen more questions formed in Robbie's mind, but the simulation forestalled him.

"You are needed now."

"Hold on!" Robbie shouted. "I want to ask something else."

Mr. Breton held his gaze and proclaimed. "Honor the covenant, Keeper. Machines are forbidden in this place. You must not forget."

He blinked.

Mr. Breton, the sea, and the plain were gone. Robbie stumbled on the metal platform like he had missed a step. He held the artifact in his injured hand. Demeter lay at his feet, unmoving. His mouth was open in a silent scream, and his eyes wept black tears.

He was dead.

Everything that happened before the entanglement crashed back into his mind. Demeter striking Blake. Gallant fending off a pack of hellcats. Valeria dropped into the abyss. The rage and fear and guilt all welled up, threatening to consume him. Breathing heavily, Robbie shouted until he felt his throat tear. With all his remaining strength, he threw the artifact off the platform. It soared through the air and down into the mists below. He shouted again and kicked the notebook off the platform. Sobbing, he stumbled away from the dead man.

A moment later, he fell to his hands and knees, the platform pushed uncomfortably against his flesh. He deserved that pain and so much more. He remained in that position and stared into the mists.

Robbie heard something in the silence between his sobs. At first, the noise didn't register in his guilt-warped mind, but then he heard it again. With great effort, he made himself look around to locate the source. A voice. He ran toward the sound, which brought him to the bridge where he had last seen Valeria. He looked down into the abyss. He watched and waited. The clouds lit up briefly, and he saw a slight silhouette against one of the platform's metal support posts.

"Valeria?" His shout was desperate and hopeful.

"Robbie," she called back, but her voice was weak, and she was far. So far.

"Hold on! I'm coming."

He looked around the platform, searching for anything he could use to reach her. He found nothing.

"Robbie. I can't hold on anymore."

"I'm coming!"

He knew he'd need all the help he could get. He took the phone from his pocket to activate his kit, but the screen was black. After several seconds of trying, the device remained unresponsive to his ministrations.

Desperate, Robbie put the phone away and climbed over the railing.

21

SO NEARLY INFINITE

Alice's grandfather stopped when they reached the stairwell to the rooftop. He turned to face her.

"Go to the Junction and take the track to Sciathe."

She grabbed her grandfather's arm and held on until he looked at her. "No! I am not leaving without you."

"Your kit is damaged. How long before it returns to full integrity?"

She flicked her eyes to the top right. A menu only she could see appeared in the air, and she selected a heads-up display with a long stare. She had several unread messages and missed phone calls but ignored them. Alice cursed silently when she saw the metric for kit integrity. She considered lying for a second but replied truthfully. "Twenty-seven minutes."

Calvin shook his head. "We don't have that much time, Alice."

"I know, Granddad, but we have no idea what's happening here. I think we're safer together."

The old man took a breath and then nodded reluctantly. "No more combat for you."

She chose not to argue with him.

"Alice," her grandfather said, voice strained, "is it real?"

The question caught her off guard. She wasn't sure how to answer. "Um, yeah, I know this feels like a nightmare, but it's real."

"The tattoo on your wrist. Is it real?" he asked again.

Oh.

She felt her face burn with embarrassment. This conversation was so much worse than fighting mercenaries.

"Ah, yeah."

"What does it say?"

Alice lifted her wrist so he could see it. He tilted his head and squinted at the text.

"'She rose to her requirement,'" he read aloud. Then he smiled proudly and hugged her. "You certainly have."

She didn't have the heart to tell him that it was meant to be ironic.

They made their way up through the stagnant air of the dimly lit concrete stairwell. The sound of the helicopter's powerful turbine grew louder with each step. Calvin stopped halfway up the stairs, squeezing his eyes shut and clutching his head. Alice expressed concern, which he dismissed immediately. They continued their ascent, and she noticed him repeatedly blinking as if trying to clear his vision.

"How many on the roof?" Calvin directed his question to the hacker.

"Four plus the pilot."

"What about armor and sword sets?"

"Just one left. Roman, the guy downstairs, and Kemper, the guy in charge, are wearing the only working prototypes.

"I will kill you if you're lying,"

Avinash gulped, then nodded.

Her grandfather sustained his interrogation. "The pilot. Mercenary or bystander?"

Alice suspected that the fate of the pilot's life rested on Avinash's answer. The hacker's face looked ashen. She worried that he might vomit.

"Mercenary. Same company, I think, but he's the only decent one of the lot."

They arrived at the door to the rooftop. Her grandfather took a moment to catch his breath. "Alice, remain here and watch the prisoner. If he tries to run, hamstring him. I want him alive for questioning, but not so much that I will risk his escape."

"Please, Granddad. If you need to do this, let me help."

"I won't endanger you any more than is necessary. These men are trained killers. At least one of them has technology to rival our own. The others can use the same tactic to get past your kit as the man downstairs."

Thanks for the reminder.

"If I fall, kill the prisoner and run. You know where to go. Your parents will find you there."

Does he really believe that I can kill Avinash? The words tattooed on her wrist came back to haunt her.

Calvin opened the door, and bright sunlight sliced into the dim stairwell. The wind caught her hair, whipping the loose strands into her eyes. Though they couldn't see the helicopter, the turbine noise and the swirling winds from the rotor blades let them know the aircraft was preparing to lift off. Her grandfather strode onto the roof. Alice conjured her daggers and approached Avinash. He stared at the dark, roiling blades as she brandished them before him.

"Neat," he squeaked barely above a whisper.

She tried to sound intimidating, though she was likely more terrified than him. "Stay right behind me. Don't shout. Don't run."

He nodded, and they followed Calvin outside. The first mercenary they encountered leaned casually against the wall near the elevator, looking in the opposite direction of their approach. Calvin walked behind her and said something. She turned, gave a startled cry, and tried to raise the gun. Despite being in his seventies, Alice's grandfather still exuded physical strength. Without his kit, the straight-armed punch he delivered to the mercenary's face was likely hard enough to break her nose. Except that Calvin's kit was active, and the resultant force of the punch was magnified many times over. The dark blue light pulsed around his fist, driving into the mercenary's skull like a sledgehammer on a rocket. She struck the wall behind her and crumpled into a lifeless heap.

Alice covered her mouth. She turned away from the stomach-churning scene.

"Oh, man," Avinash whispered and then vomited on the ground next to Alice's feet.

Calvin stepped over the dead mercenary and continued around the wall until he reached the bottom of the stairs that led up to the helipad. The helicopter had landed the wrong way, with its tail nearest the stairs. Alice had grown up around helicopters, and she knew such a landing was a safety violation due to the danger the exposed tail rotor posed to the crew and passengers as they boarded or exited the vehicle. The blood drained from her face when she saw her grandfather reach the top of the platform, inches from the spinning rotor.

The figures on the helicopter spotted him. One was

through the door with his gun raised, and the other two were preparing to disembark.

Alice knew what her grandfather intended when she saw him lift his hand toward the deadly rotor. She also knew, at least theoretically, that the strange physical laws governing their kits should protect him from the destructive force of a metal blade spinning faster than the eye could perceive. But to know something notionally was not the same as knowing it through experience.

Kind of like jumping off a 70-story building without a parachute.

"Look out!" Alice shouted so loudly that her voice gave out.

Alice, Avinash, and the three mercenaries watched Calvin Asher extend his hand into the spinning tail blades. Dark blue light pulsed one-billionth of a second before the first blade struck, and the rotor went from five hundred revolutions per minute to zero in the blink of an eye. The sound of metal twisting and tearing apart accompanied the rotor's obliteration. Debris exploded in all directions, and the main body of the helicopter convulsed on its landing skids. The cockpit's alarm began to screech a warning, and one of the mercenaries loudly repeated something in a panicked shout.

"Shut it down! Shut it down! Shut it down!"

Her grandfather didn't break stride. He reached the first mercenary to step onto the helipad from the vehicle. The man had stumbled to the platform following the chaos of the tail rotor's destruction and now stood to face the older man. Alice watched in horror as her grandfather stopped a foot away from the ex-soldier and extended his hand. The sword appeared and impaled the man through his chest.

Dead.

Another mercenary took up position and shouted. He fired his weapon, and a stream of bullets sped toward Calvin. The hot metal slugs ricocheted dangerously off his barrier.

"Get down!" Alice pushed Avinash to the ground and tried to shield him from the barrage.

A sudden shout from the front of the helicopter drew her gaze. The helicopter pilot had taken his first steps out of the cockpit just in time to take a stray bullet in the midsection. He fell to the platform, clutching at his abdomen. A figure emerged from the far side of the helicopter. The large man was covered in matte-black armor that shimmered with a sickly yellow glow. He began shouting orders over the violent cacophony.

"Hold fire! Hold fire!"

The mercenary with the gun obeyed the command, and the rooftop grew quiet. The two men appeared to exchange words over tac comms. They glanced at her and Avinash. The one with the armor, whom Avinash called Kemper, shook his head. The gesture appeared dismissive. It left Alice feeling frightened and, surprisingly, a little angry. Kemper stepped forward, flicking his arm out to his side. Metal segments poured out of the object in his hand, linking together until he held a sword.

"I guess you still have a little fight left after all," Kemper stated.

"Your bravado is in bad taste, mercenary. Are you proud to ambush a man alone in his home?"

Kemper showed no signs of emotion. He exuded a calm professionalism.

"We prefer the term *private security contractor*. A man has a duty to defend his castle. Imagine our surprise when we learned you live in your sky palace without security. You brought this on yourself, old man."

The other mercenary took up a position behind her grandfather, close enough to threaten but beyond the reach of Calvin's sword. Alice's heart almost stopped when her grandfather winced. She saw the corners of Kemper's mouth turn up slightly. Calvin dropped to one knee, and she shouted. The man behind her grandfather sprinted forward.

He's going for Granddad's phone.

Alice gripped her daggers tightly and readied herself, despite knowing she wouldn't reach them in time. Another shout, this time from Kemper. His expression had gone from triumphant to distressed, and he converged on Calvin, who remained on one knee. The mercenary approaching from behind tried to heed the warning but could not stop fast enough. Her grandfather shot to his feet, thrusting his sword outward and into the path of the mercenary's inevitable momentum. The sword tip went through the man's neck and out his cervical vertebrae, completely severing the bones, muscles, and connecting tissue. Kemper plowed into Calvin a half second too late. The corpse fell to the ground, followed by a flash that lit the rooftop.

Their two blades met. Alice's grandfather exhibited a proficiency with the sword she had never before witnessed, not even from Hamza, despite his title as the Rosewood's master-at-arms. Calvin's blade cut, thrust, and parried in precise, economical movements. Yet, her fear continued to grow as the contest wore on. Her grandfather's noticeably slower movements suggested he was attempting to strike at Kemper's unarmored back, but the mercenary did not give him the opportunity.

Alice couldn't breathe. Something sharp and clawlike gripped her heart while she watched the duel. As the seconds passed, it crystallized in Alice's mind that Kemper was not a particularly adept swordfighter, though he was stronger and faster than her grandfather. The mercenary commander was likely a veteran soldier familiar with combat. He landed powerful blows against Calvin while opening himself up to vicious counterattacks, with both men relying on their respective high-tech armors to save them. The protective lattice of Calvin's kit had flashed from dark blue to violet, while the mercenary's armor was black and smoking in five or six places.

The duel carried the two men further away from the platform stairs, where Alice and Avinash watched the deadly dance. Her grandfather almost ended the fight permanently when his pommel struck a glancing blow off Kemper's unarmored face. It spun the man around. Calvin punched the younger man's upper chest, sending him sprawling over a piece of helicopter debris, his sword clattering to the ground. Now disconnected from the power cells Kemper wore on his back, the yellow shimmer faded from the sword.

"I think that's it," Avinash said beside her as they watched Calvin approach the mercenary, who slowly backed away.

Alice dared not speak. She narrowed her gaze and strained to hear the conversation that had started between Kemper and her grandfather. The distance, the wind noise, the hum from her kit, and the whine of the coolant system on Kemper's armor conspired to keep the words a mystery.

"What's going on?" the hacker asked. "Your gramps doesn't seem the forgiving type, ya know."

Despite the distance between them and the slight tilt of Calvin's body away from her vantage, Alice saw a change in his demeanor. She suspected he looked at something in the heads-up display projected onto his retina.

A message?

Whatever caused the revelation made her stomach drop away, and she was suddenly flushed and sweaty. Calvin removed his phone from his pocket and began scrolling the screen with terrible intensity. In her mind, she could hear Hamza's admonishment when she had done something similar during her training.

Never expose your phone to your enemy.

Her grandfather's eyes shifted from the phone screen and locked on to the mercenary, who watched impassively from the ground. Calvin's jaw clenched, and his face turned a deep scarlet. She had never seen him so angry. As if to confirm her assessment, Calvin bellowed something unintelligible and charged the man.

The mercenary's foot whipped out and struck Calvin's knee. Her grandfather stumbled but held on to his phone, slipping the device back into his pocket. Kemper rolled toward his fallen sword, retrieving it with both hands and springing to his feet before Calvin recovered.

Alice saw Kemper reconnect the wire from his wrist to the sword, and the yellow glow lit the weapon again. Alice stepped backward as their weapons flashed in a series of powerful collisions. Her grandfather took an uncharacteristically wild swing that Kemper managed to sidestep. The blade sliced deep into the helicopter platform. Calvin swung his sword around for another attack when his arm wavered, and his momentum carried him sideways. He collapsed face down a second later.

Another feint?

Alice didn't know, and it seemed Kemper wasn't sure either. Her grandfather's hand spasmed open, dismissing the sword. The mercenary's hesitation ended, and he quickly sprang forward, driving his sword into Calvin's back.

Her grandfather remained still, but his kit ignited, and the two combatants remained in that position as if posing for a Jacques-Louis David painting. Then Kemper withdrew his sword, likely realizing he knew a faster way to finish off his opponent. He knelt, searched Calvin's pockets, and took the phone.

As Kemper straightened, Alice sprinted behind him and lashed out with a dagger. She felt her weapon slide through something hard, but the mercenary spun to face her before she could punch a hole through his back. She was too close for him to use his sword to any effect, so Kemper tried to create some space between them by attacking with his elbows and knees. Alice shifted around each strike and counterattacked with alternating dagger blows to different parts of his body.

One of her daggers pierced a blackened section of Kemper's armor, previously damaged in the duel with her grandfather. The man gasped. Two inches of her dagger sank into the side of his ribcage, and he dropped Calvin's phone. Kemper grunted but twisted away before the blade could inflict more harm. Her dagger caught on the inside of his armor. She released the hilt half a second too late, and Kemper's armored elbow slammed into the lattice that appeared in front of her face. Bright-red intersecting lines of protective matter obscured her view momentarily as she fell back. The mercenary's sword struck the lattice at her midsection, and then he drove his armored foot into her side. Her kit stopped the last blow before it overloaded, but the kick's force drove her to the ground.

Alice landed hard on her hip, driving the breath from her lungs and cutting off her scream of pain. Once again, everything was quiet on the rooftop. The hum behind her ears was gone. Another important sound was also absent, but she couldn't identify it. She willed herself up, fearful that Kemper was approaching her to finish the job. Instead, she saw the mercenary frantically pressing something on the inside of his forearm, his sword forgotten at his feet. His eyes were practically bulging with panic or fear or pain. He began pulling at the metal on his chest piece as if trying to remove it. Something was clearly wrong with his armor. That's when she felt the intense heat emanating from the mercenary. Instinctively, she scrabbled away from him.

To his credit, Kemper didn't cry out. He simply vanished in a conflagration of silver light. There and then not there. She covered her eyes and looked away; the afterimage of a too-bright candle flame briefly burned into her retinas. After several seconds, she opened her eyes again to see that nothing remained of the mercenary except for the segmented sword. She expected to see scorch marks where he had stood, but the ground remained unmarked. Though she couldn't know for sure, she suspected that her dagger must've damaged the coolant system when she struck the glancing blow on his back.

She sobbed suddenly and made her way on unsteady feet to her grandfather's side. Her dread subsided just a little when she saw that his eyes were open and he was attempting to sit up.

"Alice," he said her name tentatively, as if uncertain.

"Yes, Granddad. I'm here."

"My head. It hurts so bad."

"I know."

Calvin Asher looked around and then frowned. "Why are we on the roof?"

Unsure of how to respond, Alice placed a hand on his arm and tried to smile.

"It's a long story, Granddad. Take a minute to rest, okay?"

"Just for a minute, dear." He closed his eyes.

She scanned the rooftop for Avinash.

Gone. At least I don't have to kill him.

Alice's concern over the missing hacker vanished when two figures sprinted up the stairs to the helicopter platform, each bearing a darkly glowing sword.

22

NEVER LOST AS MUCH

Alice exhaled. She knew these people. Not well, but their appearance eased some of the tension in her taut muscles.

Edward Kerrick and Isilde Lloris.

Edward's long strides took him to Alice's side in seconds. Despite his dirty-blond hair and blue eyes, Alice saw the resemblance in the facial structure and tall, imposing muscularity that he shared with his son, Drake.

"What happened here?" he asked in a crisp voice comfortable with command.

Alice looked down at her grandfather and then around at the carnage across the landing platform, the bodies and blood and the smoking wreckage of the helicopter a testament to the violence of the past few minutes.

"I—" She didn't know where to begin.

Isilde knelt beside her. The sun glinted in her swept-back, long black hair. Her beauty evoked the French movie stars in the black-and-white films Alice had watched growing up, except she was no actress. She had won an Olympic silver medal in downhill skiing for France a few years prior and now ran the handbag division of her family's famous luxury goods company.

"Alice," the woman's voice, gentle but firm, cut through the haze of her shock. "Your *grand-pére*. Do you know what ails him?"

"His head, I think." Alice described the symptoms her grandfather exhibited leading up to his collapse.

"Calvin. Can you hear me?" Edward held her grandfather now, checking his pulse while he spoke. When Edward didn't receive a response, he looked to Isilde.

"He needs medical attention. We must take him to Sciathe."

Edward rose to his full height, lifting the older man with some effort. Alice suppressed a sob at the scene. Her grandfather was the bedrock of their family. Constant, steadfast, and enduring. Seeing him weak and broken shook the foundations of her existence.

Isilde frowned. "Edward, I am no medical doctor, but I think Calvin had a stroke. He may not survive the trip."

He grunted his agreement before answering. "I'm open to suggestions."

Isilde obliged him. "We are in Manhattan. Some of the world's best hospitals are just blocks away, no?"

Alice had listened to their conversation, fighting the urge to cry out at Isilde's diagnosis. She pushed through the despair and the shock.

"The condo tower is swarming with police officers, and the street is shut down."

She didn't ask how the pair had arrived on the rooftop. They must've come up the secret elevator that connected the Station hidden below street level directly to the penthouse. Again, she looked around the helipad.

"Air ambulance," Alice stated. "But I don't think it can land."

Nodding, Edward gently lowered her grandfather to the ground.

"Then let's clear the wreckage," he said.

"We must move the bodies," Isilde added.

Edward found the number for a private air ambulance dispatcher and confirmed their location.

"The crew is scrambling now. Twenty minutes."

"Stay with him," Isilde said as she stood.

Alice wondered if the ambulance would arrive in time. Her grandfather seemed so peaceful as he lay unconscious atop the helipad. The lack of any obvious physical injuries made the situation even more surreal. She leaned in close to his face. "Please don't die," she whispered and wiped the tears welling in her eyes.

Edward made his way to the wrecked helicopter, which had skittered to a stop near the edge of the helipad. He tilted his neck to one side and then the other. He flexed his hands, reached behind his right shoulder, and summoned a huge midnight-black maul streaked with deep purples and blues into existence. A long, wicked spike affixed to a large block topped the maul's five-foot-long haft. Alice doubted she could lift the weapon with two hands, yet Edward held it casually in one.

"Careful," Isilde called. "You make things harder for us if you fling a helicopter into Central Park."

Edward replied with a curt nod, then used the maul to shove the vehicle as if testing its weight to understand the force he'd need. It rocked back and forth a moment before it settled. He set his feet and swung the weapon into the helicopter's broadside. The metal closest to the impact point collapsed around the maul head, and the remaining glass that hadn't shattered during their confrontation with the mercenaries did so now. The blow propelled the helicopter off the platform's edge and onto the condo tower rooftop ten feet below. Her grandfather's prone form jumped at the clamor, then settled back into serene unconsciousness.

Isilde cleaned up the remaining debris, kicking the broken rear rotor blades off the platform. The bodies followed soon after, including the helicopter pilot, who must've taken an errant ricochet to a vital organ. The gruesome task left trails of blood across the helipad and Alice with a roiling storm in the pit of her stomach.

The air ambulance landed moments later, and the paramedics loaded her grandfather onto a stretcher, securing him in the helicopter while the three Knights of Rosewood climbed into the cabin. She peeked out the window as they rose into the sky and stared down at the rooftop and helipad. Shadows concealed most of the wreckage. If the pilot or the crew suspected that anything was amiss, they didn't say anything. One of the paramedics asked them questions about the events leading up to her grandfather's catatonic state. Alice lied, which her grandfather would've expected her to do.

Anything to protect the Rosewood.

Alice slumped in a chair, exhausted but unable to sleep or eat despite Isilde's insistence. They had procured a private hospital room and waited for the nurses to bring her grandfather back from the various imaging tests the attending physician had ordered.

"Alice," Edward intoned, "Calvin is in capable hands.

Tell us everything that happened. Did Andars Demeter attack the penthouse?"

The name triggered her memory. Heart racing, she leaped from the chair and grabbed Edward's arm. "Demeter's in Bethel."

Alice saw the confusion in Edward's eyes turn to concern.

"How do you know?" Isilde asked from behind her.

Alice recounted the day's events since the attack on the subway. She told them about Avinash and the assault on the Rosewood's private communications network. She watched their eyes grow wide with fear and anger as she described the kits the two mercenaries had worn. Finally, the big man stood and took a step toward the door.

"You mustn't, Edward. It's not the plan," Isilde said plainly, though the heaviness of her expression revealed the discord created by her appeal.

Edward stopped. His gaze remained focused on the door before him.

"Drake's my son," he responded in a voice just above a whisper. "I can't leave him to face Demeter alone."

The pronouncement seemed to pollute the air around him with shame and regret. Alice knew a little about the Kerrick family drama, mostly from her grandfather. Edward's indiscretion with the Gallant woman had resulted in a child whom Edward could never fully raise as his own —at least not without destroying his own family in the process. Edward's insistence that Drake be admitted into the Knights of Rosewood came at a cost that the Kerrick patriarch still paid to this day.

Isilde nodded. "I know," she said sympathetically. "We came to New York to check on Calvin and were right to do so. Demeter could send more soldiers."

Edward shook his head before responding. "Your blade is as sharp as mine. I'm sure you can handle it."

"*Non!*" Isilde pounded the arm of her chair, surprising Alice with the force of her resolve. "Calvin needs us both."

As a sitting member of the Conventus, Edward outranked Isilde. He possessed the authority to act without her approval, yet he remained stuck to the floor, hand outstretched to grasp the handle, frozen in a moment of indecision.

Alice broke the stalemate. "Send someone else. I mean, if you can contact them."

The adults turned to look at her as if they'd forgotten she was in the room. Isilde brightened slightly. "Alice is right. My brother and Hamza can go to Bethel."

After several seconds of deliberation, Edward moved away from the door, his phone in hand. He began to type something onto the screen.

Alice reached into her pocket for her phone. "Is the network back up?"

The device did not react to her touch.

Right. The mercenary overloaded it when he kicked me.

She rubbed at the soreness in her hip.

"It is not," Isilde answered. "Yasmin works to restore the network even now. We have switched to standard channels but cannot speak freely."

"Do you know where my parents are?" She tried to keep the worry out of her voice.

Isilde gave her a look that suggested she had failed. "I am so sorry, no. I would not worry overly much. Your parents are very capable people." She smiled, perhaps trying to reassure her.

It didn't work. Alice drew her legs up onto her chair and wrapped her arms around herself.

"What happened today?" Alice finally asked.

Edward rejoined the conversation. "You seem to know things that we don't," he growled before continuing. "Someone, likely Demeter, launched a series of coordinated attacks against the Rosewood yesterday. He hit us in Aragón first, then Montreal, Paris, Venice, and here in New York."

Dominique had mentioned her parents were traveling to Spain.

"Who's in Aragón?" Alice asked. She knew that the Rosewood was present in the other places Edward mentioned.

"The Innocenti brothers. They participated in a qualifying race," Isilde responded, somber tone unmistakable. "There was a terrible crash on the track."

Alice's heart sank. "What happened to the brothers?"

Isilde shook her head. "Antonio is injured but okay. Domenico is not."

Edward sneered. "At first, we assumed the crash was a racing accident until my family woke up to a pack of hellcats on our yacht in the Adriatic. We were fortunate that we only lost the main yacht."

Edward flexed his hands as if battling an overwhelming desire to draw a weapon. Alice knew of the hellcats from the attack on her godfather in Bethel. She had seen photos of the dismembered machine.

"Sean and Kyle acquitted themselves quite well in that fight," Edward added proudly.

The two Kerrick boys were Edward's other children. She had only interacted with them occasionally, and they hadn't left the best impressions. Still, she was relieved that they weren't harmed.

Isilde looked thoughtful before she spoke. "It appears that we have been misled by an elaborate and dangerous ruse."

Alice frowned, unsure of the conversation's sudden turn. Isilde seemed to notice her confusion and explained. "I think the attacks were meant to distract us from Demeter's target."

Edward swore and stared out the window as if hoping to glimpse something elusive.

"Bethel," Alice stated simply.

The place where her godfather had lived peacefully for ten years until Demeter found and murdered him—the place where her father had gone to treat the local kid whom Demeter poisoned with his sword.

"But why?" she asked, more confused than ever. "What's there for him?"

Edward interrupted the discussion. "Augusta will lead a party to Bethel while we stay with Calvin," he declared while he stared at his phone.

Isilde nodded, apparently satisfied with the news.

Shouts from the hallway outside the hospital room broke the relative calm of the moment. They exchanged glances, weary after a day filled with violence and grim tidings. A moment later, a man burst into the room wearing an expression of haughty outrage, followed by a doctor and a hospital administrator they had met upon their arrival. Alice recognized the angry man immediately.

How does Uncle Alden know we're here?

His eyes swept around the room, taking in its occupants and lingering for an extra moment on Alice. He didn't seem surprised to see her.

"Such an interesting collection of my father's associates gathered in one place," her uncle stated smugly. "As I was saying, Dr. Winslow, I am taking him to a private facility."

The doctor shook his head. His neck and face were scarlet with anger or frustration.

"And as *I* was saying, Mr. Asher, Calvin is in no condition to travel. The results of the imaging tests confirm he's a very sick man. He needs treatment immediately, which we've already begun to administer."

Hearing the doctor confirm the severity of her grandfather's condition tore into Alice, and this time, she couldn't restrain the tears from cascading down her cheeks.

"You will release my father into my care," her uncle demanded. "An emergency transport I arranged is en route."

The doctor stood his ground. "Once Calvin's condition is stable, we can discuss options for moving him to a different healthcare facility."

Her uncle turned to the administrator, a short, older woman wearing a black blazer and wire-framed glasses.

"If your physician does not relent, you can expect my lawyers to sue not just this hospital but you personally and every member of the board of directors."

The administrator's eyebrows shot up with alarm. "Mr. Asher, that won't be necessary," she stammered.

The woman must've known that Alden Asher was a powerful man in his own right and not just the estranged son of a legendary Manhattan tycoon. Her uncle had left home after high school, rejected his father's wealth, and carved out his own path. In the years since their falling out, Uncle Alden's telecommunications and media empire had grown into the largest in the world. He was a man used to getting what he wanted.

Edward straightened to his full height, which made him the most physically intimidating presence in the room.

"Enough, Alden."

Uncle Alden lacked his father's stature but didn't seem intimidated. Though tall, his whip-thin body indicated more time running long distances than muscle-building. Her uncle's gaze locked on to Edward.

"Stay out of my business, Kerrick." The words conveyed a threat that made Alice shrink back in her chair. Her interactions with Alden were limited, but he had always treated her courteously. This version of her uncle seemed more consistent with the man her father and grandfather had told her about.

Isilde moved between Edward and her uncle as if anticipating violence between the two men.

"Be reasonable, Alden," she said in a calming voice. "We must listen to the doctor for your father's sake."

A contemptuous smile swept across Uncle Alden's face. It looked almost feral. "Isilde Lloris, I presume."

Alice wondered how many Knights of Rosewood her uncle knew. Her grandfather had kept the organization a secret from his oldest son. Yet, the Rosewood families often moved in the same circles. They attended the same events, stayed in the same hotels, supported each other's charities, and invested in their companies. Alden would have familiarity with some of the knights, either during his childhood or as an incredibly successful businessman in his own right, though he wouldn't know of their secret association.

"*Oui*," the French woman replied proudly.

"Tell your father I'll buy his little purse company when he's grown tired of you running it into the ground."

Uncle Alden's comment shocked the room into silence. Isilde's expression shifted from conciliatory to angry, and her hands clenched into fists.

"Alden, you have no authority here," Edward declared in a voice that sounded calmer than he looked. "Check with your lawyer. Michael has power of attorney, not you."

"And yet, my virtuous little brother isn't here," her uncle

replied coldly. Something in his response sent a chill through Alice's body.

The conversation seemed to embolden the hospital administrator, who straightened her glasses and spoke.

"Without power of attorney, you have very little say in your father's matters, Mr. Asher. You can threaten to litigate against us all you want, but we are obligated to provide the best care for your father as long as he is a patient in this hospital. Dr. Winslow has already explained the situation to you; moving him now would place him at even greater risk. Calvin stays. I assure you we'll treat him to the best of our considerable abilities. As next of kin, you are welcome to stay and hear the prognosis, but any further threats will result in your expulsion from this hospital."

Uncle Alden stared at the room's occupants as if committing their faces to memory. Then he turned and left. The tension seemed to follow him out the door as everyone visibly relaxed. Isilde said something in French that sounded like a curse.

The administrator exhaled. "I better give the board and our legal counsel a heads-up that I just made an enemy of Alden Asher." She exited the room.

"Now, then," the doctor said, the red in his face already fading. "Let's discuss Calvin's condition."

The imaging tests confirmed that her grandfather had suffered a stroke. Dr. Winslow explained the treatment and suggested that the next twenty-four hours would help determine the impact on his long-term health.

Alice wept after the doctor left, and Isilde put an arm around her shoulders until she fell asleep in the hospital chair.

She awoke sometime later to a whispered discussion between Edward and Isilde. The distress in their voices and their dark expressions sent her heart into overdrive. Alice stood, and a blanket someone had placed across her legs while she slept fell to the floor.

"What's happened to my grandfather?" she asked, unable to keep the anguish from her voice.

Isilde turned, and Alice saw her wipe tears from her eyes.

"Your grandfather remains in stable condition," Edward said.

"Then what?" Alice demanded. She heard the panic in her voice but didn't care.

Edward swallowed hard as if trying to will the words out of his mouth. "Michael and Simone were in an accident. I'm so sorry, Alice. Your parents are dead."

23

———

THIS IS HOW THE STORY GOES

When Robbie looked down, all he saw were the swirling mists. The ground might be one foot or one thousand feet below the roiling, glowing clouds. Either way, it didn't matter. If he fell, he'd be dead. Robbie took several deep breaths and traced a path with his eyes along the support posts, scaffolding, and platforms from Valeria's distant silhouette to where he stood. The good news was that hand- and footholds along the surfaces he needed to traverse were plentiful. The bad news was that he needed to move quickly before Valeria fell. He set out, crossing the outside of the platform until he reached the nearest support post. Then he climbed down, grateful, at least, that he wasn't afraid of heights.

Valeria sat atop a narrow horizontal strut, tightly clutching a vertical support post. Even in the dim light of the butterflies and flashing clouds below them, Robbie could see that she was barely hanging on. Sweat beaded her brow and trickled down her face. The noticeable tremble in her arms made his heart palpitate with terror.

"I'm here," he reassured her.

Robbie hoped the struts could handle their combined weight, or they'd both learn what existed below those mists. Slowly, he climbed down until he sat beside her. He stretched an arm around her back and gripped the post beside her, doing his best to secure her in place with his own body.

She began to cry and shake.

"It hurts so much," she told him.

"Where?"

His heart sank when she showed him. Valeria could barely move her left arm. The elbow was swollen and red. She cried out when he touched her shoulder.

"You're banged up pretty bad."

She nodded. "I grabbed the bars on the way down. My shoulder feels like it's on fire."

Robbie tried not to panic. He knew she couldn't climb back up to the platform with a broken arm, and he wasn't strong enough to carry her. "Let's rest here," he said instead.

They sat like that for a time. When Valeria asked about Demeter, he spoke plainly.

"He's dead."

He didn't tell her about the underwater realm or seeing Mr. Breton or the black ink. She explained how the vibration from the explosion had almost caused her to fall. Robbie added it to the growing list of transgressions he had committed against her.

"We need to get out of here," he said. "Blake and Gallant need us."

She nodded, and they talked about what to do next.

They had only one option. Robbie needed to climb up and find a way to get her out, but the plan was flawed. Exhausted and limited to one functional arm, Valeria couldn't hang on for long without assistance. Robbie kept the other problem to himself. His right hand was blistered and raw from the sword explosion. He'd have enough difficulty climbing up to the platform on his own. When he finally willed himself to begin the climb, Valeria stopped him.

"Will you wait with me for just a few more minutes?"

He did and held her close. They looked out over the mist and stole back time from their peril to admire the moment's sublimity. Valeria was the first to break the silence.

"I'm really sorry, Robbie."

The words took him by surprise.

"Sorry? For what?"

Valeria took a deep breath, and he saw her wince with pain.

"For the last few years. For the mean jokes and the ugly things I said to and about you."

Robbie shook his head and opened his mouth to allay whatever guilt she felt, but she forestalled him.

"No, please listen. I need to say this."

He waited for her to continue.

"I— I hated that you wanted Blake and not me. It really hurt, which is stupid and childish, I know. I shouldn't have been angry, but I just couldn't help it."

He didn't know what to say, though he wanted to say something.

"Valeria—" He began, but she cut him off.

"The worst part is that I totally understand why you love her. She's pretty much the best person I've ever met. Kind, beautiful, and thoughtful. Did you know that she goes to the retirement home to play Chinchón with my Abuelita?"

Valeria had been crying but smiled when she recounted the last part.

Robbie gently drew her closer, and she pressed her face against his chest.

"I love Blake, but not like that."

Not anymore, at least.

A moment passed before she lifted her head. Touching the front of his shirt, now wet with her tears, she said, "I'm sorry— again!" and she laughed, just a little.

Robbie kissed her.

All at once, the butterflies burst into the air around them. No, not just around them. Countless glowing insects circled the platforms and bridges above. A moment later, a brilliant flash lit the air over one of the platforms adjacent to their own. An elevator car erupted from the light and rocketed down its rails, followed by a cacophonous boom. They clung to the support posts as the vibrations from above threatened to dislodge them. Robbie and Valeria looked at each other as the car came to a stop. They listened and waited.

A faint hiss broke the subsequent silence. A hatch opened, and voices, not much louder than a whisper, carried through the air to where they held on for their lives.

"What if they aren't friendly?" Valeria asked quietly.

"We don't have a choice," Robbie replied.

A commotion started above—the rhythm of action on the metal platforms and then sharply spoken words. Robbie began to shout. Valeria added her cry for help to his. The activity and the voices on the platform stopped.

"Who's down there?" a familiar male voice asked.

Relieved beyond reason, Robbie identified himself. "Hamza, it's Robbie."

What followed was an incredible demonstration of strength and agility as Hamza swiftly climbed down to the stranded teenagers. Mouth agape, Robbie watched the display without blinking.

The feat was even more impressive in that unreal place, given the constant disorientation.

"Showoff," he said under his breath, earning a laugh from Valeria.

As soon as Hamza reached them, they discussed how to help Valeria return to the platform. Her injuries remained the biggest challenge. She wrapped her good arm around Hamza's neck as tightly as possible and sat on his right arm while he climbed up the scaffolding. Robbie followed after them.

Once on the platform, Hamza retrieved a first-aid kit from one of the elevator cars. Valeria grimaced as he fitted a sling over her injured arm. Despite his bone-weary exhaustion, Robbie paced while explaining to the newcomers what had happened. He was emphatic about returning to the library immediately to help his friends. The older woman who had arrived with Hamza stared at him intently. Robbie recognized her from the day he woke up from his coma, though he had only spoken to her over a video call. She looked as weary as Robbie felt.

"We will go to Bethel as soon as the girl's arm is looked after, Robbie," Augusta Hargrave reassured him again. She had already explained that traveling in the car with a freshly broken arm and dislocated shoulder would be more than unpleasant for Valeria.

The third individual who had arrived with Augusta and Hamza snorted. He looked to be in his thirties. He had dark hair and green eyes that stared threateningly at Robbie and Valeria. He spoke with a thick accent that Robbie thought sounded French.

"She should not be here. Nor should he."

Augusta let out a long breath. "Not now, Aristide. One crisis at a time, please."

The man walked to the edge of the platform.

"The crisis, as you say, is easy to fix," the man said, nodding toward the abyss. He sneered when Robbie glared back at him.

Augusta placed herself directly in Aristide's line of sight. While she was old enough to be his grandmother, Augusta's strength of will eclipsed the much younger man. "Keep your ideas to yourself," she snapped.

"I am not of your House." Aristide's retort was more petulant than assertive.

"Thank God for small mercies."

She moved away until she stood over Demeter's body. Something made her shudder while she studied it. "When you report to your father, don't forget to tell him these two did what the rest of us could not."

Aristide scoffed again but remained silent otherwise.

"I have done my best," Hamza stated as he stood up from his position beside Valeria.

"It will have to do. Thank you, Hamza. Please, take the girl to the Bethel track. I need a word with Robbie."

"My name is Valeria Anaya, not girl."

Augusta nodded.

"Of course, Valeria. I apologize for my rudeness. I think we have all had a very bad day."

Augusta turned to Aristide. "Go with the others."

He looked as though he might try to argue, but the steely glare Augusta turned on him seemed to change his mind.

Before she said anything, Robbie objected. "We don't have time for a word. Blake and Gallant need us now!"

"We will leave shortly. Hamza needs to secure Valeria before the ride. Tell me what happened to Demeter."

"Just call Gallant," he pleaded. "My phone is dead."

She shook her head. "The Rosewood's private communication network has been compromised, Robbie. Besides, communication signals do not work here. I promise we will go when Hamza says we're ready. Do not underestimate Drake Gallant. He's an exceptional fighter who has had years of training. Tell me about Demeter."

He turned his back on her and stared at the flitting butterflies of light. "You want to know about the black tears but don't want to ask me in front of the others."

She paused before answering him. "If you insist on conducting an adult conversation, at least have the courtesy to look at me while we talk."

He turned and stared into her emerald eyes.

"William was right. You are a clever boy," Augusta admitted.

Robbie inhaled. "I want to know about the underwater place."

She stopped to consider, then nodded stoically. "When did William first give you access to the artifact?"

"I first saw it the night the hellcats killed Mr. Breton, but I didn't remember until today."

Then he told her about his fight with Demeter and what occurred after they both touched the artifact. Robbie finished his account and then asked one of the millions of questions floating around his mind. "What is an entanglement?"

"The artifact is a key. It opens a bridge to the place and time you saw. You were, in essence, in two wheres and two whens simultaneously."

He tried his best to absorb the information.

"Robbie, where is the artifact?"

He took a deep breath. "I threw it away."

It was Robbie's turn to nod at the void below. Her eyes flared wide in surprise, and then her face darkened with apparent outrage.

"What of William's notebook?" she asked, voice tight with anger.

He told her. "I, ah, tossed that too." Then he corrected himself. "Well, it was more of a—" Robbie simulated a kicking motion but broke off the action under the intense scrutiny of her gaze. He shrugged. "Sorry."

Then Augusta did something he didn't expect.

She began to laugh, and he frowned in confusion at her reaction. She snorted, and her laugh morphed into a full-blown cackle. Soon enough, she wiped tears from her eyes.

"Oh, Robbie," he heard genuine affection in the way she spoke his name. "You were in possession of the world's most powerful and most valuable artifact, and you just— *chucked* it? You threw away a hyper-advanced, five-hundred-million-year-old device that allows us to access the knowledge of a long-dead Kardashev-level civilization, and you apologize for it like you kicked a soccer ball over my fence and broke my favorite bird feeder."

"Aren't you angry?"

She shook her head. "Just as I told Valeria. I've had a very bad day, and I'm too tired to be angry."

But Robbie suspected that Augusta wasn't being honest with him. He recalled something that Demeter had said about the artifact within the entanglement.

'Hidden inside the scroll. Just one or all of them?'

Yasmin's hologram of Alexandria had shown him a cart leaving the city. She told him that the cart carried twenty-seven scrolls. Was it possible that the Knights of Rosewood possessed more than a single artifact?

"Did you—" Augusta paused, and her manner changed. She looked tired and grief-stricken. "—see William?"

Robbie shrugged awkwardly. "He called himself a simulation, but he sure looked like Mr. Breton. Sounded like him, too."

"And did he give you a title?" she asked, the anxiety plainly written across her face.

"He called me Keeper."

The answer seemed to satisfy Augusta, who nodded and looked relieved. What Robbie didn't tell her was that Mr. Breton hadn't given him a title. The librarian had referred to him by the title after the voices had named him. Three words sang like an unholy liturgy in his mind.

Keeper. Creator. Destroyer.

Robbie kept the other names to himself. They froze his blood to ice.

"Are you a Keeper?" he asked her.

Augusta's eyebrows knit together as if the question confused her.

"There can only ever be one, Robbie."

A moment later, Hamza beckoned them from the next platform. "We're ready to go."

They set off together. When Augusta spoke again, it was clear that her words were meant only for him. "Does Valeria know what happened to Demeter or about the artifact?"

He shook his head.

"Do not mention it to anyone. Not even Hamza. Do you understand?"

"What about the black tears? Hamza and Aristide must have seen them."

"They did, but they don't know their cause. Aristide will speculate, of course."

They crossed the bridge to the elevator car that would take them back to Bethel.

When they entered the car, Valeria and Aristide were strapped into seats on opposite sides of the center post. Hamza helped secure Augusta beside the control panel. Robbie sat next to Valeria. Once securely fastened into his seat, he gently took hold of her hand. The tall Egyptian man slipped into the pilot's seat a moment later.

"Keep your eyes closed during the journey. Otherwise, you'll see the infinitely possible collapse into itself, which is quite unsettling, to say the least."

The infinitely possible? Unsettling is one way to put it.

"What is all this, anyway?" Valeria asked.

"No questions," Aristide practically shouted, though they couldn't see him from where they sat.

"I am beginning to think that your father didn't send you to spy on me after all, Aristide, but rather to annoy me."

Hamza pulled the lever. As before, the interior ceiling lights flashed red, and the hatch sealed them inside. Next, the air pressure changed. Whatever mechanism held the car in place released suddenly, and the sonic boom followed the incredible acceleration. When the temperature drop came, and they were all pressed against their harnesses like bugs against a windshield, Valeria began to scream.

Mere seconds passed, and the car rocked to a halt. Hamza was the first to unbuckle. Aristide and Augusta followed. Robbie helped Valeria, and they prepared to disembark. Hamza had been right about keeping his eyes closed. The ride was much less intense than his first experience.

Hamza and Aristide activated their swords before

exiting the car. For all of Aristide's unpleasantness, he seemed brave enough as the two men took the lead. The party reached the hatch separating the cavern from the vault, passing through without incident. The vault was just as they had left it—silent and dark. He didn't know why, but the absolute stillness increased Robbie's sense of foreboding. At that moment, he reflected on how tomblike the library seemed to him now, especially since Mr. Breton's death. It was a place of dead things, its shelves filled with the words and ideas and accounts of people and civilizations that had died decades, centuries, or millennia ago.

They climbed the cramped circular staircase in single file. Hamza and Aristide remained in front, followed by Augusta, Valeria, and finally, Robbie. They emerged into the librarian's office. The room had been destroyed. The desk was flipped upside down, and the windows were blown out. Rain poured into the room, soaking the thick rug where the desk had sat. A limbless hellcat twitched in the middle of the room. Only one of its legs was visible amid the destruction. Aristide reached the hellcat first. He drove his sword through the machine's metal chest, but the twitching did not cease until the Frenchman severed its spine in half. Hamza bent down to examine something dark that had stained the carpet.

"What is it?" Augusta asked, sounding uneasy.

"Blood."

Robbie's heart raced in his chest. The silence was enough to make his head explode. The others entered the administration hallway first and then stopped almost immediately. Hamza cursed softly, which seemed wildly out of character for him. Augusta gasped. Valeria didn't make any sound at all. She just stared at something against the far wall. Robbie was stuck in the doorway behind her, his view blocked by the others. He pushed forward to see into the hall.

Drake Gallant lay slumped against the wall. Every discernible part of his body seemed to have sustained some injury. His face was caked in dried blood from vicious slashes along his forehead, cheek, and chin. Gallant's eyes were not visible beneath the dried blood. Part of his arms, left hip, and legs were missing chunks of flesh, and what was left of his shirt was plastered to his bloody chest. Blake lay unmoving atop Gallant's arms as though he held her close until his strength gave out. If not for the carnage, it might seem like the sleeping repose of two lovers.

A wet gurgle issued suddenly from deep within Gallant's chest. His lips began to move, and sounds formed into quiet but discernible words.

"Help her!" he gasped.

The adults jumped into action, rushing to aid their fallen comrade. Behind him, Valeria's heart-wrenching wail filled the air. Robbie fell to his knees, dropping his forehead to the cold stone floor and shutting his eyes to the world as if praying. And pray he did, beseeching the universe to allow him to wake up from this nightmare and forgive him for what he had done.

"Help her," Gallant rasped again.

But there was no helping her. Blake was dead.

EPILOGUE

Robbie felt sick a lot in the days immediately following Blake's death. Sick with grief and guilt, primarily, but other reasons quickly piled up. Blake's cause of death had been a broken neck. After that detail, the official record and the truth diverged. The police and the coroner had determined that Blake died accidentally as a result of Drake Gallant's motorcycle flying off the road at a high rate of speed and crashing into a ravine during the rainstorm. Blake had struck a tree after being ejected from the back of the motorcycle. She had died instantly.

Drake had also been critically injured in the accident, but the police report did not mention multiple lacerations consistent with bite marks from some large animal. None of the emergency responders at the scene of the accident had examined Drake's injuries up close. They had arrived just as a private medical helicopter lifted into the air with Drake on board. It took an hour for the police officer in charge of the accident to figure out that Drake had been flown out of state instead of to the nearest metropolitan hospital.

The motorcycle crash was the focal point of Valeria's injuries as well. After arriving at the accident scene, she fell into the ravine trying to reach her friends, breaking her arm, collarbone, and two ribs and tearing her bicep muscle. Robbie had only sustained a minor injury to his hand, which gave him no comfort whatsoever.

The tiny shred of youthful naivete he still possessed had been unceremoniously stripped away when the Knights of Rosewood so easily shrouded the truth of what happened in lies. It seemed to him that money, influence, and power could alter reality or, at the very least, the perception of reality.

His complicity in the lies only made it worse. Augusta had assured them that Valeria was safe from the Rosewood as long as she kept silent, though Aristide made no such promises. The Frenchman was the son of Christophe Lloris, who, like Augusta, sat on the Conventus, which collectively made decisions for the Rosewood. Christophe took a hard line on most things, but none more so than protecting the Rosewood from discovery. No matter what the Conventus decided, Robbie silently vowed to protect Valeria and Artie.

The irony was that Robbie had no interest in revealing the Rosewood's secrets to anyone. As far as he was concerned, the world was better off not knowing more ways to kill people or creating more conflicts that got them killed. On the other hand, his conscience struggled whenever he thought about Mr. and Mrs. Brooks. Not only did they have to live with the soul-crushing grief of losing their child, but Robbie consigned them to believe a lie about how their daughter had died. He tried to assuage his guilt by telling himself that the details didn't matter. Blake was gone, and the person responsible was dead. The mirror reminded him that Demeter wasn't the only person responsible. It made him sick.

He missed Valeria. Part of him wished that he could see her. Another part of him knew that he should stay away. She had almost died because of him. She had been released from the hospital the day after Blake's death. Valeria's parents had whisked her home, and it seemed they planned to keep her sequestered for the rest of her life. Since Robbie no longer had a functioning phone, he had been messaging her from the family computer, which seriously limited what they said to each other.

Artie came to visit him two days after Blake's death. Robbie's parents were happy to see him, as they were justifiably concerned about how their son was handling another tragic death of someone close to him. Artie's family had returned to Bethel when they heard the news of the accident. The boys talked quietly in Robbie's bedroom about what had happened. Though Artie was also distraught about Blake, his eyes lit up excitedly when Robbie described traveling in the elevator cars. He didn't mention anything about the entanglement.

"Dude! I'm pretty sure you went through a wormhole!"

"That's ridiculous."

"Wormholes are theoretically possible according to science. Here."

Artie took out his phone, searched for something, and showed his friend.

"Check it out. It's called an "Einstein-Rosen Bridge.'"

Robbie nodded. "I think Demeter said that Feist built it."

"As in Gerhardt Feist? The dude who built the reference library?"

Robbie sighed and shrugged.

"I can't believe I wasn't there to see it. We have to go back so you can show it to me."

The look that Robbie gave him caused Artie to raise his arms in a gesture of peace. "I'm sorry, Robbie. I just—"

"I don't care about Einstein's bridge or wormholes. I saw her die! Just like that. I held her hand one second, and she was dead the next." Robbie turned away and wiped his face with his sleeve.

The enthusiasm Artie displayed just a second ago had drained away.

"I may not have been there, Robbie, but Blake was my friend, too."

Neither spoke for several seconds. Finally, Robbie sighed and said, "I'm sorry, Artie."

Artie waved a hand as if to say it's okay. "Have you heard from those Rosewood people about how Gallant's doing or if they found Piranha?"

"I haven't heard from them at all," Robbie said bitterly.

A few minutes later, Artie stood and moved toward the door. "I'm gonna head out. My mom is taking me to buy some dress socks and a black suit jacket that fits me."

For the funeral, Robbie knew.

"You can't tell anyone about what happened," Robbie pleaded. "I need you to promise me."

Artie used his index finger to draw the shape of an X over his chest. "You don't have to worry, Robbie. I won't say anything."

"Okay."

Artie turned and left.

Robbie threw himself down on his bed and stared at the ceiling for a long time. He might have dozed, vaguely recalling his mom calling his name, opening and immediately closing his bedroom door. When he grew restless again, he looked for something to preoccupy his mind and wished, not for the first time, that the artifact hadn't broken his smartphone. Robbie fished the device from his nightstand and was surprised when the screen turned on.

He quickly lost himself in the many worlds the gadget offered. The games and sports highlights, his friends and total strangers from around the globe sharing everything about their lives, from crazy opinions and film theories to travel photos and lifehacks. It anesthetized him to his pain, but it was only temporary. When his mind returned from the paths of meaningless diversions, the truth of what happened stared him in the face. He came across the group message Blake sent at the library right before Demeter and Pirhadi had sprung their trap.

Blake: (Thumbs-up emoji). Be there in a few.

The Rosewood had deleted all messages from or about the library from Blake's phone. Not only were the circumstances of her death a total fabrication, but they had wholly erased the last few hours of her life.

He read the few text messages he hadn't seen yet. Then he made the terrible mistake of searching for information about Blake's death in the news. The results led him down a rabbit hole of such baseless accusations and profoundly stupid speculation that he could almost wish Demeter had succeeded in taking the scroll and the notebook. Articles, videos, and hot takes (whatever those were) had collectively judged and condemned Drake Gallant as an entitled, selfish rich kid and typical star athlete whose recklessness had cost Blake her life. Some called on the big college where Drake was supposed to play football in the fall to rescind his scholarship.

The false narrative was mainly driven by the revelation that Drake was the illegitimate son of billionaire real estate developer Edward Kerrich. Kerrich's other two children, and Drake's half-brothers, Sean and Kyle, were infamous social media stars who spent their days and nights partying in exotic locations and taking shirtless pictures of themselves with expensive cars and aspiring supermodels. Not a single post mentioned that Drake had been raised by a working single mother who never took so much as a coin from Edward Kerrich or that Drake rarely ever spoke to his half-brothers. Amid all the self-righteous indignation, none referred to the dozens of hours Drake spent at the hospital talking to lonely geriatric patients, the holidays he spent helping out in homeless shelters, or even his stellar grades. The injustice haunted Robbie in another way. He had known some of these things about Drake but ignored them because of his own petty jealousy.

Robbie's stomach hurt. His head pounded. He cried then in his room, sobbing into his pillow. When he heard the click of his bedroom door, he didn't look up. He didn't look up when he felt his bed shift from the added weight, not once, but twice. Nor did he look up when he felt the strong hand on his back or the gentle kiss on his head. He lay there and wept while his parents sat silently at his side.

A day before Blake's funeral, Robbie sat in the kitchen with his mom when her phone rang. Something in her tone —solemn and overly sincere—made him look up. Her eyes filled with tears almost immediately, but her voice remained steady.

"Of course, Rachel. Just a moment."

She held the phone out to her son without saying anything. He took it.

"Hello?"

"Hi, Robbie. This is Rachel Brooks."

"Hi, Ms. Brooks."

A pause, then a sniffling, but sounding far away. "I wondered if you would be a pallbearer at Blake's— at the funeral."

The voice wavered. Each word was heavy with barely restrained emotion.

"I, uh, yes, Ms. Brooks."

A longer pause.

"Thank you."

Robbie returned the phone. "Blake's mom asked me to be a pallbearer."

Lauren Noble nodded.

"I don't think I can do it."

He looked away, unable to meet his mom's eyes. Lauren pulled out a chair beside him. She exhaled before speaking. "Robbie, I can only imagine what you're going through. I know how you felt about Blake. You grew up together. She was your best friend, and— " His mom seemed about to say something else but stopped herself.

"Losing people close to us can make us feel like we're adrift on an endless sea of grief. As someone who loves you more than anything in all the universe, believe me when I say that if I could take that pain from you, I would."

He turned to look at his mom, and he knew without a doubt that she spoke true.

"Blake's memory will be with you for the rest of your life. Her death will always make you sad, but slowly, in time, that sea of grief will get smaller and smaller until the memories of your time together will become an island of solace in ways unexpected."

He didn't believe her, of course, but he nodded anyway. Tears rolled down his mom's cheeks now. She let them fall and spoke to him with unwavering certainty. "Carrying Blake to her final rest is an honor, and it means a great deal to Rachel and Mark. I know it won't be easy for you, but if you refuse, you'll always regret it."

She hugged him comfortingly and then left him alone with his thoughts.

"Blake's parents would feel differently if they knew she died because of me," he whispered.

The pews at St. Boniface Catholic Church were packed for the funeral. When the church was at capacity, the mourners lined the street outside, standing in the blazing sun of a hot, cloudless day. It seemed to Robbie that the entire town of Bethel was paying their respects to Blake Brooks. Artie was there with his parents and two sisters. Valeria, her arm in a black sling to match her dress, was there with her parents and sister. Robbie and Valeria shared a few looks across the pews but didn't get a chance to speak.

He sat near the front of the church during the service. His parents flanked him on either side. When Mr. and Ms. Brooks entered, he forced himself not to look away, even though their sorrow threatened to devour his soul. Father Flynn delivered the Funeral Mass. The old priest, who Robbie knew had been quite fond of Blake, lost his composure. His voice cracked more than once, forcing him to pause each time.

Drake was not present at the funeral. Robbie didn't know if he was still too injured to attend or if his absence had anything to do with the public sentiment blaming him for Blake's death. Drake's mom attended, though. Robbie saw people staring at her and knew she saw them too. She came alone. Ms. Gallant was respectful and perhaps a little defiant in her prideful posture, though she broke down in tears a few times during Father Flynn's sermon. Some photographers and members of the press were outside, trying to get a salacious story on Edward Kerrich. Robbie was glad they were disappointed.

He performed his duty as a pallbearer without incident. After the interment at the cemetery, he told his parents he wanted to stay for a while. They nodded and left with the procession of mourners. He stood alone and stared at the temporary grave marker beside Blake's final resting place. He decided at that moment that the saddest thing in all the world was when a person's birth year and death year were chronologically close. The grave marker was a reminder that Blake's were just fifteen years apart.

"Robbie?"

He turned and saw Augusta Hargrave, dressed all in black, standing at a respectful distance. Two figures stood behind her. A tall man in a black suit and a girl about his age wearing a black dress.

"Can I share a word with you?" Augusta asked him.

He shrugged. She led him for a walk among the gravestones. Her companions did not follow.

"Why are you here?" he asked.

"To pay our respects," she continued, "and because Drake cannot."

"How could you let them do that to him?"

Robbie was referring to the media blitz painting Drake as a monster. Augusta understood what he meant immediately. Her expression turned sour.

"We aren't sure who exposed that Drake is Edward's illegitimate son. That poor boy has been through a great deal, indeed."

"How is he?" Robbie asked.

"Physically, he should recover." She inhaled. "I am here for another reason, Robbie. The Knights of Rosewood need you. You must take your seat on the Conventus."

He stopped and stared at the woman. "What do you mean?"

"The night William died, he used a loophole in our laws to make you a knight so that his kit could protect you from Demeter. In doing so, he also made you his heir."

"Why me?"

She shook her head. "Pragmatism, given the circumstances. And to save your life."

"Oh," Robbie replied, looking down at the gravestones around them.

Augusta waved her hand dismissively. "Don't be sullen. William spoke highly of you and your family. Besides, what's done is done."

They stood in silence for several seconds before Augusta spoke. "The Rosewood is in a terrible place, Robbie. Without William, only five houses remain. Two of the five suffered catastrophic losses during Demeter and Elaheh Pirhadi's plot."

"Where is Pirhadi?"

"In a holding cell. The FBI arrested her for us at an airport, though her lawyers are working hard to have her released. Regardless, we need you. Houses Hargrave and Breton were a united front. Currently, the Conventus lacks — equanimity, which is something you can help us achieve."

"But how would it work? I'm a kid, remember! I go to school. I have homework and parents who need to know where I am. I know nothing about whatever you do on a secret council."

"Yes. It's a challenge, but not an insurmountable one. Holding a seat on the Conventus will position you better to protect your friends."

His eyes widened in panic at the insinuation. "My friends? You mean Valeria."

Augusta tilted her head slightly. "You know exactly who I mean, Robbie."

His heart fell as he realized they knew about Artie. "I guess I don't have much choice."

Augusta didn't argue with him.

"Why was Mr. Breton's notebook so important?" Robbie asked, suddenly changing tack. "It looked like a bunch of gibberish to me."

Augusta exhaled, then was silent for several heartbeats. "I certainly expected this question, though I am reluctant to tell you. It is a secret known only to the Conventus."

"You just asked me to claim my rightful seat," he stated, perhaps more forcefully than he should have.

For a moment, Robbie expected her to ignore his question about the notebook, but then she relented. "You must never discuss this information with anyone outside the Conventus. Do you understand?"

"I do."

"The first Keeper was a fisherman from the southern part of Mesopotamia. His name was Ziusudra. He was literate in a proto-Sumerian dialect that existed in the region during that era. Each time Ziusudra emerged from the entanglement, he wrote down the things that he learned, whether he understood them or not. Subsequent Keepers did the same. In time, those records became the scrolls the Knights of Rosewood are sworn to protect."

The revelation hit him like a flash of lightning and scoured his mind of all other thoughts.

"Mr. Breton wasn't translating the scrolls. He was recording the information he learned from the entanglement into his notebook."

Augusta nodded. "An arduous and imprecise process, yes. And then Isa would scan the information, upload it into a database, and find practical applications for whatever he learned."

Lightning struck a second time at the mention of Isa, triggering the memory of what must've been a warning from the simulated Mr. Breton. *'Honor the covenant. Machines are forbidden in this place.'*

Robbie wanted to ask Augusta if she knew what the warning meant, but the woman had started walking back toward Blake's grave. Robbie caught up to her a moment later, but the proximity of the woman's companions, who stood vigil beside the grave, forestalled any further questions. The man saw them approach. He met them halfway to the grave and offered his hand to Robbie, who obliged with his own.

"Hello, Robbie." The man's thickly accented English made him think of Aristide. "My name is Antonio Innocenti."

He seemed familiar, but Robbie couldn't place him.

"I understand that Blake was your friend. I am deeply sorry for your loss. I have no words of comfort, and for this, I am dismayed."

Antonio bowed his head. Then he returned to the other figure standing beside the grave. The man walked with a noticeable limp. Augusta spoke quietly.

"Antonio and his younger brother, Domenico, were targeted in the plot to destroy the Rosewood. Antonio survived. Domenico died a few days ago."

"Oh. I'm sorry to hear that."

The girl also looked familiar but in a different way than Antonio. She looked like someone he had met before.

"And the girl?"

Augusta closed her eyes, seemed to compose herself, and then answered him.

"That's the girl who saved your life, Alice Asher. If not for her, who knows when we would've come back to Bethel."

"Dr. Asher's daughter," he stated.

"Her parents—" Augusta trailed off, and Robbie thought he understood.

"Both?" he asked.

She gave him a look that confirmed the worst.

It was Robbie's turn to compose himself. He swallowed hard. "I should say something to her, right? Condolences or something."

Augusta shook her head. "Some other time, Robbie. Today, she is here to share in Drake's grief. She is not yet ready to share her own."

Later that night, Robbie lay in his bed. His house was dark and quiet. His parents had bid him good night, but not before assuring him that he could wake them if he needed company. Thoughts swirled around his head in a torrent. He thought of Blake, of course. The life that was stolen from her. He thought about Mr. and Ms. Brooks and their unending grief. He felt a growing conviction in his heart that he owed Drake a debt he could never repay. He thought of Antonio Innocenti, who lost a brother, and of Alice Asher, who lost both parents. He thought of the Rosewood, returning to summer school, and everything Augusta Hargrave had told him about the underwater place.

The entanglement.

The smartphone lit up on his nightstand. He had been careless and forgot to put it away.

He looked at the screen and frowned. The device was in the process of rebooting, which he'd never seen before. The home screen appeared a few seconds later, followed by a system message.

Recompile complete.

That was odd. He'd need to message Yasmin and ask her about it in the morning.

"Good evening, Robbie."

He almost dropped the phone. The female voice was loud enough for him to hear but not loud enough to wake his parents.

"Ah, hello?"

"I am quite sorry I have been away for so long."

"Isa?"

"We have much to discuss."